# CAGED

## Sheppard & Sons Investigations, Book 5

## Eveline Rose

Sword & Rose

# Dedication

This book is dedicated to all the women who are stronger than they think are, and the men who love them.

# Also by

# Acknowledgements

Thank you, Reader, for choosing to spend some time in my world. I hope you enjoyed it.

I want to thank my Proof Reader, Nina, and my Beta readers, Gigi, Kirsten, and Shauna'h. Your feedback was invaluable in helping me polish my story. A big thanks to Maria Secoy, and the mentor team at All Write Well–this book wouldn't be in your hands if I hadn't found them!

A special shout out to my coach, "Flyin" Brian Akins, who helped me with the boxing scene.

I also want to thank my friends, who have surrounded me with love and support while listening to me chatter on endlessly about my characters and plot lines over many glasses of wine.

Thank you all!

About 84,000 words

EvelineRose.author@gmail.com
CAGED
Sheppard & Sons Investigations Book 5
by Eveline Rose

# Chapter 1

## Cate

I was having a shitty day and knew if I didn't clear my head and focus, I'd have an even shittier night. Tonight was the monthly Sheppard & Sons Investigations (SSI) group training session, and I had a black eye courtesy of my boxing coach. That's what I get for moving too slow during a sparing session.

Now I have to face Jaden Sheppard, the youngest son of my boss and the bane of my existence. He had a chip on his shoulder the size of Texas and blamed me for his lack of "quality jobs"—his words, not mine—at Sheppard and Sons.

I rolled my eyes as I parked in the back lot of the office building. The only reason Jaden had issues in the office was because he acted like a jerk. He thought his last name, Marine Raider experience, and three months on the job qualified him for the top PI jobs. *At least that's my interpretation.* But it was the state of Texas that required him to do a year of on-the-job training to become a full-fledged private investigator. Only those of us with law enforcement backgrounds were exempt.

I grabbed my gym bag from the back of my hunter green SUV and mentally prepared myself for the razzing I was about to get. I usually didn't mind; the guys at SSI were good-hearted. But today, I was in a mood.

When I walked into the office, the receptionist/human resource rep/executive assistant to the owners, and Jack's wife, Meg, greeted me with a smile.

"Hey Max." Her eyes rounded as her mother-to-be instincts kicked in. She stood up and rushed over. "Are you okay? Who do we need to kill?"

I laughed. "I'm fine." I almost admitted to not moving fast enough while training, but didn't want to risk one of the guys overhearing and thinking I'd be an easy target. Because of the physical, and occasionally dangerous, demands of our jobs, we met once a month to spar. It kept us in fighting shape and was a good team building exercise.

*Or maybe I do.* It was always fun to beat down guys who underestimated me. At five-foot-seven, I was at the tall end of average, but hours spent training in the gym meant I was anything but average in build or skill.

Meg's eyes roamed up and down, making sure I was indeed fine. Apparently, the guys had a history of downplaying their injuries, so she insisted on verifying.

"It's from training," I admitted, in a whisper.

"Don't let the guys hear that." She looked around the spacious, well lit reception room. "They'll start betting against you."

The guys always placed side bets on who'd win. No one bet on me the first time, and I doubted they would anytime soon. Because of assignments, this would be my second time attending.

I'd held my own against Jamie and Jack, the eldest Sheppard sons. But AJ and Doug, the two non-Sheppard full-timers, were both significantly bigger and better trained. They'd kicked my ass without much effort.

It wasn't unexpected, but I still didn't like it. Refusing to suffer a repeat, I'd hired a personal trainer. *I might still lose, but it won't be nearly as embarrassing.*

I hadn't seen Jaden fight yet, so I had no idea what to expect from him. Like AJ and Doug, Jaden was built like a brick house. He was three inches shorter than Doug, who at six-four was the tallest guy at SSI. Thanks to Meg, I wasn't the shortest person in the office, but I was the shortest person required to train.

"I don't think they'll ever bet on me," I said, keeping my tone light and friendly. Someday, I'd bet on me and if I was lucky, I'd win.

"No, but someday you'll show them what a badass you are and kick all their asses."

If I didn't know any better, I'd think she wanted me to do just that.

"I just hope I'm there to see it," she added with a laugh.

"Likewise." The phone rang, ending our talk.

When I walked into the office I shared with Jaden, he glance up just long enough to verify it was me before saying. "Hey."

"Hey." I mimicked his bored tone.

The clicking of our keyboards was the only sound as we worked. At five-forty, I went to the bathroom to change into leggings, a padded sports bra, and my well-worn, fitted marine t-shirt.

As expected, the guys all asked about the black eye, except John, who just raised an eyebrow and observed. Since it hadn't happened on assignment, they started wondering, loudly, what kind of things I did for fun.

Like I'd ever tell. They didn't need to know my life was boring compared to theirs.

Jaden was the last to arrive.

John looked at his watch. No words needed.

"What, I'm on time." Jaden defended himself.

"Barely," Jack said, taking a dig at his younger brother. "Didn't the Marines teach you that on time is late?"

"They did." I answered, drawing Jaden's attention.

He did a double take when he noticed my black eye.

"What the hell happened to you?"

I didn't have time to answer before AJ asked, "Dude, you share an office. How the hell didn't you notice before now?"

Jaden cringed at the question. "I was busy working."

What he didn't say was, in an attempt to avoid conflict, we ignored each other as much as possible when we were in our office. It irritated me to no end that he couldn't act like a professional, instead he acted like a brat mumbling comments about my organized desk, lunch habits, and work methods.

Just yesterday, he'd given me shit for thinking.

"Must you do that?" His voice thick with irritation.

"Do what?"

"Tap your pen like that?"

Tap my pen on my chin? How much noise could I be making? "How does this," I tapped my pen on my chin, "annoy you?"

He turned, giving me a dirty look as he answered. "The tap tap tap is annoying." He accented each tap with a slap on his desk.

"Fine. I'll stop."

"Good."

"Good."

I hadn't realized how often I tap my pen against my chin while thinking until he called me out for doing it again. He huffed and walked out, saying, "I can't work like this."

Back in the present, Doug said, "Apparently, the Marine Corps doesn't teach their spec ops guys to be aware of their surroundings." As the only Air Force veteran, he took advantage of the few opportunities he had to make fun of the other branches.

"Watch it, Sharpe," John said, defending the Marines. The branch he, Jaden, and I had in common.

"Even we learned that, and we were Army infantry," Jack said while fist bumping AJ, celebrating their shared time in the trenches.

"Let's get to work," John said in his fun-killing tone.

Protocol was for us to work out for thirty minutes to warm up before sparring.

I snagged one of the two treadmills, grateful Jaden's entry had taken the focus off me and my black eye.

AJ grabbed the other one. "You ready for another ass kicking?" he asked.

Unlike the stick-up-their-ass dickheads I'd worked with at the FBI, AJ's energy was more frat boy military brotherhood than corporate sexism.

I held onto the anger that always surfaced when I thought about my former co-workers, knowing it'd serve me well on the mat.

When it was time to face off, John pulled Jaden's name from the hat. When no one volunteered to be his first challenger, John picked a second name.

Mine.

Not for the first time, I noticed the tattoos covering Jaden's arms. The short sleeves of his tight t-shirt showed off more of his inked up, muscled arms than I normally saw. Giving me an eye full of art to appreciate. The only color, at least that I could see, was the American flag on his right upper arm. It was a reversed, or fighting forward, flag military personnel wore on the right arm of their uniforms. Among the black and white art on his left bicep was the Marine Ranger insignia.

I put my guard in my mouth and strapped on my headgear. *Focus.* Tonight wasn't just the first time Jaden and I would spar, it was the first time any of us would see him on the mat. No one doubted he'd be hard to beat, having just returned from the Special Forces and still in a fighting mindset. Not to mention full of piss and vinegar.

My anger didn't serve me as well as I would've liked. It might have against his brothers, but not Jaden.

He was all speed and fury.

Unlike the others, he didn't wait for me to make the first move—he charged.

I braced myself too late for the impact and we stumbled back. When I fell back, he landed on top of me, catching himself on his hands before flattening me like a pancake. I managed to buck my hips and throw him off, but that small victory was short-lived.

I rolled and sprung to my feet, but he was already up and ready. He feigned a punch before sweeping my legs and dropping me back to the mat—pinning me in the blink of an eye.

John counted down as I struggled against Jaden's hold. As soon as John reached one, Jaden jumped up.

In complete contradiction to how I felt, I held my head high as I stood and walked to the edge of the mat.

"Looks like the Raiders taught me a thing or two you can't learn in a classroom." He shot me a dirty look I didn't think I deserved. It wasn't my fault I had an advanced college degree or law enforcement experience, and he didn't. He seemed determined to blame me, nonetheless.

# Chapter 2

## Jay

They didn't call me Taz for nothing. The military was all about nicknames, and mine was Shep until Ranger School when an instructor referred to me as the Tasmanian Devil. I was a tornado, attacking every task and challenge with a whirling fury. He'd warned me to be careful, saying I'd burn out if I didn't slow down.

He had no way of knowing I'd always been like that; driven by the need to prove myself, to prove my worth.

Rather than burning out, I thrived. The constant challenge was exactly what I needed, because, for me, boredom was the enemy.

I called out, "Next!" after beating Maxwell in what had to be record time. It felt good to knock her down a peg or two. She walked around like a fucking know-it-all, and I was sick of it. She'd been at SSI, my family's business, a couple months longer than me but kept herself separate, like she was too good for us.

Because of her FBI experience she didn't have to mentor for a year before becoming a licensed private investigator, like I did. And she had a fucking Master's degree, while I only had an Associate's.

And don't even get me started on knowing I'd have to salute her overly organized, never late, nary a fiery red hair out of place, uptight ass at Marine functions. Not that I planned on attending any. Reunion with the team guys? Maybe. As long as Henderson wasn't there, because if we were ever in the same room again, one of us would die.

When no one volunteered to challenge me, Dad had them face me in order of seniority. Poor Jamie never stood a chance. Jack didn't do much better. Then I faced off against AJ. Fucker was big and might have been a real challenge, but he'd recently fallen in love and was losing his edge. I wondered if he'd get it back once the honeymoon phase was over.

If Blake ever fucked AJ over, and the only thing keeping him warm at night was the hatred burning through his veins, he'd probably be able to kick my ass. That'd be a fun day. Not that I wanted Blake to hurt AJ, I didn't. But going head-to-head against a pissed off AJ was a challenge I wanted.

Doug, on the other hand, was calm as fuck and hard to predict, which only fueled my fire. If I hadn't gone bat shit crazy on his ass, I might have lost.

"Jay, you good?" Jamie asked as we filed into the locker room.

"Yeah, why?"

"Because we don't usually try to kill each other on the mat," Jack answered for him. My brothers were close in age and had always been friends. But not me. I was several years younger. The black sheep. The mistake. The one they never invited to play in their reindeer games.

*Maybe working here is a mistake.*

"Just wanted to win, that's all." I shrugged it off, knowing I'd been more aggressive than necessary.

"That you did. But be warned, I'll be ready for you next time," AJ said as he rubbed the bruise forming on his arm.

"You got anything to add?" I asked Doug.

"Jaden," my father said, his tone reminding me of when I got in trouble as a kid. "Get cleaned up. I want to see you in my office." He didn't wait for an answer before leaving the small locker room.

"Man, I hate that tone," Jack whispered.

*I'm definitely in trouble.*

"Only because you have to hear it so often," Jamie said with a laugh. Jamie was the oldest son and perfect in every way.

It surprised me to hear that. Jack wasn't a perfect rule follower like Jamie, but he'd never gotten into much trouble.

Not like me, I was the problem child. *And we all know it.*

"Not as often as Jay," Jack said, proving my point.

"Whatever. Not everyone wants to be perfect and boring." They didn't see me roll my eyes as I stripped down for a shower.

"He must be talking about you," Jack teased Jamie as I stepped into the steaming spray. "I'm definitely not boring." I shut them out as the hot water washed over my tense muscles.

After dressing, I headed to my father's office. At the door, I said, "You wanted to see me, sir." I didn't have to use sir with him, and given his tone earlier, I probably shouldn't have, but I was in the mood to play with fire.

"Have a seat." He pointed to a chair in front of his big wooden desk.

I brushed my wet hair off my face and dropped into the chair. "What's up?"

He raised his left eyebrow without a word. Then he shook his head and chuckled. Which scared me more than the silent eyebrow.

"Since this is your first time attending a training session, I'm giving you the benefit of the doubt."

"For what?"

"For not realizing we don't go full-out on the mat. It's meant to be challenging, not a death match."

"I didn't hurt anyone." Defending my actions felt as shitty at twenty-five as it had at fifteen.

"No, you didn't, but your anger was palpable."

He gave me a chance to deny it, but what was the point?

"Want to talk about it?" he asked, leaning back in a relaxed position.

I didn't. "About what?"

"Jay, your mother and I are worried about you." I forced my eyes not to roll, a bad habit I'd broken in the Marines, but had picked back up after coming home. "You've had an attitude since you came home. Does it have anything to do with your canceled backpacking trip?"

He'd nailed it. "No." *Yes.* "I'm fine." Talking to my father about what happened was the last thing I wanted to do. I doubted it'd change his opinion of me; I was the family screw up. And, despite the promise I'd made to myself before coming home, I was still playing the part.

"Okay. My door is always open if you want to talk."

"Thanks, Dad," I said as I stood. "Anything else?" I asked as I turned to the door.

"You coming to dinner Sunday night?" Ma was so excited three of her four cubs were home, she started hosting weekly family dinners. I didn't mind. In fact, I preferred it over meals with just Jamie and his fiancée, Emily. They were too sweet for my bitter heart to handle for prolonged periods.

Not that I wasn't happy Jamie had found someone to share his life with again. I was. But witnessing it felt like salt being poured on my wounds.

"Yeah, I'll call Ma and let her know."

"Good. Go home and get some rest."

I nodded and walked out.

"Jay, you want to come over for dinner tonight?" Meg asked when I walked by her desk. She and Jack were as bad as Jamie and Emily when it came to open displays of affection—worse now that they were expecting their first child in December—and I couldn't handle it.

Ma desperately wanted grandchildren, and they'd be the first to give her one.

It would have been Jamie and Isabelle, his first wife, if she hadn't been killed. Her murder was the reason Jamie and Dad left the police force and started SSI. They invited Jack and me to join as silent partners while we finished our time in the military.

Jack said yes. I said no.

At the time, I'd still planned on becoming a firefighter when I left the Marines.

But over the last five years, I'd watched too many buildings burn and seen too many innocent people die in the flames. Fearing I couldn't handle fighting a fire without tossing my cookies, or worse, freaking out and endangering others, killed my career before it began.

So, I joined the family business.

In some ways, it wasn't a hard decision because I'd always wanted to serve my community after serving my country. Becoming a firefighter was supposed to be my way of being true to myself without inviting direct comparison to my law enforcement family.

Which makes me a fool for joining the family business where I get compared to them every fucking day, just like when we were kids.

Unable to say no to Meg, I forced a smile and said, "Sure, can I bring anything?"

"Just your charming self," Jack answered from behind me with a clap on the shoulder.

"You're just jealous." I said. Of what I couldn't imagine; he had a great life.

"You keep telling yourself that."

"Be nice you two," Meg scolded us, practicing her mom voice. I had to admit, she was pretty good at it. "You don't need to bring anything. Dinner's at seven."

"Okay, thanks. See you then." That gave me just enough time to pick up a six-pack, so I didn't show up empty-handed. Ma taught us better than that.

Maxwell was straightening up her desk when I walked in to grab my laptop and gear. "You know the world won't come to an end if the edges aren't lined up, right?"

Her piercing blue eyes bore holes in my skull. Her cheeks turned a vibrant shade of pink, causing her scant freckles to stand out. Her teeth clenched.

*God, it's fun to mess with her.* I shouldn't have watched her ample chest rise as she breathed in slowly through her nose to calm herself down before responding, but I did. There was nothing I wanted to see more than Catelyn Maxwell losing control.

Something told me it'd be magnificent. *It'd probably rock my world.* I shook my head to clear out the thoughts.

"Why does it bother you?" she asked, her tone cold enough to freeze the bottle of water on her desk.

"It doesn't," I lied. My desk would never be called neat or tidy, but it wasn't trashed, either. I preferred to think of it as organized chaos, and it worked for me. It only looked messy because it was in the same room as hers.

"Then shut up," she said.

"Yes, ma'am." I saluted before draining the water on my desk. After tossing my laptop in my backpack, I walked out without another word.

Remembering the frustration in her eyes when I pinned her to the mat, and ignoring how good she felt under me, I grinned. Maxwell was brilliant, and if I was being honest with myself, gorgeous. There was no way I'd ever measure up to her, except on the mat.

*I'm an ass.* I chided myself for gloating about beating a woman six inches shorter and at least sixty pounds lighter.

# Chapter 3

## Cate

"He's such an asshole," I complained to Charlie during our weekly Sunday morning zoom call. We met during Marine boot camp and became fast friends; our friendship grew to sisterhood when we served together overseas, and survived our transition to civilian life. Like me, Charlie went into law enforcement, much to her mother's disappointment, when she returned to her small town. Her mom was proud of her, but had hoped Charlie would finally be out of harm's way after leaving the Marines.

Not like my dad. He was thrilled when I joined the FBI. But not so much so when I left to join Sheppard & Sons. I had my reasons, but I couldn't tell him. He wouldn't understand and end up being even more disappointed.

"I thought things were going well at SSI?" she asked instead of fueling my fire.

"They are. It's a better fit than the FBI. Except for Jaden, he's an ass." I considered myself a calm person, and hated myself for letting him get to me.

"So you said. What'd he do now?"

"He took out his anger issues and embarrassed me on the mat."

"Are you sure you're not just upset you lost?" Humor danced in her eyes.

"Yes. I've lost before, so that's not it. It's supposed to be a training session, not a violent take down and embarrass your teammate session. He set out to make me look bad."

"Did he beat everyone else?" she asked, her even tone helping calm me down.

He had. I knew where she was going—maybe I was taking it too personally.

I replayed the other fights in my mind on fast forward, ignoring my body's reaction to watching him—his sexy forearms and arrogant grin—as he beat every opponent.

"Not gonna lie, Char. It helped my bruised ego when Jamie went down almost as fast as I did."

AJ gave Jaden a run for his money, and Doug almost beat him. No money changed hands because no one had ever seen Jaden fight, so they hadn't bet on him. *I doubt anyone bets against him next month.*

I made a mental note to schedule extra sessions with my coaches. I still trained regularly in boxing and had added Brazilian Ju Jitsu to my schedule so I could learn the fine art of grappling. The Krav Maga I'd learned in the FBI didn't help me against the guys at SSI. I justified my decision with the reminder that in my line of work, learning another defensive skill never hurt.

"So maybe it wasn't so much about beating you as it was about proving himself."

"Maybe." I still believed he had a personal vendetta against me. Though I couldn't understand why.

"If your assessment, that he doesn't think he measures up to his father and brothers, is correct, then it would make sense."

My assessment was spot on. His rebellious attitude was textbook. "You're right." I conceded.

"Of course I am." She laughed. "So, what are you going to do about it?"

When I told her I'd train more, she called me out for not addressing the real issue. Jaden Sheppard challenged me in ways that rattled my nerves. Knowing she was right, but not wanting to think about it, I changed the subject.

"How's the planning coming along?"

Charlie was happy to oblige and fill me in on the latest wedding planning drama. She wanted a simple wedding, but her fiancé was torn between pleasing his betrothed and pleasing his mother, who wanted a big, lavish event.

"I wouldn't care if we weren't paying for everything," she said, explaining the latest battle over the size of the guest list.

There wasn't much I could do to help, but as her maid of honor, I could listen when she needed to vent.

I wondered how I'd deal with family drama around planning a wedding. First, I'd have to find someone I wanted to spend my life with. *And someone willing to spend the rest of their life with me.*

After what happened with Gavin at the FBI, I doubted it'd ever happen. He hadn't only destroyed my trust in him, but in all men. At least at the romantic level.

I had an hour to kill before the Women's self-defense class I was helping teach at SSI, so I refilled my coffee and sat down to read. My newest obsession was regency era romances. I loved the handsome rogues who were actually good guys under their rakish exteriors.

I made sure my navy SSI polo was tucked properly into my khaki cargo pants before walking into the training room. It was the only finished room in the training building at the back end of the property. According to the last update, the jointly owned SSI/Law Enforcement Training Center would be up and running shortly after Jamie and Emily got married in July. *If nothing goes wrong.* The project was ambitious, with a covered outdoor range, an indoor range, a kill house, and several training classrooms. Because the joint SSI/LE training center acronym, SSILETC, reminded of me FLETC (the Federal Law Enforcement Training Center), where I'd done my FBI training, I referred to it as SLETC (pronounced Slet-C). It stuck.

Today's Women's Self Defense class would be the first official class held in the new space. I helped set up chairs in the freshly painted but still undecorated room before helping Meg sign in students. Including Emily, her best friend, Ashley, and AJ's fiancée, Blake.

"What happened?" Emily asked, indicating my eye.

"It's nothing." I shrugged it off.

"Tell me the other guy looks worse," Ashley said, making everyone laugh.

Including me. "Of course." Meg knew it was a lie, but I didn't think she'd throw me under the bus. "Meg, go sit. I've got this."

"Are you sure?" Meg asked. She was taking the class with her friends as a refresher.

"Positive. Go." I ushered them away. "Have fun."

Once everyone settled in, John began the lecture. He explained the importance of paying attention to your surroundings and trusting our intuition. He demonstrated how easy it was for someone to sneak up on us by stepping into the space of a high school student staring at her phone and not paying attention.

The class laughed when he cleared his throat, causing her to yelp. The laughter didn't last long because John, a great instructor, covered the girl's embarrassment by thanking her for providing the perfect demonstration. She blushed and nodded before putting her phone away.

John explained different strikes, while the rest of SSI demonstrated them and their effectiveness. He paired me with AJ to show the class how simple moves could help overcome size disparity. I couldn't help but notice Jaden was always on the opposite side of the room. *Probably for the best.* We'd end up arguing and embarrassing ourselves. And worse, making SSI look bad.

Something neither of us wanted to do.

"Remember, you're not trying to win a fight. You're trying to buy enough time to get to safety," John said when someone asked how realistic it was for someone without years of training to beat a bigger guy in a fight.

We held pads and coached students through a few simple moves, including eye gouges. By the end of the class, everyone was having fun hitting the bag like it represented an ex-boyfriend who'd cheated on them.

Near the end of class, Jamie and I demonstrated how to break free if someone used duct tape to bind their wrists. Apparently, it was a running joke to bind Jamie's wrists with bright pink tape.

"They get nervous about this bit, so we like to loosen them up with a good laugh," Jack said as he wrapped baby vomit green tape around my wrists. I'm sure the company had a better name for the color, but it was the ugliest shade of green I'd ever seen.

The guys collected discarded tape while Meg and I handed out information packets to the students. They received a certificate for attending, handouts with tips and tricks, plus additional resources, and business cards for SSI.

"You don't need to help," Jack insisted when Meg picked up a chair.

"I'm pregnant, Jack, not broken," she argued without any zeal.

It took about two seconds for the women to gang up on Jack; myself excluded. Though I agreed. Meg was perfectly capable of folding a few lightweight metal chairs.

"Fine." Jack gave up and threw his hands up in front of this chest. "But don't overdo it."

When Meg stuck her tongue out at Jack, Ashley got a case of the giggles. "I bet if you flutter your eyelashes, he'll leave you alone." Emily and Meg joined in, leaning on each other and laughing until tears rolled down their cheeks.

"Do I want to know?" Jaden asked.

"No." Jamie, Jack, and AJ said together.

"You don't know why they're laughing, do you?" I asked.

"Nope," AJ said.

"Not a clue," Jack said.

The girls must have told Blake, because her eyes rounded in shock before she bent over laughing.

"I know." Jaimie gloated. "But Em swore me to secrecy." The guys turned on him, demanding he spill his guts, but he wouldn't budge.

Meg called me over and explained. Last summer, Ashley told Emily to flirt with Jamie by batting her eyelashes at Jamie, but Emily immediately had images of cartoon characters fill her head, so now any time one of them brought up fluttering eyelashes, they all devolved into giggle fits.

I appreciated her sharing the story, but I still felt like an outsider. *It's my own fault.* I've kept myself distant to protect myself.

Times like this reminded me just how lonely playing it safe could be.

"Alright, ladies, class is over. Time to go," John said with a smile, his love for them shining in his eyes. He turned to the guys and said, "Back to work. You don't want me to keep your mother waiting, do you?"

"No, sir." They said in unison. Even AJ and me, because no one wanted to upset Mary Sheppard. She was the team Mama Bear, but wouldn't think twice about giving us a talking to if we fucked up.

"Max," Meg was the only person from the office who chose to call me Max instead of Maxwell. "We're going to Em's to hang out and order food. Want to come?" Meg asked. *Funny how she refers to Jamie's house as Emily's.*

"I'm sure she's too good-" Jaden corrected himself, "too busy to join us." His insulting words and tone hit the mark. They probably all thought that was the reason I always said no.

I wouldn't have accepted, not because I thought I was too good for them or even too busy, but because I felt out of place in the tight-knit group.

And I'd learned the hard way not to get too close to my co-workers.

But I didn't want them thinking he was right, so I accepted. *One hour can't hurt.* "That sounds fun. Can I bring anything?" I asked.

Jaden's 'fuck you' expression felt satisfying in a way I hadn't anticipated.

"Whatever," Jaden said before lifting a rather large stack of chairs, making his biceps bulge under his tight navy polo. Refusing to think about his tattooed forearms flexing, I turned away and asked Meg to repeat herself.

"We'll probably order out, so you only need to bring the usual," she said, like I should know.

*I'd know if I accepted her invitations more often.* Ignoring my embarrassment, I asked, "What's the usual?"

"Whatever you want to drink," several voices answered.

I resisted the urge to look at Jaden while we finished packing up. Watching his muscles flex as he carried heavy things was not something I wanted to get caught doing.

*I may not get along with him, but he's damn easy on the eyes.* And I had a thing for muscles and tattoos on guys.

I grabbed a twelve pack of a local amber craft beer and a bottle of sparkling grape juice before going to Jamie's.

When I first came to Weatherford for a case, Jack and Meg lived with Jamie. SSI had called my boss, Agent Jones, and asked for his help finding Chase, Beth's son and John and Mary's godson. *And soon to be Doug's stepson.* Jones thought my profiling skills would come in handy, so he'd asked me to come as a favor. Luckily for everyone, Chase was kidnapped by a distraught mother, not a hardened criminal. Rescuing him was relatively easy.

During our drive back to Dallas, I'd grilled Jones about his connection to SSI. That was how I learned Meg was a victim of trafficking. Jones was the FBI agent who'd helped her relocate and get the help she needed to start over.

Emily moved in with Jamie as soon as Jack and Meg moved out. *And now Jaden lives here.* It was a step up from living with his parents, but it said a lot about his maturity that he lived with his soon-to-be-married big brother.

*I'm a hypocrite, judging Jaden but not Jack.*

Meg greeted me at the door and invited me in.

After greeting her, I handed her a bottle of sparkling grape juice. "This is for you."

"Thank you. Now I can have bubbly in my wine glass instead of water."

"You aren't planning on drinking all of these yourself, are you?" Jamie asked as he took the twelve-pack from me.

I laughed. "No, I figured I'd bring extra as a gift for the host."

"Much appreciated," he said with a nod.

I hovered near the edge of the crowd and observed as we talked in the kitchen.

I told myself I wasn't annoyed that Ashley openly flirted with Jaden. Rationalizing my irritation by questioning why she'd want to hook up with him.

Maybe it was the lop-sided grin he kept flashing her.

Maybe it was the way his amber eyes sparkled as he flirted.

Maybe it was his stupidly sexy body.

# Chapter 4

## Jay

Maxwell accepted the invite just to prove me wrong and then showed up with a twelve-pack of craft beer and a bottle of sparkling grape juice for Meg. Which thrilled Meg, who was drinking "plain old boring water".

*A gift for the host.* I mimicked her in my head. Of course she brought a gift. *What a kiss ass.*

When Emily said, "We're ordering pizza, wings, and salads. Is there anything specific you want?" Maxwell shrugged and said she wasn't picky.

"The military does that to a person," Jack joked. He wasn't wrong. You learned to eat what you could, when you could. But Maxwell was an officer and had never seen combat, so I doubt she really understood.

Maxwell acted relaxed, but I could see the tension in the way she held herself. Not that I paid that much attention to her body, or the curve of her shoulders, or how she absentmindedly tapped her fingers on her legs when she was tense or nervous.

Just like the irritating way she tapped her pen to her chin when thinking.

*That's what she gets for accepting an invitation just to spite me.*

I downed my beer and got a second one from the fridge.

"Blake, what'd you think of the class?" Maxwell asked.

"I learned a lot," Blake answered. "But I'm not sure how much I'll remember."

"I'm sure AJ will help you with that," Meg said. "If not, I'm sure Jay can."

AJ growled in my general direction. No doubt the exact response Meg wanted.

"Dude, I didn't say anything. Growl at Meg." I twisted the cap off a bottle of Maxwell's fancy beer. She had good taste, but I'd ever tell her.

"If he does that, Jack'll growl back." Meg laughed, "It'd be chaos."

Maxwell watched the verbal sparing with a half smile. It was like she didn't want to let herself enjoy the banter.

"Best let them get it out of their systems now," Ashley said with a grin. She loved watching us bait each other, and occasionally egged us on. "Jay, who are you going to growl at?"

"Leave me out of it," I said, saluting her with my beer.

"Smart man," AJ said.

"Whatever, dude." I flipped him off before asking, "Anyone else want one?"

"I'll take one," Jack and AJ said together.

I still couldn't believe AJ was engaged. I thought we'd be drinking buddies, being the only two single guys at SSI, but he'd put a ring on Blake's finger before we had a chance to become friends.

I made a mental note to reconnect with some of my friends from high school. We'd lost touch after graduation, most of them going to college while I joined the Marines.

It was hard maintaining long-distance friendships. While they were getting married and starting families, I was doing my best to not get killed in the desert.

"Jay?" Jamie's voice cut off my thoughts.

"What?"

"What kind of wings do you want?" he asked.

"Buffalo's fine. With blue cheese." Ranch dressing was the standard, but I didn't care for it.

"Told you," Jack said. *Like he knows me so well.*

I was always the odd man out, and they'd never really taken the time to get to know the adult me. Jack was three-and-a-half years older and Jamie and his twin, Madi, were five years older. Mom and Dad were done having kids after Jack, so unlike my older siblings, I wasn't planned.

*A mistake.* Something my brothers had reminded me of often when we were kids.

A happy accident is what my mother called me, but it didn't help. I was nothing like my siblings; something none of them were shy about pointing out.

Jamie and Madi were typical type A personalities. Smart, over-achieving, popular. Jack wasn't as bad, but he was clever and easy-going, and everyone loved him. He was also the spitting image of our dad, only taller. The only attribute I got from my father was his amber eyes.

I wasn't as smart as any of them, and couldn't stand sitting still in the classroom. I wanted to run around and play. Even in high school, I preferred classes where I could learn by doing not by reading. I squeaked by with low passing grades, falling short whenever my teachers compared me to my siblings.

The only place I made a name for myself was on the field. I was big and fast, qualities that helped me lead our varsity football team to the championship. I was the third Sheppard to lead the team, Dad and Jamie having done so before me, but I was the only left tackle ever voted to captain. I grinned at the memory. *No one ever sacked our quarterback if I was on the field.*

I was scouted my senior year and offered more than one football scholarship, but my grades sucked and I would've failed in college. Much to my mother's disappointment, I declined the offers and joined the Marines instead. Me joining didn't disappoint her; she was proud of her children for serving. She just didn't want another cub to leave the nest for dangerous places unknown.

But, I couldn't stay in Weatherford.

Joining the Marines gave me an opportunity to crawl out from under my brothers' shadows and grow into the man I was meant to be. I didn't regret choosing the military over college or a pro football career. And when I was finally ready to earn my degree, the Marines paid for it.

Stuck in my head, I'd missed most of the conversation, but the doorbell, alerting us to the pizza being delivered, caught my attention.

"Of course that got your attention," Jack said.

"Fuck you, Jack." It wasn't my fault I was always hungry; it took a lot of effort, and a lot of calories, to stay in top fighting condition. I couldn't best my brothers in any category, so I prided myself on being the biggest.

That, and being able to kick both their asses.

*I guess there's one category I can best them, unarmed combat.*

Jack raised an eyebrow. "Who pissed in your beer?"

"No one. What do I owe you?" I asked, pulling out my wallet.

"Twenty each," Jamie answered. "You can give it to Em."

"Hell yeah, we should plan a girl's night out with Jamie's money." Ashley chimed in as she grabbed the twenty out of my hand.

"That's my twenty," I teased her.

"Not anymore," she teased back.

Ashley was hot, but knowing she'd hooked up with AJ made her a no-go for me. That, and I didn't want a relationship, so sleeping with her would get me in trouble.

*But it's fun flirting with her.*

# Chapter 5

## Jay

I got up early Monday to pick up coffee. "Hey Ma," I said as I walked into Grannie's, the coffee shop she owned. "Can I get eight coffees, make that seven and one decaf Mocha?"

I figured I owed everyone an apology after no less than four people pointed out to me, over the weekend, that my behavior was excessive and uncalled for.

Guys from my Raider team thought it was cool I'd be working with my family when I returned to civilian life, but that's because they'd never suffered through the same lecture from their father and two older brothers, who also happened to be their bosses.

As if that didn't suck enough—Dad told Ma.

The only thing worse than having my father correct my behavior with a stern, yet concerned, heart-to-heart, was sitting across the table from my mother and having her peer into my soul as she said, "I'm disappointed in you."

I wasn't proud of my behavior or putting myself in a position where they all felt the need to lecture me. One thing I'd promised myself when I signed on to work at SSI was that I wouldn't fall back into my old negative patterns.

*Doing a* bang-up *job of that, Sheppard.*

At dinner, I admitted I'd gone into the training session feeling like I needed to prove myself, but I refused to talk about why I felt that way. *The mat is the one place I don't feel 'less than' my brothers.*

Or why I've seemed angry since coming home.

Six months earlier than expected. It had nothing to do with my family.

I was fairly confident my dad knew I felt like I didn't measure up, but he never mentioned it. Not directly. Instead, he constantly reminded me I didn't have to prove myself.

I didn't necessarily feel the need to apologize to everyone for kicking their asses. Losing was part of training, but how I did it was over-the-top. The coffee was my olive branch.

"Want some pastries, too?"

"Sure. Can you include some blueberry muffins?" I'd already eaten breakfast, but couldn't say no to my favorite fresh baked pastry.

"I can." She smiled.

"Morning Jay," Beth said as she joined my mom behind the counter. "Doug said you've got, and I quote, 'mad skills on the mat'." She laughed.

"Thanks, Beth. I'll be sure to remind him of that later," I teased. Beth wasn't just the store manager, she was Ma's best friend and Doug's fiancée.

Ma came around the counter to hug me goodbye. Her head barely reached my chin, so I couldn't miss the new gray in her wavy, dark brown hair. Hair I'd inherited from her. Jamie and Madi inherited her expressive hazel eyes.

"Behave today, okay?"

I laughed. "Of course." *With any luck, I'll have an assignment while the dust settles.*

As expected, the coffee and treats were a hit. And lucky for me, Ma included half a dozen blueberry muffins because everyone wanted one.

"The new guy gets it," AJ said, getting the keys to one of the company cars from Meg and grabbing a muffin before leaving. He had an executive protection gig babysitting an actor's pre-teen daughter all week. I didn't envy him that detail.

New guy gets the coffee was SSI's version of hazing. It started with AJ, because Jack wanted to welcome his friend with a little good-natured ribbing. He decided daily trips to Ma's coffee shop were the way to do it.

"Thanks, Jay." Doug said before leaving to meet with a person of interest in the case he was working.

The front door opened, prompting Meg to stand and greet the guest.

"You must be Mr. Darling. If you'd like to have a seat, John will be right with you."

That was my cue. I grabbed Maxwell's coffee and headed for my office. I was behind on paperwork, and today was as good a day as any to catch up.

"Thank you," Maxwell said, without looking up, when I set her coffee, with cream but no sugar, on the corner of her desk.

"You're welcome."

I hadn't gotten far when an alert from Meg popped up, summoning Maxwell and me to the small meeting room upstairs.

We didn't speak as we closed our laptops and grabbed our coffees.

"After you," I said, letting her walk out first.

"Now you want to be a gentleman?" she asked. I could practically hear her beautiful blue eyes rolling, even though they didn't move.

"If you can't take the heat…" I left the rest of the quote unsaid just to irritate her.

"What, can't remember the rest?" she asked. Her smarter-than-thou tone grated on my nerves.

"Get out of the kitchen." I huffed out the rest. I made eye contact before adding, "Or in your case, the gym."

Her cheeks turned pink as she glared at me. I couldn't help but notice the freckles dotting her nose stood out more when she blushed.

*No, she's not blushing; she's turning red from anger.* I had to give her credit. As pissed as she was, she didn't rise to the occasion. She ran her hand over her hair, making sure her fiery red hair was in place, and walked away.

I followed as she marched up the stairs to the conference room.

*It's going to be a long day.*

At the door, she tugged her suit blazer to remove any wrinkles, and smoothed down her skirt. Always a perfectionist.

Not wanting to look like a slob, I tucked my SSI polo tighter into my steel grey khakis.

We ignored each other from opposite sides of the table as we waited for my father.

When the door opened, he wasn't alone.

"Mr. Darling, this is Catelyn Maxwell and Jaden Sheppard." We stood as he introduced us and shook Darling's hand. "Have a seat."

Darling's eyes darted nervously between Maxwell and me as he sat. Something about his demeanor felt off. *What's he hiding?*

Dad and Darling filled us in on why he needed our help; his nineteen-year-old daughter, Wendy, had been missing for three days.

"At first, I thought she'd gone away for a long weekend. But then I found this when I heard the alarm going off." He put a cell phone, protected with a colorful flower case on the table. "It's Wendy's; she never leaves home without it."

*No one ever does.*

He'd already reached out to her friends, but no one had seen her.

"Mr. Darling said we can search the phone," Dad said.

Maxwell put on gloves before picking up the phone and examining the case.

"Has she taken off like this before?" I asked.

"She doesn't always tell me when she's going out, but she usually texts if she'll be gone overnight."

Which she couldn't do if she didn't have her phone.

"Can you think of anyone who might want to harm her?" The question always sounded stupid to me in movies, but it turns out it was a necessary one. People weren't always forthcoming with details, even when they were asking for help.

"No, she's a good kid." Darling looked genuinely concerned, but there was something about his demeanor that nagged at me.

"Any reason someone might use her to target you?" I asked. We'd seen firsthand how easy it was for a bad guy to use a child to get to the parent when Blake, AJ's fiancée, was kidnapped because of her father's connections.

Darling broke eye contact and stared at his hands, playing with a non-existent wedding ring. "I can't think of anything."

He was hiding something; I just didn't know what.

# Chapter 6

## Cate

The phone case was typical for a nineteen-year-old. So was the picture she used as a background on her home screen, a group shot of her with her friends at a party.

I half listened as John and Jaden asked questions while I scanned Wendy's texts.

"Who's Mr. R.?" The name showed up in a text thread. And Wendy bragged about gifts, including jewelry, a new cell phone, and fancy dinners.

"I don't know. I assumed it was a nickname for one of her friends."

"Does she have a boyfriend?" I asked. Mr. R could mean Mr. Right. But why keep it a secret? *Older man? Teacher? Married?*

"No, she broke up with the last guy a couple of months ago." I didn't put much stock in his answer; teenage girls weren't always forthcoming with things like whom they were dating. *Especially if they're using an initial with their friends.*

"Do you know his name?"

"Bill, I never knew his last name." He looked embarrassed and then defended himself. "They didn't go out long."

I nodded as I typed Bill's name into the contact search bar. Bill McCray was the only result. *Not Mr. R.*

My gut was telling me Mr. R. had given her a second phone. That kind of behavior didn't bode well if he also insisted she leave her other phone at home when they went out.

"Are any of her things missing?"

Darling fiddled with his ring finger and avoided making eye contact. "I'm not sure. I didn't really look."

"If it's okay, I'd like to see her room," I said.

He hesitated, but then said, "Of course."

"Mr. Darling, Meg has some paperwork for you to fill out. I'll walk you down," John said as he stood.

"Is that it?" Darling asked.

"For now, we'll be down in a minute," I answered.

Meg met Darling outside the door and escorted him downstairs.

"What do you think, Jay?" John asked.

"There's something he's not telling us, but I don't think he knows where Wendy is, or the identity of Mr. R," Jay answered.

I nodded my agreement. "My gut says Mr. R gave her a phone for private contact."

"My gut agrees," John said. "Go to Fort Worth and check out Wendy's room before he changes his mind."

Jaden closed his laptop and rested his heavily inked arms on the table. He looked like he wanted to say something, but I answered before he could.

"Yes, sir."

"Take Jay with you." He turned to Jay. "You're not a PI yet, so it's Maxwell's case, but I think it's a good one to start honing your skills."

"Yes, sir." He didn't sound any happier than I felt knowing we'd be working the case together. His icy stare confirmed my suspicions.

I didn't know if he was upset because he didn't like working with me personally, or because he had to learn from a woman.

I didn't really care. As long as he didn't do anything to get in my way or fuck things up, I could deal with his shitty attitude.

*God knows, I've dealt with worse.*

"I'm driving," Jay said as we walked out the door to the secured lot in the back.

"That's fine." I could give him that minor victory if it soothed his ego.

He turned to me as if surprised, then marched towards his truck. Of course, it was huge and black. It would've shocked me if he drove anything else. The four-door, extra-wide truck had a lockbox in the bed and tinted windows.

He entered the address on his navigation system and shoved the truck in gear.

"When we get there, I'll ask Darling to take us directly to Wendy's room. I'd like for you to hang behind and-"

He cut me off. "Look for clues. Thanks, but I know how to do my job."

An exasperated sigh wouldn't help, so I held it back and forced myself to respond calmly.

"I know that, Sheppard. But I'd like for us to be on the same page. To do that successfully, we need a game plan." So, calmly, but not entirely without snark.

I waited for a smartass remark, but he shocked me by dipping his head once in acknowledgement.

"I think he'll feel more comfortable talking to me when you're not around, so give us a few minutes before you come in." People, especially men, often underestimated me. Which worked in my favor. It was amazing how often they'd let important details slip because they'd let their guard down.

"Can you do that?" I asked when he didn't answer.

"Yes, Maxwell, I can do that." His answer was so heavy with snark it was practically a third person.

"Don't go anywhere, not on the direct path to Wendy's room."

"Follow you like a puppy dog. Got it."

*Sweet baby Jesus, this man tries my patience.*

"It'd be best if you hover near the door instead of coming in."

"You want me to just stand there and look pretty?"

"No, Sheppard, I want you to observe Darling while I'm analyzing the room. I need you to see what I can't."

"No need to get snippy." He grinned, goading me into a reaction.

I tapped my fingers on my thigh. *I won't let him get to me. I won't let him get to me.*

"Once I'm done in her room, I'll ask to use the bathroom."

"You're assuming she doesn't have her own."

"No. I'm making an educated guess based on his clothes, car, and greasy fingernails." I held up my phone and turned the screen towards him. "And Google Maps." Darling was a working class man, and the house was far too small for more than one bath.

"It's not like I could look it up." He held his hands up and pointed at the dash.

"You do understand the concept of teamwork, don't you?" I huffed out. So much for not letting his shitty attitude get to me.

"I'm a Raider, a team guy through and through. Or have you forgotten?"

I wanted to say, 'could have fooled me', but let it slide. I'd never seen a Special Forces guy so reluctant to work with or trust others.

*I bet someone seriously fucked him over.*

"Then act like it," I said.

"Yes, ma'am." He saluted with two fingers.

*God, I hate it when he does that.* I didn't care that I was a First Lieutenant in the Marines and he was enlisted. We were civilians, which meant he did it to annoy me.

Jaden parked on the street, giving us a chance to observe the neighborhood and yard as we approached the front door. The house fit in with the rest of the neighborhood. Darling had a clean yard but no landscaping, and the house could use a coat of paint. Unlike the others, there were two cars in his driveway.

*Was one Wendy's?*

Darling opened the door before we knocked. "Come in."

"Thanks." Jaden stepped back and held his hand out. "Ladies first."

He was working the plan in the most irritating way possible.

"Thank you."

*Did he just fucking wink at me?*

I made a mental note to stop at the gym before going home. Hitting a bag would work off my frustration. *And help me keep my sanity.*

After leading us down the short hall to Wendy's room, Darling stepped back. I observed the room from the doorway to get a general feel for her environment and mindset.

Unfortunately, the only thing that stood out was how little her room stood out. If she'd left for the weekend voluntarily, she would've taken her phone, clothes, and makeup, and maybe her laptop.

But she hadn't.

There were a few posters on the wall—Wendy had a thing for Taylor Swift—but nothing else. She'd pulled the floral comforter up to the pillows, but the bed wasn't made. Dirty clothes were piled up in the far corner near the closet. Her closed laptop, a reusable water bottle, a pink make-up train case, and at least a dozen bottles of fingernail polish cluttered her small desk.

Wendy's room was disorganized, but not dirty.

"Mr. Darling, have you moved anything?"

"I looked around her desk when I heard her phone alarm this morning, but I haven't touched anything else."

"Was the door open or closed?"

"Closed, why?"

"Just curious." If she'd left it open, he probably would have noticed she was gone sooner. By closing it, she'd bought herself some time. *If she left voluntarily.*

"Are you okay with me looking around?"

He looked at Jaden, then back at me before answering. "If you think it'll help."

I put on rubber gloves and got to work. I started with her small closet. It was packed to bursting with shirts, dresses, costumes, and a cheerleader's outfit.

"Was Wendy a cheerleader?" I asked.

"All four years of high school." His pride filled the room.

"Did she have plans to attend college?"

"She did. She took this year off to work and save money."

I nodded. "Thanks."

The necklace compartments of her jewelry box were full. I pulled out a few pieces and examined them. Given the cheap clasps and tarnished metal, I figured the stones were fake. The top two drawers were more of the same, only with earrings, rings, and bracelets.

The bottom drawer was completely empty.

*Interesting.*

Usually, I dictated my notes, but not wanting Darling to overhear, I typed them into my phone.

Out of the corner of my eye, I saw Jaden leaning against the hall wall. To an untrained eye, he'd looked like he didn't have a care in the world, but I could tell he was watching Darling. *At least he's doing what I asked.*

I opened the dresser drawers and looked inside.

"What's she looking for?" Darling asked Jaden.

"Maxwell is a profiler. She's looking for clues about Wendy's state of mind."

*I couldn't have put it better myself. Thanks, Sheppard.*

There was nothing to note in Wendy's dresser, so I moved on to her desk.

"Sheppard, can you give me a hand?"

"Yes, ma'am," he said, exaggerating his southern drawl.

*And he's back.*

"What do you need me to do?" He asked as he slipped on a pair of large rubber gloves, snapping the wrists of each one.

"We need to look through her trash and read the notes." Her floral bin had a lot of crumpled up scraps of paper. I'd expect to see that in John's office, he was old school, but not in the bedroom of a nineteen-year-old.

"Good times." He didn't sound thrilled, but he didn't hesitate to get on his knees and start grabbing slips of paper from the small can.

"Take a look at this." He handed me a post it with nothing but a street address. "No city, but if it's in the area, it shouldn't be hard to narrow down."

He was right. "Bag it."

I moved on to the desk while he finished looking in the bin.

It didn't surprise me to find out her laptop was password protected.

"I'd like to take Wendy's laptop back to the office." I left out the fact we'd have to hack into it before I could start my research. "This and her phone are the best options we have for finding her." I'd scour her phone while Doug unlocked her laptop.

"What if she comes back?"

"Call us and we'll return it to you immediately. I promise you, we're not looking for anything other than clues to where she might be," I reassured him. *Or whom she's with.*

"Okay. Will I get a receipt like they do on TV?"

I held back my laugh. "Yes, would you like it on paper or electronically?"

"Paper is fine."

Electronically was easier and faster, but for some reason people always wanted paper.

I grabbed the laptop and put it in a large plastic bag.

"Sheppard, will write you a receipt for the phone and laptop?" I asked, handing him the bagged items.

"Can we go to the kitchen?" Jaden asked as he exited the room.

"Sure."

"Is it okay if I use the restroom?" I asked as I snapped off my gloves and put them in my pocket.

"Of course, it's just down the hall."

# Chapter 7

## Jay

I took advantage of the time alone with Darling to ask him a few conversational questions while I methodically filled out the receipt. Contrary to what Maxwell said, he seemed more comfortable talking to me without her.

"I'm sorry you have to go through this. How is Mrs. Darling holding up?" From the photos I'd seen in the living room, I guessed she was no longer in the picture. I wondered if he'd told her Wendy was missing; surely she'd be here if she knew.

"She thinks I'm over-reacting." He played with his finger where his ring had been. "She left me for another guy a year ago."

My gut twisted into a thousand knots. *Cheating bitch.* I forced my jaw to relax before saying, "I'm sorry to hear that." I didn't have to feign my empathy.

Maxwell returned from the bathroom, but instead of interrupting, she watched from the edge of the room. When I raised an eyebrow in question, she signaled for me to keep going.

"How did Wendy handle it?"

He laughed. "She said she's fine, but you know what it means when a woman says she's fine."

I laughed with him. "Yeah, she's anything but."

"She admitted to not liking the guy her mother moved in with, which is why she lives with me." I considered asking the man's name, but didn't want to sidetrack him. It'd be easy enough to find out.

"Do you think he's dangerous?" I asked.

Maxwell and I looked for clues in his answer.

"What? No, he's a jerk, but I don't think he'd hurt Wendy."

Maxwell walked in and asked, "Almost done?" I took it as her signal it was time to go.

"I just need your John Hancock here." I pointed to the line. After he signed, I gave him the top copy and put our copy in my backpack. "Thank you, Mr. Darling. If you hear from Wendy, or think of something else that might be helpful, please don't hesitate to call."

I shook his hand before handing him a business card.

"Thank you." He extended his hand to shake Maxwell's.

"We'll keep you updated on our progress," she said.

"Do you think you'll be able to find her?" he asked.

"We'll do our best," Maxwell answered.

Unfortunately, we couldn't promise any more than that.

"Nice job getting him to open up like that," Maxwell said after we got back in my truck.

"You say that like you're surprised." I was tired of her treating me like an idiot.

"Learn how to take a compliment, Sheppard."

I turned over the engine and revved it instead of answering her.

She sighed.

"What did you find in the bathroom?" I asked.

"Two toothbrushes and a hairbrush," she said. "What else did you learn from Darling?"

"He hasn't taken down the family photos. In fact, he picked up a wedding photo more than once, and there are tracks in the dust near the other photos."

"He misses her," Maxwell said. It felt more like she was thinking out loud than talking to me, but I answered anyway.

"No shit, Sherlock."

I didn't have to turn my head to feel the heat of her glare.

"Continue," she said through gritted teeth.

"Wendy's an only child. As you so cleverly stated, he's still pining for his ex. He also confirmed the second car in the driveway is Wendy's."

"Anything else?" she asked as she typed notes on her phone.

"That's not enough?"

She rested her hands in her lap, the tension in them obvious from her white-knuckle grip on her phone. She turned to me, and said, "If it's all you have, then it's enough. It was a question, Sheppard, not a judgment."

What was it about her that made me so defensive?

"You heard the rest."

"Did you pick up on anything while I searched?"

"He watched you like a hawk, but not like he was worried you'd steal something. More like curiosity. He reached for his ring a lot, he did it at the table, too. I think it's a combination of nerves and missing his ex."

"Thank you," she said, sounding more exasperated than mad.

"You're welcome." My tone matched hers.

After a few minutes of nothing but country music filling the cab, I asked, "Do you think Darling has something to do with her disappearance?" I didn't get that vibe, but Maxwell was the profiler.

"What's your gut tell you?" she asked.

*I didn't expect her to ask my opinion.* Or was she testing me, waiting for me to fuck up?

"I don't think so. He seems genuinely concerned, and I think he feels guilty for not realizing she was missing sooner." Not that he was to blame. I couldn't imagine many nineteen-year-olds giving their parents a play-by-play of their weekend plans.

Not that I'd know from experience. I was serving my country at nineteen, and the only time I spoke to my parents was when I had down time and a signal strong enough to call from a computer. Not exactly typical.

"Agreed." At least we agreed on something.

"Is that your gut talking or your degree?" It came out snarky, out of habit. But I really wanted to know which it was.

She barely turned her head when she looked at me. "Both."

"What'd you notice in the jewelry box?" I asked, remembering she'd spent a lot of time examining one of the small drawers before making a note.

"Wendy had a lot of costume jewelry crammed in the box, but the bottom drawer was empty. I don't know what it means yet, but it doesn't fit."

The idea didn't hoist a red flag for me like it did for Maxwell. "She could've been wearing whatever was in there."

"Maybe, but she'd crammed every other drawer without care. It doesn't make sense for one drawer to be empty."

"I'll have to take your word for it." I didn't own any jewelry besides my watch and dog tags, but Maxwell probably did.

She always wore the same diamond earrings and a watch, but no rings or bracelets, and only occasionally wore a necklace. Which fit her severe work style.

"Was anything else you saw useful?"

"Not really. So far, she seems like a typical nineteen-year-old living at home. Because most kids live in the digital world, I won't know any more until I look through her phone and laptop."

What she didn't say, what neither of us was saying, was that from what we'd seen so far, it looked like Wendy went out with the mysterious Mr. R. and never came home.

The question of the hour was, did Wendy choose not to come home or did someone decide for her?

I hated that we still had more questions than answers.

We couldn't ignore the possibility Wendy had left this life behind and run away with Mr. R. If he lavished her with gifts, an assumption I made based on Maxwell's cell phone theory, then he may have promised her an easy life.

"Do you think she ran away with her mystery guy?"

She thought about it a good minute before answering. "Maybe. But I don't have a good feeling about it."

When she didn't continue, I asked, "Care to elaborate?"

"What would you pack to run away?" she asked instead of answering.

*Great, another test.*

"Clothes, wallet, phone, laptop–"

She cut me off, "Exactly. Wendy left her phone, makeup case and laptop. And Mr. R giving her a cell phone is a controlling move."

I was afraid she'd say that. We might not have a lot to go on, but my gut was telling me something had gone wrong and Wendy was in trouble.

# Chapter 8

## Cate

Back at the office, I asked Jay to look up the address he'd found in the trash and do some online digging while I went through Wendy's phone.

I completely lost track of time as I read through dozens of text threads and hundreds of emails. Wendy had been socially active until about six weeks ago, when she slowly faded away from her friends before disappearing altogether.

"Sheppard."

"Yeah?"

"Did Darling say anything about Wendy quitting her job?"

"No, I would've mentioned it." He sounded offended.

"I was afraid you'd say that. According to one of her friends, she quit last week. All communication from Wendy stopped Thursday night, at least on this phone."

I went back to reading the texts, forming a time line as I did.

Jaden stood up and stretched loudly, breaking my concentration.

"Must you do that?"

"Do what?" he asked. His lop-sided grin reminding me of his father and brothers.

"Make so much noise?" I couldn't hide my irritation.

"Whatever. I'm getting lunch. Unless that's a problem, too?"

It wasn't. In fact, it was a blessing.

"It's not."

I'd brought leftovers, so I warmed them up in the employee kitchen and ate at my desk while I checked Wendy's call log and listened to her voicemails. Making a list of any number not listed in her contacts for Jaden to research when he got back.

A glance at my watch told me he'd be back soon.

Wendy's voicemails didn't have anything to help find her, but a friend had left several messages. The messages made it seem like this wasn't the first time Wendy had ignored her friends for a day or two (her friend's words, not mine).

I had just opened Wendy's laptop when Jaden's voice disrupted my train of thought. He was talking to Meg from our doorway.

*Seriously? He can't stand by her desk like a normal person?*

"Thanks, Meg."

When he came into the room, he asked, "Have you moved at all since I left?"

I held up my bowl. "I warmed up my lunch."

"But you ate at your desk."

"What do you care?"

"I don't. I guess I just forgot I work with a robot."

*Don't let him get to you. Don't argue with your boss's son.*

I mumbled, "I'm not a robot," as I straightened the stack of papers on my desk. Was it a crime to like my desk neat and organized?

"You know you don't get a gold star or extra credit for working yourself to death, right?"

"Yes, Jaden, I do. But unlike you, I'd like to find Wendy sooner rather than later."

He didn't have to say it; the fuck you was written all over his face.

Accusing him like that wasn't fair, but at least it put an end to his bullshit.

"Did you at least find anything useful?" he asked.

"No, but I have a list of recurring numbers from her call log that aren't in her contacts. Could you look them up when you get a chance?"

He walked over and held out his hand. "Sure."

He looked up the numbers as soon as he sat down.

"Dead end. They belong to restaurants."

"Hmm." It made sense for the outgoing calls, but not so much for the incoming ones. Unless she knew someone who worked there.

But if that were the case, wouldn't they use their cell phone? How often did a restaurant call to confirm an order or a reservation?

I rarely ate out, so I didn't know.

I gave up trying to guess Wendy's laptop password and messaged Doug, asking him to help us when he got back to the office.

"Let's piece together a timeline," I said, standing and walking to the large whiteboard I'd hung on the wall. Jaden had made some snarky comments about joining the twenty-first century when he first moved into the office, but seeing things mapped out helped me, so I'd kept it.

I drew a time line along the top and started filling it in while I waited for Jaden to gather his sloppy notes. *How he gets anything done, I'll never know.*

I left room at the far left for anything on social media that predated the texts. "Can you start with the oldest, please?"

"Ten weeks ago, she posted from a party that she was single again."

That coincided with the information we had about her breakup with Bill.

"The following week, Wednesday, she posted, and I quote, I met the most amazing man. Not only is he gorgeous, but he's charming and sophisticated, end quote. She didn't use his name, and she never mentions him again."

It wasn't much, but the words charming and sophisticated were pretty telling when being used by a teenaged waitress.

"Did you happen to look into her last boyfriend?" I asked. It wasn't necessarily something a new PI would think to do because Bill wasn't a person of interest.

"I did. He's a college freshman living the frat-boy dream. His posts are mostly about parties, and after a few posts about getting dumped, he started playing the field."

"So neither charming nor sophisticated."

"No." He laughed. "I found a picture that might be Mr. R." The picture he handed me wasn't the best quality.

"I asked Doug to clean it up."

"Good," I said absentmindedly, while sticking the picture to the whiteboard with a magnet.

It looked like they were at a college party, based on the decor and the few guests I could see. Wendy and the unidentified man were in the background. She faced the camera, but he was looking to the side. We had more than a profile but less than a full face. The image was too dark and grainy to get a read on his expression, but his body seemed stiff. Wendy, on the other hand, looked relaxed. Probably a combination of the party being held by her friends and a healthy dose of alcohol. They both held beer bottles.

If Doug could clean it up, we might get some hits with facial recognition.

I crossed my arms as I stared at the picture. "He fits the profile, scant as it is. Suit, gold watch, slicked back hair, stiff demeanor," I mumbled to myself.

"What was that?"

Lost in the puzzle, I'd forgotten Jaden was standing there. "Sorry, just thinking out loud." I repeated what I'd said, filling in the gaps, so he'd know the character profile I was building.

"Possessive asshole or fucktard groomer?" he asked with a lift of his chin.

I laughed. He'd nailed the two directions I was leaning in the least professional way possible.

"I'm not sure."

Both would be on their best and most charming behavior in the beginning. Both would lavish her with compliments and attention. Neither would reveal their true personalities or intentions until it was too late.

Zeroing in on Wendy's neck, I remembered the empty jewelry drawer.

I looked closer at the picture. "When was this taken?"

"Three weeks ago. Why?" They'd only been dating six weeks.

"I didn't see that necklace," I pointed, "when I was in her room."

"It's not like you were looking for it."

"No, but I'd remember it." The stone-studded chandelier necklace in question stood out from the others.

"Right, like you could remember every detail." I could have done without his sarcasm.

Taking a deep breath, I refused to take the bait. Keeping my tone neutral, I said, "My point is, I doubt she bought it for herself."

"Maybe it's fake," he argued.

"Fair point, but she had nothing else like it. And that necklace," I pointed at it, "would fill the empty drawer."

We finished filling in the pieces with minimal arguments. *I don't know why Jaden takes pleasure in riling me up, but I refuse to give him the satisfaction.*

Over the last eight weeks, Wendy had slowly faded away from her former life.

We compiled a list of people to question and messaged Doug, asking him to pull the GPS history from Wendy's phone. It was possible she'd carried it while she was with Mr. R, even if only in the beginning. If we could ID a few places they'd gone, we might get a better photo or our mystery man. I crossed my arms, tapping my fingers as I stared at our notes, trying to connect the dots. There was something I was missing, something that was probably staring me right in the face.

*But I can't see it.*

"Catie!" Anger welled up at Jaden's use of the nickname I hated with every cell of my being. He knew, like everyone at SSI, that I preferred they use my last name. And I wouldn't have reacted so strongly if he'd used Catelyn.

Spinning, I barked, "Don't." I fisted my hands to channel the anger.

"Don't what? Call you Catie?" He said it again, his eyes sparkling with mischief, just to piss me off.

*Don't let him get to you.* Through clenched teeth, I said, "Do not call me that." Only two people had ever called me Catie. My mom, before she left us, and Gavin Nielson, when we were dating.

*Before he fucked me over and destroyed my career.*

# Chapter 9

## Jay

I'd struck a nerve when I called her Catie. Not that I could have known she didn't like it. I was simply trying to get her attention. But the daredevil in me enjoyed pushing her buttons, so seeing the anger flair in her intense blue eyes was all the encouragement I needed to pour gas on the fire.

"Aw, why not? Don't you like it?" I teased.

Refusing to take the bait, she turned her back on me. Her perfect, tight bun, so unlike my unruly wavy brown hair, taunted me.

I should've let it go, but I was itching for a fight and knew Maxwell could hold her own in a verbal match. *Hell, she'll probably wipe the floor with me.* Which was part of the problem; I was tired of her, and everyone at SSI, treating me like I was stupid.

Just because the state of Texas required a year of on-the-job-training didn't mean I didn't have experience.

I might not have a fancy degree, but I'd spent years in some of the worst hellholes imaginable. Environments where misreading body language or missing a clue resulted in death. Being observant was literally a matter of life and death.

I stepped up behind her, easily seeing over the top of her five-foot-seven head, and laughed. "What's the matter Catie Cat, cat got–"

Before I had time to react, she spun and swung, landing a solid right cross to my jaw. The familiar taste of copper coated my tongue.

*Holy shit. She just fucking hit me.* Little Miss I-never-break-the-fucking-rules just hauled off and punched me.

Unable to help myself, I grinned. When I wiped the side of my mouth, my hand came away wet with blood.

Then I did the dumbest thing I could've done and laughed.

This time, I was ready when she swung. Grabbing her right wrist, I stepped behind her and twisted it behind her back.

"Let go of me!" she yelled, swinging her left fist.

I pulled her close to my chest so she couldn't turn and use her left fist against me. I'd egged her on and deserved the punch, but that didn't mean I'd let her keep striking.

She answered with her left elbow.

Strong and fueled by a fuck ton of hatred, her elbow did some damage. Not broken rib damage, but I'd have a bruise. Reminders of the day I'd crossed the line and made my partner lose her shit. I grabbed her other wrist and wrapped her in a bear hug. *Holy shit, she smells good, like strawberries and champagne.*

As irrational as it was, her smelling good pissed me off. Instead of apologizing and putting an end to the madness, I said, "You only get one freebie, Catie Cat. After that, I fight back." I wouldn't. Not really. But I was more than capable, and willing, to restrain her so she couldn't hit me again.

She went perfectly still. I should've sensed the calm before the storm, but I was too busy gloating.

Maxwell corrected my misperception by head-butting me, making my head snap back. *She might drive me crazy, but I had to respect her determination.* I was still off balance when she hooked her foot around the inside of my ankle, yanking my leg out from under me.

*Impressive.* Before I could put my foot back down, she hooked the other ankle.

*Very impressive.* Reacting instinctively, I tightened my grip as I fell to make sure I landed on my back, ensuring I'd cushion her fall.

When we landed, I slammed into her trashcan and sent it crashing across the room.

Maxwell elbowed me as soon as I released her hands.

We thrashed on the floor, each trying to get up but getting caught on the other.

"ENOUGH!" My father's voice echoed through the room.

I pulled away from Maxwell and stood up. It'd be a miracle if he didn't fire us. *No, just me. I won't let him fire Maxwell because of my stupidity.*

Maxwell stood right beside me.

Neither of us made eye contact.

"What the hell is going on in here?" he demanded.

I doubted Maxwell had ever heard that particular question from my father, but I had. Which meant I knew it was rhetorical, and it was best not to answer right away.

And under no circumstances should you defend yourself or blame the other person.

At first, neither of us spoke. We stood at attention, arms rigid by our sides, our focus straight ahead but not making eye contact with my father. At least I assumed she'd also reverted to what they'd taught us in boot camp.

My father waited in the doorway, arms crossed and a scowl on his face.

Maxwell gave in first. She lifted her head and squared her shoulders. "I'm sorry, sir. I lost my temper and hit Jaden. I was out of line."

"Is that true, Sheppard?" Hearing my father call me Sheppard solidified just how much trouble I was in. Shadows moved beyond my father's shoulders. *Great, just what I need, an audience.*

Something I said sent her way over the edge. If I'd known that'd happen, I would've backed down. It was fun pushing Maxwell's buttons, riling her up, but I didn't want to get her in trouble.

Following Maxwell's lead, I made direct eye contact. "Partially, sir, I pushed her buttons relentlessly, trying to make her act out. I deserved the hit."

Her head whipped about forty-five degrees before she recovered from the shock and turned forward again.

*I'm not the asshole you think I am.*

"Give me one good reason I shouldn't suspend both of you right now."

I didn't hesitate to answer, "Because Maxwell is the best chance we have for finding Wendy."

Dad asked, "Maxwell?"

"Because Sheppard's intuition and insights are invaluable. The case will suffer if you pull him from it."

It was my turn to be shocked.

We waited while my father stared at us, deciding what to do. I relied on my training to keep my muscles from twitching at the discomfort of being in his crosshairs.

"Consider this your first, and only, warning. If I so much as see one of you give the other a dirty look, I'll suspend you both."

"Yes, sir." We answered in unison. *The Marines trained us well.*

"Clean this place up." He looked at his watch. "I want you both in my office in an hour with an update."

"Yes, sir." We waited for him to leave before moving.

Dad turned around and yelled, "Get back to work, all of you!"

If it weren't for the sound of the trash clinking as we tossed it in the bin, you could have heard a pin drop in our office.

Before getting back to work, I washed my face with the water from my bottle. There was no way in hell I'd risk leaving the office and having to face my brothers after what had just happened.

The side of my mouth was tender where she'd split my lip.

If I wasn't worried about starting another fight, I might have complimented her on throwing a hell of a punch.

Out of the corner of my eye, I saw her stretching her right hand. It hurt like hell to punch someone and her hand would swell before long, but she didn't need me telling her that.

I typed up my notes, creating a timeline with links and photos, and emailed them to Maxwell.

"Thank you." My mail icon alerted me to an incoming message. "I'll combine these tonight and we-"

Her phone alarm went off. Because, of course, she set an alarm for ten minutes before we had to be in my father's office.

Her printer whirred to life and started spitting out pages.

I'd thought she was crazy when I realized she'd bought a printer for her office when the company had a fancy one for everyone to use. When I'd asked her why, she explained it made her life easier and kept her from losing her train of thought while she worked.

After sharing an office with her for eight weeks, I could see the benefit. I'd never dared to use it, but for the first time, I was grateful she had it. If she'd had to wait for the shared printer, she might be late.

No. We might be late; because, like it or not, we were a team.

And I wasn't about to fuck up twice in one day.

*Everything she does makes sense, in hindsight.*

"Ready?" she asked as she grabbed the papers and put them in an orange file folder. Everything about this case was color-coded orange. Post-it notes, highlighters, folders.

Catelyn Maxwell was one well-organized, extremely efficient pain in my ass.

I knocked on my father's closed door two minutes before our scheduled time.

Jamie opened it and moved off to our right. Jack leaned against the filing cabinets to our left.

*Great, do they think we need chaperones for the meeting*? Or were we about to get three versions of a lecture?

"Have a seat," my father said.

Our asses hit our seats at the same time; we held the same 'at attention' postures and neutral facial expressions.

"We're going to have a little chat before you give us your updates." Dad leaned forward on his desk and folded his hands together.

We gave identical micro nods.

"Your little display earlier was unacceptable."

"Yes, sir," we answered together.

"We know there's tension between you, but this." He shook his head. "I'm disappointed in you." He said it to both of us, but I knew it was directed at me. The family mistake. I'd bet my left lung Jamie and Jack had never gotten into a fistfight in the office.

"Sorry, sir." For two people who couldn't stand each other, we were shockingly in sync. The Marine in us wouldn't let us hang our heads in shame, but it was obvious we both felt it.

"It surprised me to hear you defend each other," my father said, leaning back.

Jamie picked up where Dad left off. "It gives up hope the two of you can sort out your shit and work together like mature adults." Just because I deserved the less-than-subtle insult, didn't mean it didn't hurt.

I had every intention of being a mature adult when I returned home and took the job at SSI. *So what the hell happened?*

I had to share an office with an intelligent, red-headed perfectionist who drove me crazy. The way she never had a hair out of place. The way she straightened her desk every time she left the office. The way she tapped her pen on her chin when she was concentrating.

The way I felt when I was near her. Like I'd never be good enough.

"We need to know if we can trust you to work together without creating a mess and destroying the company's reputation," Jack added his two cents.

"You tell us, do we need to reassign the case?" Dad asked.

Neither of us rushed to speak. I didn't know if they'd see it as a good sign or a bad one, but I took a moment to think before answering.

*Could we?* I wasn't so sure. Maxwell was brilliant, but everything about her rubbed me the wrong way.

# Chapter 10

## Cate

Could I work with Jaden Sheppard? That was the million-dollar question. He was smart and insightful, but he had a chip on his shoulder and seemed hell bent on taking his frustrations out on me.

*I still can't believe I punched him.*

My unprofessional behavior was inexcusable. I believed myself to be a better person, one capable of handling workplace bullshit.

All that time taking shit from the jarheads in the Marines. All that time taking shit from the frat boys in the FBI. And not once had I lost control and hauled off and hit someone.

Not even when Gavin started the rumor that I purred during sex and convinced everyone to call me Catie Cat. Not when printouts of raunchy memes, with Catie Cat written in marker, started showing up on my desk and around the office.

Reporting Gavin was out of the question, and I couldn't prove anything, anyway. *Going to HR would have made things much worse.* I learned a lot of things during my time with the FBI, the most important being—never date a co-worker.

I was already looking for another job when Jones asked me to consult on a missing child case in Weatherford. When I first met the SSI team, I thought they were a little rough around the edges, but they gave off strong family vibes. *And not just because it's a family business.*

When I saw they were hiring, I didn't hesitate to apply. I had zero regrets about leaving the FBI.

Until today.

*Hell no. I'm not giving up another good job because some asshole can't handle working with a woman.*

"Sir, what happened today was a mistake." No excuses, no explanations, just owning my shit. "And it won't happen again." I made eye contact with each of my bosses. "If you give us a second chance, I believe we can work together and find Wendy." I refused to say bring her home, because none of us could guarantee that.

They nodded. Then John asked, "Jaden?"

After Jaden echoed my sentiments, we updated John on the case. Afterwards, he told us to go home, making it clear it was an order, not a suggestion.

Since I couldn't stay at the office, I took a picture of the whiteboard and packed up my notes so I could work from home. But first, I had to blow off some steam.

Once my phone connected to the car's speaker, I called my coach, Brian.

"Hey Cate, how's it going?"

"It's been a day. You available tonight?"

He mumbled about wanting to get home early.

"I'll double your hourly fee," I offered.

"That bad, huh?"

*You have no idea.* "Yeah. What do you say?"

"I'll see you in the ring at seven."

"Thanks, Brian. I appreciate it."

An hour in the ring with Coach Brian was just what I needed. I'd get in a workout, hone my boxing skills, and work off my anger. My right hand would suffer for it, but at that moment, I didn't care.

I got to the gym early to warm up. After five minutes on a treadmill, I wrapped my hands and put on my favorite gloves; the Marine logo faded from use. I put in my earbuds, pulled up my workout playlist, and faced off against the bag.

I let the upbeat tempo of the music set my rhythm as I set the bag swinging with punch after punch.

By the time Brian showed up, I was dripping in sweat.

I worked harder than I should've, knowing I had an hour with my coach, a two-time, lightweight national champion.

"Thanks for meeting me," I said as he wrapped his hands.

"No problem. Want to talk about it?"

"No, I want to hit shit," I said with a laugh. My hand was already throbbing, so I took two ibuprofen, knowing I'd need more later while I iced it. *I've boxed through worse pain.*

I'd been boxing most of my life. I was a hurt, angry five-year-old after my mother left us, and my father thought it'd be a good way for me to channel my aggression.

He was right. I thought about quitting as a teen, but boxing brought me closer to him, so I stuck with it, boxing through high school, college, and the Marines.

Brian started off slow with basic drills: blocking, high and low. Each block followed by a three-punch combo.

Before long, he called out longer, more complex combinations, testing my speed, accuracy, and concentration. I messed up more than once, but understanding my need to go fast and hard on the pads, he never slowed down.

He called out strikes, "Jab, jab, uppercut." I slipped right and left. "Three, two, three." I slipped and landed two body shots to his padded body protector before rolling under his hook. "Cross, hook, cross." I landed the last punch with a solid thud.

After twenty minutes, I asked him to take off the pads and glove up so we could spar. I didn't stand a snowball's chance in hell of beating him, but the workout would drain the last of my frustration.

At first, he went easy on me and I held my own. Slipping out of the way of jabs and crosses, returning blows, rolling under hooks, and connecting with my elbows.

But Brian was fast and was soon dancing circles around me. The fight turned one-sided as fatigue got the best of me and all I could do was duck and block.

Brian stepped back and dropped his hands, signaling the match was over.

"Nice effort." He held his glove up for a fist-pump. "You good?" he asked with a laugh. He'd just kicked my ass without breaking a sweat. Meanwhile, I was bent over, panting like a dog left in a car on a hot day.

"Yeah. That was exactly what I needed," I said, wiping sweat from my forehead with my equally sweaty forearm. "Thanks."

"Glad I could help."

We chatted for a few minutes while we chugged water and cooled down. It wasn't always easy finding a new coach, but I lucked out finding Brian when I moved to Weatherford. He was a good guy and a great coach. And he'd hooked me up with a friend of his when I wanted to add Brazilian Jiu Jitsu, or BJJ, to my training schedule.

"Our normal time Saturday?" he asked as we packed up.

"Yeah." I held my fist up. "Thanks again, Bri. I owe you one."

"You owe me double, but who's counting?" he laughed, knowing I was good for it.

"Cash okay?" He'd bill me for the hour at the gym, so I only owed him for the extra amount.

"Cash is always okay."

On the way home, I grabbed a salad with extra chicken so I wouldn't have to cook. That way, I could start working right after my shower.

Combining our notes into a coherent document was easier than I expected, thanks to Jaden's notes being clear, concise, and neatly organized.

Nothing like the chaos of his hand-written notes.

I quit researching around midnight. Before crawling into bed, I put eye drops in my tired eyes to soothe them and reminded myself that tomorrow would be a fresh start.

*And come hell or high water, I won't let Jaden Sheppard get to me ever again.*

# Chapter 11

## Jay

I declined Emily's offer for dinner, earning an undeserved scowl from Jamie. My answer was polite and appreciative, so I figured it had more to do with me depriving him of an opportunity to lecture me than being rude to his fiancée.

"It smells delicious." I asked, "Can you save me some leftovers?"

"Of course." Emily was all smiles. She was good for Jamie, her love helping him heal after the devastating loss of his first wife.

Jamie was born to be a family man, so getting a second chance at love was exactly what he needed. Emily, too. Her abusive ex was six feet under after being dumb enough to point a gun at Dad.

Dude got what he deserved. *Karma's a bitch.*

I wondered if karma would serve my ex-girlfriend, Sara, and my ex-best friend, Henderson, what they deserved. I hoped so.

*I need to burn off some energy.* I changed into my running clothes, put on my weighted vest, and ran until everything hurt.

The run was supposed to be therapeutic, clearing my mind of the memories of Sara's betrayal and my fight with Maxwell.

Instead, I couldn't stop thinking about how incredibly fucking sexy Maxwell looked when she was angry. Or how she accepted full responsibility for our scuffle and defended me when given the chance. She may have done it to save face, given the circumstances, but I didn't think so. Maxwell was a lot of things, but I'd never seen her kiss ass or lie.

I wasn't proud of myself for pushing her that far, but I couldn't deny how much I enjoyed watching her lose control. Or how my body reacted to having her in my arms, the scent of her sweet strawberry shampoo filling my nose. Even if she was only there so I could prevent her from hitting me again.

*I bet she's a hellcat in bed.*

Oh, hell no! No way was I letting my mind wander down that path. Maxwell and I were like fire and ice, bring us together and we'd destroy each other.

Ignoring the pain, knowing I deserved it, I pushed myself harder, running until my stomach threatened to purge it contents.

Still ashamed and not ready to deal with Jamie's disappointed big brother attitude, I showered in record time and ducked out to go to a bar for dinner and a beer. *Great, now I'm acting like a coward.*

I was half done with my burger and had just ordered my second beer when a Quick Wash commercial caught my attention, triggering the memory of the business card on Darling's refrigerator. One I hadn't given a second thought. Until now.

A piece of the puzzle snapped into place. What middle-class mechanic used a laundry service?

Maybe it was Wendy's? Which made even less sense. I know my perception of nineteen-year-olds was skewed because I was in the military, but I didn't think teenaged waitresses used laundry services.

I pulled out my phone and looked it up. The longer I stared at their website, the more convinced I was that something was hinky.

I chugged the last of my beer, paid my bill, and raced home.

Searching the company's website would be easier on my laptop. At first glance it seemed typical; they had industrial sized do-it-yourself machines, drop off wash and fold services, and same-day dry cleaning.

Something nagged at me as I clicked through the images, but I couldn't put my finger on it. Leaning back in the chair, I stretched with a giant yawn.

"What are you working on?" Jamie asked from behind me.

"Darling case. A commercial I saw triggered a memory." I pointed at my screen. "He had a Quick Wash laundry service business card on his fridge, which doesn't fit with what we know about him. I think there may be a connection to Wendy's disappearance, but I can't put it together."

"What's your gut say?" he asked as he leaned over my shoulder to read my screen.

"It's connected." *Even if I can't tie it together yet.*

"Walk me through it."

Not knowing if he'd read our full report, I summed it up. Because the report only contained the facts, I added my observations and impressions along the way.

My eyes kept going back to the address on the webpage, because I was so engrossed I didn't hear Jamie's question.

"That's it!" I pointed at the address on the screen as it clicked together.

I pulled up the photo of the slip of paper we found in Wendy's trash.

"I couldn't find the address earlier when I searched because it's off by a digit. But there's no way it's a coincidence." The address on the slip of paper had a suite number that didn't exist, at least not in Fort Worth.

"In our line of work, there's no such thing as a coincidence. Talk to Maxwell tomorrow and figure out your next steps," Jamie said. "Good catch."

"Thanks." For the first time in a long time, there was no sarcasm in my voice.

When my toothbrush rubbed the cut on the inside of my cheek, I winced. Then I smiled. *Maxwell throws a mean punch.*

The thought of getting punched by a co-worker shouldn't have turned me on, but it did.

How the hell was I supposed to work the case when my partner pissed me off as much as she turned me on? *Or does she turn me on as much as she pisses me off?*

It didn't matter. I had to figure out a way to ignore her attitude, and my suddenly intense physical attraction, so I could work with her. Her holier than thou attitude was a pretty good mood killer. *Maybe it won't be a problem.*

I also needed to apologize without starting a fight.

# Chapter 12

## Jay

Having discovered an important piece of information, possibly even a case breaker, I woke up Tuesday morning in a good mood. I left early enough to grab Grannie's coffee and treats for the office and still arrive before everyone else.

My first step towards making amends.

The rich scent of freshly brewed coffee brought back memories from high school. How many girls had I hit on from behind that counter? How many coffees had I given away before Mom caught on and started charging me?

I shook off the memory. That felt like a lifetime ago.

"Jay."

I turned towards my mom's voice. "Morning, Ma."

"Looks like you and Cate had the same idea."

*What the hell?* The smile melted from my face faster than chocolate on a sidewalk in the middle of July.

Maxwell walked out of the hall leading to the bathrooms, and just like that, my good mood deflated. When she saw me, anger flared in her eyes before she forced herself to smile.

"What's the matter?" My mom asked. There was no way in hell Dad hadn't mentioned my fuck up.

"Nothing," I grunted.

"Jay, come here." She led me to a booth at the far side of her coffee shop. "Sit."

I sat and stared at the dark wood tabletop.

"Is it really so bad you both want to make amends by buying coffee for the office?"

Classic Ma. She didn't ask if that was my plan or what had killed my smile. *She didn't have to.* All that time away and she could still read me like an open book.

"No, but-"

"No buts. You both made a mistake, and you both want to make amends. Neither of you had any malicious intent in coming here."

*Am I really so transparent?*

I nodded. "You're right."

She reached across the table and squeezed my hand. "Go figure out a compromise with Cate." Mom didn't like calling Maxwell by her last name, like we did at the office, claiming it sounded too stiff. Meg, Emily, Beth, and Blake used the shortened version, Max, but Ma didn't like that either, so she called Maxwell "Cate".

*I wonder what her friends call her. What about her boyfriends?*

Nope. It didn't matter, and it was none of my business.

"Yes, ma'am." I stood up and accepted her hug. I didn't feel close to my family, always feeling like the black sheep and believing I didn't measure up, but I'd never say no to one of my mom's hugs. "Thanks."

"Today's a fresh start. Now go."

"Hey, Maxwell. Great minds think alike, huh?" I put too much effort into sounding cheerful and ended up sounding deranged instead.

I took it as a good sign when she half-chuckled and said, "I guess they do."

*Look at us not fighting.* I got an image of us throwing down in my mother's coffee shop and broke out in a cold sweat. I'd take Dad threatening to fire me a thousand times over before intentionally doing something to incur the wrath of Mary Sheppard. Or worse, the disappointment.

Her verbal smack downs were legendary in our family. Having earned more in my teen years than my three siblings combined, I never wanted to be on the receiving end again. Of course, that was nothing compared to hearing her say, "I'm disappointed in you."

Those words shredded me every time I heard them.

Not that I'd stopped doing the stupid shit that earned them.

With any luck, this was the last time I'd do something stupid and have to see that look in her eye, or hear that tone in her voice.

"Any objection to me picking up apology muffins, since you beat me to the apology coffee?"

"No."

"What's your favorite?" I asked. It never hurt to extend a tasty olive branch.

"Cinnamon," she answered, lifting her hand to look at her phone.

Her right hand was swollen, and she had small cuts on her knuckles. Courtesy of my teeth.

"Morning, Beth. Can I have a dozen muffins, at least four blueberry and three cinnamon?"

"Coming right up."

Mom handed Maxwell her coffees. "See you at the office," Maxwell said as she headed for the door.

I nodded and paid Beth.

When my mother handed me the bag, she said, "Remember what I said; let go of yesterday and start fresh."

"Thanks, Ma. Bye, Beth."

Before the masses could ransack the bag, I made sure Meg and Maxwell got their choice of muffin.

Luckily, no one mentioned the previous day's fight. *Luck has nothing to do with it.* I could imagine the carefully crafted email my father sent, warning everyone to let it go. Otherwise, my split lip and Maxwell's swollen hand would have sparked good-natured ribbing.

Nothing like the black sheep of the family spinning out of control and living up to his team nickname, the Tasmanian Devil, and fucking shit up in the family business.

Back in our office, before we got down to business, Maxwell walked up to me and stuck out her hand. "Truce?"

I grasped her hand in mine, keeping the pressure light so I didn't hurt her swollen hand. But not so light she could accuse me of going easy on her. "Truce."

She nodded and turned, mumbling, "I won't lose another job because of another asshole."

*What the hell does that mean "another job"?* Had this happened before? And who was the other asshole? Did I have to go kill someone? What? No. Why would I even think that?

I was dying to know if Maxwell had hit a previous co-worker. Before this moment, I would have put all my money on no.

Remembering our truce, I bit my tongue and filed the information away for later.

# Chapter 13

## Cate

Of course, Jaden stopped by Grannie's to get coffee. At first, it pissed me off, which was completely irrational, but it wasn't the first time he'd pissed me off without trying.

Then I remembered he was the new guy, so it was his job to get the coffee. Getting coffee for everyone at the office was the SSI version of new-guy hazing. When they'd first told me, it pissed me off, thinking they were giving me shit for being a female, but that didn't last. AJ was the first person hazed, and everyone hired since had gone through it. When Meg told me about the SSI discount, and the office coffee fund she'd started, so newbies didn't go broke, I'd apologized for over-reacting and paid for the first round.

*Plus, it shouldn't surprise me we want to apologize the same way.*

Seeing Jaden with Mary was interesting; he seemed calmer. Not superficially; his whole demeanor changed as they talked.

Mrs. Sheppard had some mad mama bear skills. She'd dress you down for being stupid while confessing how worried she was. She'd tend your wounds while threatening to kill you if you ever got hurt again.

She loved her family with a fierceness that shocked me. Scared me a little too, because one of her cubs had it out for me. I didn't think she'd judge me based on Jaden's dislike of me, but if push came to shove, she'd kick me to the curb in a heartbeat. So would his father and brothers.

It didn't matter that Jaden wasn't as close to them as they were to each other. *I'd bet my next paycheck that bothers him.* They'd always have his back.

As they should.

*Who'll have mine?* Not for the first time, I felt lonely despite being part of a team. The only person truly on my side was Charlie, but she'd have a husband soon. And probably little ones soon after they got married. Eventually, she'd be too busy with her own family to keep up our Sunday morning video chats.

*Get out of your head and get back to work.*

"I found the address last night," Jaden said after he got settled in at his desk. "I'm sending my notes now."

"Why didn't you send them last night?" It wasn't fair to accuse him; he couldn't have known I was up late working.

"I knew if I did, you'd stay up late working." He shrugged, like it was no big deal he'd decided for my benefit.

*Busted.* I would've stayed up late following the new lead, or at the very least, updating our collective notes.

"Can you sum it up for me?"

He told me about the commercial tripping his memory, and how he connected the Quick Wash business card on Darling's refrigerator to our mystery address.

I pulled up the website while he explained, so I had a visual.

"I can't put my finger on it, but something's hinky." He'd walked over and stood behind me. The smell of his bourbon vanilla cologne reminded me that Jaden was all man. There was no denying his good looks or sex appeal. *Well, not until he opens his mouth.* His shitty attitude killed any chance I had of being attracted to him.

*Thank God for that.* I'd sworn off office romance forever.

I turned my focus back to the screen. Before I could ask, he told me he'd emailed Doug and asked him to look into the shop.

I shared his gut feeling, though I wouldn't have called it hinky.

"We should talk to Darling again, see what he knows," Jaden suggested.

"I agree, but he's at work. We can pay a visit later if you don't have plans."

"I'm free."

I nodded, a plan forming. "How do you feel about having the Quick Wash in Fort Worth clean your clothes?"

"Why mine?"

My father's voice popped into my head: A good leader never asks someone to do something they aren't willing to do themselves. He was right; it wasn't fair of me to volunteer Jaden's clothes if I wouldn't volunteer my own.

"Sorry, that wasn't fair. Let's go to the thrift store. We'll buy a bunch of clothes and take them in to be cleaned."

"Sounds like a plan," he said, returning to his desk to grab his coffee and muffin.

"You can't eat that in my car."

"No, but I can eat it in my truck."

Why did men always insist on driving?

Reminding myself of the truce, I grabbed my laptop. "Fine. Let's go."

On our way out, I stopped by the office Doug shared with AJ. Their office looked like ours; two desks shared the space with seats for clients in front of them, two lockers sat in the back corners, and filing cabinets lined the back wall between them.

The main difference between our rooms was the whiteboard and printer I'd added to ours, and the extra computer gear Doug needed as our tech guy.

"I'm good, Maxwell, but not that good," Doug answered my knock on the frame.

I laughed with him. "We're checking out the cleaners. Call us if something pops up."

"Will do."

When we got to Fort Worth, Jaden drove through the cleaner's strip plaza so I could take video footage. One end housed a liquor/convenience store, the other a Chinese restaurant. In the middle was the Quick Wash, surrounded by two smaller boarded-up shops.

*Interesting.* I made a note to research the history of the shops.

"Those spaces were occupied on the cleaner's website," Jaden said, confirming my suspicion that it was worth noting. "One was a nail salon, the other an insurance office."

"We'll look into the previous tenants later."

"First impressions?" he asked.

"There's more to see here." My gut screamed that it was all related, but the pieces didn't fit yet.

"Agreed." Jaden parked at the far corner, on the end near the convenience store, giving us a chance to observe the area as we walked across the parking lot. We strolled down the sidewalk, in front of the empty store, to the cleaner's door.

"Remember, we're friends and you're helping me move," I said before we reached the door. "And let me do the talking."

He bit back what I could only guess was a snarky reply before saying, "Yes, ma'am," and opening the door for me. "After you."

*God, I hate it when he calls me that.* I plastered a smile on my face as I walked by.

"Good afternoon." The clerk looked us up and down through the plexiglass window separating him from the rest of the store. "How can I help you?"

His lingering gaze on my breasts made my skin crawl. So much so I changed the game plan.

"Hi. My husband and I are new to the area, and the washing machine in our new place doesn't work. We saw your flyer at the store and want to ask about your services."

Jaden and I had changed out of our work clothes, a pantsuit for me, a habit from the FBI I was still trying to shake, and a polo and khakis for Jaden. Our jeans and t-shirts making us look more like people in the middle of moving than two PIs.

He ignored Jaden as his eyes roamed over my body, forcing me to hold back a shudder. "Ask away," he said.

"I saw on the website that you offer same day services, but I didn't see any prices listed."

Jaden walked over to a corkboard on the wall and checked out the notices.

"Hey Babe, looks like there are some good restaurants in the area," he called over. I assumed his use of the pet name meant he was on board with my change to our cover story.

I smiled and turned my attention back to the clerk, taking the flyer he handed me through the cutout in the plexiglass. *Is it bulletproof?*

I rolled my eyes, earning a smile from the clerk. "Thanks, Hon."

Behind the clerk was an open office door, but I couldn't see anyone.

"Do you want those washed?" the clerk asked, pointing to the bag of clothes we'd bought on our way here.

The prices listed seemed high, but then I'd never had a service wash my clothes. Except for dry cleaning my uniform, and I always had that done on base.

I nodded and asked, "How long will it take?"

"I can have them done today." His eyes roamed my body. "For an extra fee."

I repressed the shiver of disgust. *God, I need a shower.*

"That won't be necessary." I gave him my biggest smile. "I'm sure it's more than we can afford." I looked around.

"Let's just use the machines," Jaden said from the back of the room. He rested his strong, tatted forearms on the top of a large washer.

"We don't really have time," I said. I bit my lower lip and made a big show of contemplating our options.

"Tell you what, I'm feeling generous today so I'll give you a new customer discount; twenty percent off."

I didn't have to fake it, as my eyes widened in surprise. He had to be high on the food chain to off such a large discount.

"Really? That'd be great. I wasn't expecting to replace an appliance so soon after moving. And of course, it's the washing machine, so I have to pay for cleaning now, too." I added a hint of hysteria to my voice. "I haven't even unpacked yet."

"It's the least I can do for a new neighbor. What'd you say your name is?"

"Charlie." I made like I'd shake his hand, but the glass was in the way. "Charlie Bishop." I chose my best friend's first name and her soon-to-be last name.

"I'll come around, Charlie," he said, getting up and walking to the door. Jaden was in the perfect position to see inside the office from where he pretended to read a poster.

"I'm Adam. Adam Parker," he extended his hand. The watch on his right wrist was either the real deal, or it was doing a great impression of a Rolex. *Maybe he's the owner?* That would explain the overly generous discount.

"It's nice to meet you. You have no idea how much I appreciate your generosity." I left my 'husband' out of my answers, knowing it never hurt to play up the flirty female card.

"Here, let me take those." He held his hand out for the clothes.

Openly flirting with my fake husband in the room wasn't a good idea, but a few bashful glances might serve us well. A guy like Adam wouldn't care about my marriage vows if he thought I'd sleep with him. I repressed my shiver and focused on the job.

I looked up at him through my eyelashes. "Thank you."

"I'll put these in the back and get you the customer form."

"Okay, thanks."

I walked over to Jaden and pointed at a flyer. Without moving my lips, I whispered, "You get all that?"

He nodded, then said louder, "Let me snap a picture so we don't have to take the flyer."

"Ms. Bishop," Adam called out, subtly ignoring my married status and confirming my suspicions.

I ignored Adam's slip up, took the form, and asked, "Will cash be okay?"

He pointed to a metal sign above his window with a greasy smile.

Cash is King.

And a PI's best friend. Or worst enemy, depending on who was using it.

I handed him the form, the address and phone number sections blank, and a twenty.

"Can I pay the balance when I pick up my order?"

His sleazy smile widened. "Of course. I'll have your clothes ready by five. It's a pleasure doing business with you, Ms. Bishop."

"It's Mrs." Jaden half-growled as he walked over to stand beside me. Playing the jealous husband, he placed his left hand on my lower back and stuck out his right hand. "I'm Henry Bishop."

"Right, my apologies. I use Miss as a general nicety."

*Sure you do.*

"Oh, it's okay. He gets grumpy when he's hungry," I said, patting Jaden's rock hard abs.

# Chapter 14

## Jay

"Let's check out the Chinese restaurant while we're here," I suggested while forcing myself not to react to Maxwell's warm hand on my stomach. Even through my t-shirt, it sent a zing to all the wrong places. It didn't help that her tight jeans showed off her perfect ass and her low-cut t-shirt did nothing to hide her impressive cleavage. Her shirt was almost the same shade of blue as her eyes, and accented her fiery red hair. She'd replaced her usual strict bun with a high ponytail that bounced as she walked.

It practically begged me to wrap it around my hands and pull her head back. *Nope. Not going there.* Maxwell might be hot, but she'd probably lecture me on my kissing form or some other stupid shit, killing any and all desire.

"Okay. Thank you again for all your help, Adam. I really appreciate it," Maxwell said.

"My pleasure. I'll see you in a few hours," Adam said while smiling at 'my wife' and ignoring me. His actions shouldn't have invoked anger or jealousy.

But they did.

We left and walked to the restaurant in silence. I played my part and put my hand on the small of her back. She played her part and didn't threaten to break the offending appendage. Judging from the tension in her muscles and the clench in her jaw, she wanted to break more than my hand.

I smiled, wondering how far I could go before she hit me again.

*Don't be stupid, Sheppard.*

Not wanting to push my luck, risk losing my job, or disappointing my family, I dropped my hand before opening the door.

The restaurant looked more upscale than I'd expected. The interior was dimly lit; there were colorful murals on the walls, and dark wood chairs surrounding tables covered in contrasting white tablecloths.

"How many?" the hostess asked.

"Two, please," I answered. "A corner booth, if that's okay." I nodded to the far side of the restaurant.

She nodded as she grabbed two menus. "This way."

We sat close to each other on the curved bench, giving us both an unimpeded view of the restaurant.

"I hope you like Chinese," Maxwell said.

Did I detect a note of teasing?

"I'll eat just about anything." It wasn't a lie, and I was always hungry.

After we ordered an appetizer platter, lo mein with chicken for Maxwell, and a Kung Pao Chicken for me, Maxwell got up to use the restroom. On her way back, she took her time looking over the ads and notices on the bulletin board.

"What caught your eye?" I asked after she sat back down.

"Another restaurant to try," she answered as she showed me the image.

The business card she'd snapped a photo of was odd in its ambiguity, but the image reminded me of a flyer I saw in the Quick Wash. I pulled up the photo I'd snapped.

"What do you think they're hiding?" she whispered, her eyes darting between the two images. Our server brought our appetizers, so we put our phones away and played at being a married couple who still needed to unpack while we ate. I thought the egg rolls were good, not Michelin Star good, but better than average. Maxwell disagreed.

After polishing off more than my fair share of the appetizers, at Maxwell's insistence, I visited the men's room, stopping to examine the bulletin board on my way out.

I paid cash for lunch so we didn't leave a paper trail, and carried our leftovers as we walked back to my truck.

Deciding we 'needed' gum, we ducked into the liquor store to see what we could see.

A flyer, like the one in the cleaners, was taped to the window.

Back in the truck, I asked, "Do you think they're all involved in something shady? Or are they just being neighborly by hanging the flyers?"

"That's one of the many questions we need to answer," she said.

"Why the attitude?"

"What attitude? All I did was answer your question."

"As condescendingly as possible."

"Christ, Jaden, get over yourself," she huffed. "I don't know the answer and was thinking out loud. Not attacking you."

"You could have said that."

"Shall I preface every comment with whether or not I'm trying to insult you?"

"Fucking smart ass," I mumbled.

"Better than being a dumb ass." She turned and cleared her throat to get my attention. I instantly regretted it when I made eye contact. The glint in her eye and the wicked smile on her lips terrified me. "That was a general statement, a typical response to being called a smart ass, not a direct statement directed at you."

"Thank you," I said, hating that I couldn't think of a snappy comeback. Much to my surprise, my bland thank you took the wind from her sails.

"Can you drive around back?" Maxwell asked.

Just like that, we were back to business.

"Yeah. Was it just me, or did the interior of the laundromat seem too short?"

"I noticed, too, but didn't see any doors. Did you?"

"No. I wish I could have seen more inside the office, but my line of sight wasn't good."

"Neither was mine," she said.

Around the back, we spotted several cameras pointing at the back door of the cleaners.

"A back door with no door handle, surrounded by cameras." I pondered out loud. "Nothing to see here, folks."

Maxwell held her phone to her ear like she was on a call, but in reality, she was filming as we drove by.

"That was interesting," I said, pulling out of the parking lot.

Maxwell finished typing before answering. "Very."

"Do we need to work locally so we can pick up the clothes?"

"No, I'll call later with an excuse and tell Adam I'll pick them up tomorrow. I want go back to the office."

"Your wish is my command, wife." I laughed.

"Sorry about dropping that on you. I know we agreed on being friends for the op," she said. "Thanks for rolling with it."

Why wouldn't I? We had our differences, but we were still a team. At least for this assignment.

"No worries. I'm adaptable." After a short pause, I asked, "Why'd you change it?"

"Parker gave me the creeps, and I wanted to see how he'd react when I called you my husband."

"He did his best to pretend I didn't exist."

"That he did," she said. "We'll use it to our advantage."

I had no intention of letting Maxwell return alone to see Adam, a guy who gave off serious creepy stalker vibes. She might not like it, but I wouldn't budge and risk something happening to her.

"You okay with me recording while we hash out what we saw? It's faster and easier than typing."

"That's fine." I made a mental note to be on my best behavior.

After setting her phone between us, she asked, "What's your gut telling you? Start with the big picture."

I organized my thoughts before answering. "The laundromat is a front for whatever business they're running from the back." Succinct.

"Agreed." She tapped her finger on her leg. "The cleaners is too short for the space. Did you notice anything that hinted at a hidden room?"

"No, there was no disruption in the paint along the back wall and the random posters weren't big enough to hide a door."

"And the back door is suspicious," she added. "Too many cameras for a half empty plaza. Add in a door without a handle and it's–"

I cut her off, "Hinky."

"I was going to say suspicious."

"Tomato, tomahto. Regardless of what we call it, it can't be a good thing, right?" I asked as a joke.

"No, probably not."

Returning to work mode, I said, "There isn't room for more than a small office back there."

"No, but if they're laundering money or acting as a loan shark, they wouldn't need more than a small desk and a chair."

"True. We have a laundry list of things to do." I grinned when she made eye contact and shook her head at my stupid pun. *At least she smiled.* "What do we tackle first?"

Maxwell fired off the list. "We need to find the last tenants for the two spaces next to the laundry, and find out who's currently leasing them. I want to talk to Darling again, find out his connection to the Quick Wash, if there is one. Run facial recognition on the guy in the picture. Check out the end businesses to see if anything stands out. Oh," she turned to me, "we should buy cheap wedding rings. I saw Adam check out our hands."

I covered my flinch at the words 'wedding rings' with a cough.

I'd shopped for an engagement ring not so long ago. Luckily for me, Sara drove the stake through my heart before I dropped the three grand I'd saved up.

The memory still stung enough that the thought of shopping for wedding bands, even fake ones, made me want to hit something. Or someone.

Two someones, actually.

I forced myself back to the topic at hand, asking, "You think he doubts the cover?"

"No, that alone wouldn't be enough. We're still unpacking, after all." She smiled at me.

"I'll buy you the ring, but I'm not getting on one knee."

"Thank God for that." This time, she laughed. "And your father will buy the rings. Get used to expensing things, Sheppard."

Her phone rang. "It's Doug." She accepted the call. "You're on speaker."

"It was buried deep, but I found the owner of the Quick Wash."

"You going to tell us, or do we have to guess?" I asked, not bothering to mask my impatience at his long pause.

"Sorry, we'll fill you in when you get here. What's your ETA?" Doug asked.

"We're ten out."

"John said to meet us in the conference room when you get here."

"Copy that," Maxwell answered as the call disconnected.

"Well, that can't be good," I said.

"No." She was already emailing the photos and videos she'd taken.

I pulled my phone from my pocket. "Can you send the ones I took, too?" I typed in the pass code and handed it to her.

# Chapter 15

## Cate

When we walked in, Meg told us everyone was waiting for us upstairs. *Everyone? Whatever they found must be bad.* I grabbed my white board and files from our office before rushing to the conference room where Doug had the images we'd sent projected on the big screen. I set my whiteboard on the floor for quick reference.

"What'd you find?" Jaden asked. Patience was not a virtue he possessed.

"The Quick Wash is owned by Roman Enterprises, and so is the building," Doug said.

"Roman? Please tell me it's not Richard Roman," I said.

"One and the same," John answered.

"Shit." Roman's name came up a lot when we investigated the threat against Blake, now AJ's fiancée. We suspected he blackmailed Blake's father, but the connections were circumstantial at best. And Roman was a slippery bastard who paid smart people with questionable ethics to bury his connections deep, making what little we had on him useless. The few thugs who'd survived when we rescued Blake had protected Roman by naming a dead man as their boss.

Her father's gambling debt was the reason Roman had Blake kidnapped. He wanted the millions she inherited from her grandfather, on her twenty-fifth birthday, to settle her father's debt, and then some.

Looking at Jaden, I could tell he was thinking the same thing. The back room wasn't big enough for a gambling den, but either of the two spaces beside it were.

"What'd you find?" John asked.

I nodded for Jaden to start.

"The Quick Wash has a hidden room in the back." He stood up and pointed at the still I screen capped from the video. "The back door is under surveillance and can only be opened from the inside. The address we found in Wendy's trash should be in the same plaza, but doesn't legally exist."

After a pause, Jaden said, "I noticed a Quick Wash business card on Darling's refrigerator during our visit. Something's hinky."

"Hinky?" Jack asked.

Ignoring him, Jaden continued, "We'll talk to Darling again, see what he knows. With any luck, he'll spill his guts about his connection to the Quick Wash and Roman."

"When we pick up our laundry, we'll look around the building some more," I said.

Eyebrows around the room went up when Jaden told them we were posing as a married couple. I couldn't blame them. We weren't exactly the poster children for workplace camaraderie.

"Has anyone told AJ?" I asked. If we were investigating Roman, he'd worry about Blake.

"I called him," Jack answered. "He was ready to quit so he could race home, but I convinced him to stay. We've assigned Eric to watch Blake, and she'll stay with us until AJ gets home."

I nodded.

"Any thoughts on how this connects to Wendy?" Jamie asked.

"No. When we're done here, I'll update our notes. Jaden will go back through Wendy's socials and see if anything stands out now that we have more info. We'll question Darling again after he gets home from work."

"Let us know how we can support you. I have a meeting at three, but I'm all yours after that," John said.

Jaden looked shocked when he said, "Thanks."

Doug chimed in, "I haven't identified Wendy's Mr. R from the picture yet, but I'll keep looking. Let me know if there's anything else I can do."

Jamie and Jack had full calendars for the afternoon, but said they could help later. I didn't think we'd need to disrupt their evenings, but it was good to know they were available.

"When you've organized your notes, CC the team," John said with a smile. No one at SSI teased me for my near obsessive need to organize my notes. Except Jaden.

"Will do." I gathered up my files and whiteboard and went back to the office.

Jaden and I worked quietly until four-thirty, only talking when we needed to verify information.

"You good if I call Darling to see if he can meet with us tonight?" he asked.

"Yeah. Thanks." My stomach rumbled. I'd eaten a good-sized lunch, but was hungry again.

"Copy that." He pulled out his phone. "I'm starving. You want to order a pizza or something before we go?"

"Let's find out what time he's available and plan around that."

He pointed at me with his phone. "Good thinking." He opened his drawer and pulled out a protein bar.

*That man is always hungry.*

My stomach chose that moment to growl, making me laugh at the timing.

"What?" he asked.

"Nothing, just realized how hungry I am."

He held the half-eaten bar out. "Want a bite?" He grinned, the specks of gold in his amber eyes sparkling in the light from his monitor.

*He's a good-looking guy.* Luckily for me, his attitude made it easy for me to appreciate his good looks without being attracted to him.

*I made the mistake of getting involved with a coworker once, and I'll never do it again.* Especially not with my boss's bad boy son.

# Chapter 16

## Jay

We stopped at the local big box store and bought two cheap fake gold bands, foregoing the engagement ring.

"With this ring," I joked as I handed her the ring, sticky tag and all.

"Funny, Sheppard." She smiled, but didn't laugh.

*She does that a lot; I wonder why.* Did she go home and tell her friends how exasperating it is working with us? *With me?* Did she journal about the men at work driving her crazy?

Or was she afraid to get too close?

"I'm Mr. Bishop now." I doubled down with a smirk.

Without missing a beat, she answered, "Funny, Bishop."

A thin layer of ice melted from my heart at her attempt at humor.

Nothing to write home about, but I disliked her a little less hearing her lighten up and seeing her smile reach her eyes.

Her beautiful blue eyes. They reminded me of a cloudless sky on a perfect June day. But they usually stared at me with impatience or disgust so I rarely appreciated how striking they were.

"Let's go. Darling's expecting us," she said.

"After you, Sweetums."

"No."

"Sugar pie?"

"No."

"Snookems? You can't say no to that."

"Hell no." This time she laughed. Maxwell didn't have a dainty laugh. It was more like a hyena cackling, at least that was what it sounded like when she huffed it out at me. But it was still a laugh.

"I feel like I'd have a pet name for my wife."

*But not Catie.* I'd learned the hard, bloody way not to call her by that nickname.

Maxwell chose not to respond, instead giving me some talking points and asking me if I wanted to take the lead.

I did. We hadn't formed a lifelong friendship or anything, but I felt like I'd connected with Darling.

"Thanks for meeting with us again," I said when he answered the door.

"No problem, I'll do whatever I can to get Wendy back."

"We appreciate your time and will keep this brief," Maxwell said.

"Have you found anything yet?"

"Not yet, but we have some leads," I answered as he led us to the kitchen.

Instead of sitting, I stopped at the refrigerator and pointed at the Quick Wash business card. "Do you use the Quick Wash?"

"No, I did some work on one of their company vans. Why?"

"What about Wendy?"

"I suggested them when she spilled something on her favorite dress. But I don't know if she used them."

He played with his finger, where his wedding ring used to be.

Maxwell noticed it, too.

"Do you think they have something to do with Wendy's disappearance?"

Interesting, he made the connection before we mentioned it.

"We think she was there recently, so we're checking it out."

He nodded and looked at the business card while playing with his finger.

"Have you ever been to the room behind the cleaners?" I asked.

Maxwell and I had talked about how to handle Darling, and had agreed to take it slow and lead up to the secret room. Instead, I charged out of the gate with it. His reaction told me everything I wanted to know.

His head snapped up as he asked, "How do you, I mean, no, what room?"

"Mr. Darling, you obviously know about it. The sooner you tell us, the better." I hadn't meant to act like the bad-cop half of the team, but since I had, I went with it.

"We're not here to accuse you of anything, we just want to find Wendy," Maxwell played the good cop without missing a beat.

"I want that too, but-" he said.

"But you don't want to tell us you've been gambling?" *Maxwell is going to kill me.*

"I. I." He hung his head. "No."

"It's okay. Like I said, we're not here to accuse you of anything, and we understand things can get out of control," Maxwell soothed him. "Do you owe them money?"

"Yes," he finally admitted. "Do you think that's why they took Wendy?"

"We don't know if they're involved," Maxwell answered.

"Have they threatened you in any way?" I asked.

"No. We have an agreement. I've been working off my debt, and I haven't gambled in weeks."

"How did you find them?" Maxwell asked.

"They found me. Like I said, I worked on their company van. One of the guys overheard me talking to a friend at work about taking a trip to Vegas. I wanted to go, thinking it'd be good to get away, but couldn't afford it. I'm a casual gambler, so I was as interested in the change of scenery as much as the casinos."

"So he approached you?" I asked, pushing him back on track.

"Yeah, he was real nice, apologized for interrupting us and eavesdropping, but since he had, could he offer us a local solution."

"If Vegas wasn't about the gambling, why'd you say yes?" I asked.

"I wouldn't have if it'd been just me, but my friend wanted to go, so we made a night out of it."

"Did you both lose?" Maxwell asked.

"No, only me. I'd been on a winning streak, and my hand was a sure thing. Or so I thought, but I didn't have enough money to call. They offered to let me bet with money I didn't have."

"Like a loan, if you lost?" I asked. Poor guy, they set him up. No doubt the house cheated.

"Exactly. I made the first payment with no issues. But then I got sick-" he cut himself off. "I sent Wendy to the cleaners with the second payment. I assumed all she did was drop it off to Adam at the front counter." Guilt washed over his face.

Maxwell and I made eye contact; we could now connect Wendy to the Quick Wash. And Roman. Unfortunately, that connection didn't bode well for her.

"Did she say anything afterwards? Has she mentioned the cleaners since then?" I asked.

"No. Nothing. But she's a teenager." He broke eye contact. "She doesn't talk to me much about anything anymore."

We got more information on his payment plan, which sounded generous given what we knew about Roman.

Back in the truck, Maxwell said, "I have a feeling Wendy is the reason for his generous repayment plan."

"That doesn't sound ominous at all." I said, turning the key and bringing my truck to life.

"Yeah, until we know the why we'll assume the worst."

"Sexual favors?" I asked, feeling gross just for saying it.

"Maybe, but it could be voluntary on her part. I doubt she would've mentioned Mr. R. the way she did if she was being coerced or forced."

"Good point. You think Mr. R is related to Roman?" I asked. We knew from the picture that Mr. R. wasn't Richard Roman, but that didn't mean he wasn't a Roman.

"It's possible, but we can't assume."

I wasn't assuming. I was thinking out loud, but didn't think it was worth arguing over. Not when we were more or less on the same page and getting along. "Fair enough. Where to next?"

She pulled up the ex-boyfriend's information. "Let's surprise Bill with a visit. I'd like to find out what she said when she broke up with him."

She typed the address into the dashboard GPS.

Fortunately, Bill was home and happy to tell us all about how Wendy trampled his heart by pulling a one-eighty and dumping him for an older, richer, better-looking guy.

"Her words, not mine." He looked Maxwell up and down. I noticed that happening a lot during this investigation. *No wonder she dresses in suits and plays down her beauty.*

"Did she tell you his name?" I asked, forcing his attention back to me.

"No, she just described him like he was her meal ticket."

"Thank you for your time," Maxwell stuck out her hand, which he eagerly shook.

"Can we call you if we have any more questions?" I asked.

"Sure." His attention still on Maxwell.

Wanting to stop the ogling, I stepped between them and handed him my business card. "If you think of anything else, please don't hesitate to call."

Back in the truck, Maxwell turned on me. "What the hell was that all about?"

"What?"

"You know what? I don't need you protecting me from someone looking at me," she huffed.

"What, you like that shit? Guys drooling over you while you question them?" I knew it wasn't true, and I really shouldn't have said it.

"Fuck you, Sheppard." She slammed her seatbelt to lock it in place.

I stared. I hadn't expected that reaction. Anger, yes, but I figured she'd fight back, not close down.

The click as I secured my seatbelt set her off.

"I'll have you know. I can handle myself."

I opened my mouth to apologize, but she started again.

"I fucking hate it when men treat me like I'm an object to stare at. But you know what, Sheppard, it serves a purpose!" she yelled.

"What purpose could it possibly serve?" I yelled back.

"They underestimate me and I learn a lot more because of it. Just because you think a woman can't do this job doesn't make it true."

What the hell? Where'd that come from? I'd been an ass on more than one occasion—this occasion being the most recent—but I'd never been a sexist ass.

*Have I?* No, I hadn't. Just an every day, run-of-the-mill ass.

"You know what, next time I'll just let them drool and leer and strip you naked with their eyes while you're talking to them. Maybe I'll even encourage it."

*Now I'm being a sexist ass, with a capital A.* At least I sounded like one.

"What the fuck does that mean?"

"Just trying to help."

"Well, don't."

"Don't what?"

"Don't help."

"Fine." *You're acting like an idiot, Sheppard.*

"Fine."

We drove the rest of the way in silence, Maxwell working on her phone, while I drove. I had a feeling we wouldn't get much more work done tonight. At least not together. And the lion's share of the blame was mine.

What was it about Maxwell that made me act like a raging lunatic?

# Chapter 17

## Cate

We'd have to talk eventually, but I was so annoyed with Jaden I worried I'd break our truce if I tried before cooling off.

I don't know why Jaden thought he had to step in to protect me from the stares of a kid barely out of high school. Bill laid it on pretty thick, trying to present himself as a player, but he was insecure. He wasn't a threat. Not even close. The last thing I needed was Jaden getting in the way and making him clam up.

It was almost eight by the time we got back to the office.

"What do you want to work on tonight?" I asked Jaden as he walked towards the door.

He glanced over his shoulder, then turned to face me. "Maxwell, it's after eight. I haven't had dinner. I plan on eating and getting some rest so I can think clearly tomorrow."

"Okay."

"Okay?"

"Yes, okay."

"What does that even mean?" he asked.

"What do you mean, what does that mean? What does okay ever mean?"

"What's with the attitude?"

"I don't have an attitude."

"You do," he said. "Maybe if you got some rest once in a while instead of trying to prove how smart you are, you wouldn't be so bitchy."

"I'm not bitchy, Sheppard. I want to find Wendy."

"Are you implying I don't? 'Cause that's bullshit."

"No, I'm…"

"I'm not a robot. I need to sleep. So do you."

"I get plenty of sleep." I just didn't get a lot.

"I'm going home Maxwell, I suggest you do the same." He sounded exasperated.

"You know you're not my boss, right?"

"Yeah, I know. I'm the expendable Sheppard," he muttered as he turned towards the door.

*What the hell does that mean?* We might not get along, but I knew better than to kick a man who'd just dropped a mind-fuck of a revelation, when he was down.

The expendable Sheppard. Did Jaden really think that? His family loved him without fail. It'd devastate them if something happened to him.

*Why doesn't he think so?*

"Good night," I said. "We'll regroup in the morning." I grabbed my bag and followed him.

"Good night." After ushering me out the back door, he turned off the lights, locked the door, and set the alarm.

He waited for me to pull out before leaving. It was something his father and brothers did, too. Hell, all the guys did it. At first it annoyed me because they didn't do it to each other. *But they do it for Meg.* It was one of the protective things I didn't argue about. Partly because I did it to my friends, and partly because it was a southern gentleman thing and therefore not personal. Also, partly because they didn't treat me like a girl when it came time to do the job.

Needing someone to talk to, I called Charlie on my way home. Unfortunately, she wasn't available. After leaving a voicemail, I treated myself to a burger, fries, and a chocolate milkshake.

I spent the rest of the drive thinking about what Jaden had said. No matter how hard I tried, I couldn't let a statement like that go. I wanted to know what was behind his line of thinking.

I spent more time thinking about that, and other things he'd said, than working on Wendy's case. Feeling guilty, I stayed up later than I should've to get my notes updated and organized.

When I finally stood and ordered myself to go to bed, the voice in my head sounded a lot like the youngest Sheppard.

I refused to think about what it might mean.

# Chapter 18

## Jay

We met with the team early Wednesday morning to share new updates. By that time, Wendy had been missing at least four days, and our chances of finding her dropped with every passing hour.

"I didn't find anything new," Maxwell said, staring at her whiteboard.

"I did."

Maxwell turned towards me, her raised left eyebrow the only sign of her shock.

She wasn't the only one who'd worked late into the night. And it wasn't because I felt guilty knowing Maxwell kept working—I could hear the clock ticking down for Wendy.

"What, you think you're the only one who works on cases at home?"

"I thought you were too tired to work after we left."

I didn't miss the snark in her voice. Sighing, I changed the subject. "My gut wouldn't let me sleep, so I researched the plaza and the empty suites." I opened my laptop and signed in. I mistyped my password, and had to try again.

Her patience ran out. "Well, what'd you find?"

*Christ, it's not like I did it on purpose.*

I opened my file. "Both tenants were bought out of their leases early by a shell corporation. I don't have a name yet, but I'm guessing it's Roman."

"We don't guess," she said. "We research, we dig, we verify."

*Don't roll your eyes. Don't say anything you'll regret.*

"I know that, Maxwell. But I also know when to trust my gut. And my gut is telling me Roman is expanding his business into the surrounding spaces."

She stood, rolling her shoulders back, trying to be taller than her five-foot-seven inch frame, crossed her arms over her chest, and stared at me.

I could see the thoughts swirling as micro expressions flashed across her face.

She finally said, "Tell me more."

"Can I use your printer?" I asked.

"Of course. It's available to anyone on the server." She didn't roll her eyes, but her tone suggested she wanted to.

I sent the docs to the printer as I continued, "Roman owns other properties, a lot of them, but what if he wanted to use the Quick Wash to consolidate his gambling ring?"

She grabbed the papers from the printer. "Continue," she said as she started reading.

"The Quick Wash plaza is a relatively new purchase and six months after buying it, he bought his neighbors out of their leases."

She glanced up.

"For the sake of my theory, let's assume it's him."

She nodded. "Okay, go on."

"The previous plaza owner filed for bankruptcy after sinking into sudden debt."

She stopped and looked at me. "Good work." This time, the compliment didn't offend me, but I couldn't leave well enough alone.

"You don't sound surprised."

"Should I be?" She looked me up and down, then looked down at her usual attire, a black pantsuit. "Did you bring a change of clothes?"

It didn't take a fancy degree to know what she had in mind. "Yeah, fancy a trip to Fort Worth, Mrs. Bishop?"

She sighed. "I do."

I rapped my knuckles on my father's door.

"Come in." He looked up from his monitor. "Jay, Maxwell." He nodded in greeting.

I looked at Maxwell. She was the lead, after all, but she nodded, deferring to me. I saw the slightest lift of my father's left cheek, the start of the lop-sided grin, just like the one I'd inherited from him.

Dad was a pro as schooling his features, and I would have missed it if I hadn't been looking right at him.

"I, we, have reason to believe Roman is running his gambling ring in the plaza."

He leaned back and crossed his arms. "How's it tied to Wendy?"

"Her father owed Roman money, and he sent her to the cleaners to drop off a payment when he was sick," I answered.

"The timing lines up with her breaking up with her now ex-boyfriend and the appearance of the mysterious Mr. R," Maxwell picked up where I left off.

"Next steps?" Dad asked.

"We'll pick up our laundry," I shrugged. "And while we're there, I'll let slip that I want to go to Wynd Star in Dallas to win some money to pay for our money-pit of a new home."

"Play it cool. Let them come to you," Dad mused. He'd done his fair share of undercover work when he was a detective with the Parker County Sheriff's office. He looked at Maxwell and asked, "You think it'll work?"

"I do, though it may not happen right away. I'll grab a burner so we can give them a contact number."

"Good. Let me know if you want back-up. I'd be happy to take a break from all this paperwork."

I laughed. While I occasionally regretted not buying into the business in the beginning, I didn't envy the stacks of paperwork and bureaucratic bullshit they had to deal with to keep the business running.

"Is that what you're wearing?" Maxwell asked when I walked back into our office after changing.

"Yeah, what's wrong with it?"

"You look like a slob." She wrinkled her nose at me.

"I've been working on a money pit, remember?"

She looked at me as it sunk in. I was better dressed for the role than she was. Her leggings and t-shirt looked new.

"Shit. Can we stop by my place before we go?"

I laughed. "Sure." She'd taken all the fun out of teasing her. "I'm driving. You ready?"

Maxwell hesitated when I asked if she wanted me to wait in the truck. She clearly had reservations about letting me see her apartment, which only made me want to see it more.

"It's not like you haven't seen my place," I said.

"It's not yours; you live with your brother."

"For now. I haven't found the right place yet," I defended myself. It wasn't like I was jobless and living in my parents' basement. Besides, Jack had lived with Jamie. So had Meg, before she and Jack got married and bought their own place.

"Fine, you can come in." There was a very strong 'don't touch anything vibe,' coming off her.

"Thank you." I oozed southern charm, tipping the brim of my baseball cap.

Maxwell's apartment looked like it belonged in a magazine, not because it was artfully decorated, it wasn't, but because it looked so organized and clean. Like photo shoot ready clean. Like she didn't live here clean.

Everything on her shelves sat at matching angles. The pictures, the books, the awards and trophies. Even the boxing gloves were propped up to look like they were modeling.

There were several pictures of her with a man who, from the looks of it, was her father. Several of her and her father wearing boxing gloves at various ages, them at her high school and two different college graduations, and several of them together in Marine uniforms. I picked one up and examined it closer; they had the same piercing blue eyes and severe expressions. Christ, even as a kid, Maxwell had a stick up her ass.

I scanned the shelves but didn't see any pictures of her mother. *I wonder why.*

I couldn't imagine living like this. The house I shared with Jamie and Emily was clean, but it looked lived in, relaxed, and welcoming. There were pictures of both families everywhere, including loved ones they'd lost. The same was true at my parent's house.

Hell, even as the black sheep, I carried pictures of my family with me in the Marines.

Unlike Darling's shelf, there wasn't a speck of dust on Maxwell's. There was nothing to guide me, so I'd probably put the frame back in the wrong spot.

*Does she ever relax?* I'd long thought Maxwell had OCD, or at least had OCD tendencies, but now I knew. *What caused it?* I had a buddy who'd suffered extreme PTSD, and one of his symptoms was OCD behavior. PTSD wasn't the only reason a person might need such an extreme level of control, but knowing she was an FBI profiler, I had to wonder what kind of heavy shit she'd seen.

"I'm ready."

I stepped away from the shelf as she came into the room. Her eye twitched ever so slightly when she looked at the shelf.

"That's much better," I said, hoping she wouldn't yell at me for daring to touch a photo. "You look like you've been helping fix our disaster of a home."

"Thanks." She walked over and fixed the frame.

"Your dad?"

"Yes."

"Is he still in the Marines?" I asked. He was in uniform in most of the photos.

"Yes. He's a three-star general, stationed in DC."

*Impressive.* I let my whistle do the talking. Until it clicked and my jaw dropped. "Wait. You're General Maxwell's kid?"

There weren't a lot of three star generals in the Marine Corps, and even fewer in the Capitol, so of course I knew who he was.

"Yes. Let's go." She said, eliminating my chance to ask more questions.

The chime on the door alerted Adam to our presence as we walked in.

"Good morning, Adam." Maxwell, *no Charlie*, greeted him.

"You remembered." He smiled, obviously flattered by her attention.

I pretended not to care.

"Of course I did." She flashed a toothy white smile. "Hopefully our clothes are done?" She looked down at herself and chuckled. "We'll have more for you soon."

"I'll go get them," Adam said.

When I saw a shadow in the office, indicating he was coming back, I asked, "So what do you think, want to go to Dallas this weekend and see if our luck will hold out?"

Maxwell didn't miss a beat. "I don't know, what if you lose this time?"

"I won't, Lady Luck is on my side," I puffed out my chest like I was special.

She raised her eyebrows and crossed her arms. "I'm just not sure it's a good idea. We need to save money for all the stupid house shit we weren't expecting. You know, like buying a new washer and dryer."

"Charlie," Adam used her first name as he came out the door. "Silly me forgot there was an issue getting everything done. We would've called but you didn't leave a number."

"I didn't? I'm so sorry." She walked up to the window. "Are our clothes okay?" She added a little panic to her voice.

"Yes, yes, no need to worry. Your clothes are fine, but our machine went down and we didn't finish them. I'm sorry for the inconvenience."

*I bet he is.*

"Oh man, you had me worried." She put her hand over her heart. "I don't think I could handle any thing else going wrong."

*She's good.*

"They should be done tomorrow. And for the inconvenience, we'll take another ten percent off."

"Thank you. Here, let me give you my number, just in case."

She rattled off the number like she'd known it her entire adult life, rather than memorizing it less than an hour ago.

"I'll call if we have any other issues." He looked at me. "I don't want to overstep, Mr. Bishop, but I heard you talking about going to a Dallas casino. If you want to avoid the big city, we have a friendly local game you might be interested in."

*Jackpot.*

"Oh, I don't know." I paused and put my arm around Maxwell's waist. "The old ball and chain doesn't think I should."

"It's a friendly game, low stakes. Surely that'd be okay," he said, addressing Maxwell. "Come on Charlie, let your old man live a little." I didn't miss how he referred to me as Mr. Bishop but he called Maxwell, Charlie.

"Maybe," she said. Then turned to me, "We'll talk about it later. Okay?"

"Okay." I gave a very good impression of being a whipped husband. "Maybe we can get some Chinese while we're here."

She smiled and patted my stomach. Wanting to impress her, my ab muscles flexed of their own accord. *Traitors.*

"He's always hungry," she said to Adam.

"I'm a big boy," I straightened to my full six-foot-two height. *Take that, Adam.* He didn't stand a snowball's chance in hell of winning over Maxwell when I was his competition. "And you know how much I love Chinese food."

"Fine, we'll get Chinese. Again," she said, rolling her eyes.

Maxwell turned back to Adam and said, "Thanks again, Adam." She flashed her mega watt smile. "I'll stop by tomorrow, unless I hear from you."

# Chapter 19

## Cate

I had to admit; it was a smart choice to stay in the plaza for lunch. It gave us a chance to re-evaluate the flyers we'd seen with fresh eyes.

At least, that was what I thought until we were walking back to Jaden's truck and without warning, he pushed me against the empty store's front window and kissed me.

*What the fuck?*

One hand cupped the back of my neck while the other held my hip. His big, rock hard body pushed against mine, trapping me against the wall. It was the kind of toe-curling kiss that might have turned my insides to mush if I hadn't wanted to punch him.

When I tried to push him away, he held on tighter, crushing his lips to mine.

Focusing on the anger, and ignoring the fact that he was turning me on, I poured all my energy into pushing him away.

Someone whistled from the parking lot. Someone else laughed.

"What the fuck, Sh–"

He cut me off, a wicked grin on his face. "What? I can't kiss my wife?" Emphasis on the word wife.

*Shit. Pull yourself together.* I'd almost let my personal feelings blow our cover. What was it about Jaden that always made me so crazy?

I corrected my expression and looked around, feigning embarrassment. "You know I hate public displays of affection," I slapped at his chest as I scolded him, hoping to cover my blunder.

"I couldn't help it. You had a little sauce right there," he touched the edge of my lips, "and I couldn't resist the opportunity to kiss it off."

He grinned. I plastered a smile on my face while internally seething.

Jaden was having a little too much fun at my expense.

And his kiss, his touch, had turned me on a little too much for my comfort.

"Come on, Charlie, don't be embarrassed." He reached for my hand. "It's not like we've never kissed in public before." He winked.

*God, I hate him and his smug attitude and his sexy grin and his flirty wink.*

It took everything I had to not pull my hand away.

His voice irritated me. His arrogance infuriated me.

But his touch, that confused me because I wanted more.

Unwilling to make the same mistake twice, I focused on my anger.

Keeping my head down, I looked around shyly, using my faux embarrassment as cover while we walked to the truck. The instant both doors were closed, I turned on him.

"What the fuck was that?"

He smiled, "People can still see you, Snookems."

*At least they can't hear me.* "Jaden," I warned through gritted teeth while forcing my lips to lift in a smile.

"Bill's here. I didn't want him to ID us."

*Shit.* I hadn't seen him.

"Where'd he go?" I scanned the area, hoping he couldn't see us.

"You're welcome." He started the engine and backed out of the parking spot.

My sigh was involuntary. "Thank you. Where'd he go?"

"The convenience store. He's still there."

"How do you know?" I asked, annoyed that he'd seen something I'd missed.

"His car is still here."

Ignoring my irritation, I reminded myself we were a team. "You think he's involved?"

"I didn't get that vibe. It's probably a coincidence." I didn't believe in coincidences, but Bill lived close enough for this to be convenient. He continued, "No offense to Bill, I'm sure he's a smart guy." Jaden rolled his eyes. "But I think we would've picked up on something if he was involved with Wendy's disappearance."

I chuckled at Jaden's choice of words. "Agreed. I didn't pick up anything except frustrated young adult from him." Thinking back to the two empty plaza spaces, I added, "Might be worth checking his financials anyway. He might have ties to Roman and unknowingly be involved."

# Chapter 20

## Jay

What was I thinking, kissing Maxwell? I did it for the right reason, but there were other ways I could've achieved the same thing.

Kissing her crossed the line.

*But damn, it felt good.* I shifted to look out the window so I could adjust myself without being too obvious. The kiss sent most of my blood to the part of my body that needed it least.

Maxwell drove me crazy and made me feel like a failure. There was no way I felt anything for her. So kissing her shouldn't have stirred up anything.

Who was I kidding? I was a healthy young guy who'd just pushed a gorgeous, feisty woman against a wall and kissed her like my life depended on it. Of course, it stirred things up.

Like the stupid sensations in my chest I refused to give words to.

*Nope.*

And the fire in her eyes when she yelled at me wasn't a turn on. Neither was the color in her pale, sparsely freckled cheeks when she blushed.

Nope.

Not even a little.

Not at all.

I had zero intentions of catching feelings ever again. And there was no way in hell I'd allow myself to catch them for the woman sitting in my truck, the co-worker who irritated the fuck out of me every day.

Awkward silence filled the cab as I drove back to the office.

Until my phone rang. "Sheppard. You're on speaker."

"We found something you need to see."

Before Doug could say anything else, I said, "We're fifteen minutes out."

"Meet us in the conference room."

I barely had time to say, "Copy that," before he disconnected the call.

"Just what we need, more good news." I said, laying the sarcasm on thick.

Maxwell nodded, but didn't answer as her fingers tapped a nervous rhythm on her thighs.

The sinking feeling in my gut encouraged me to press the accelerator and push the boundaries of what the local cops considered "acceptable" speeding.

Back in the conference room, Doug had a bunch of images up on the big screen. He'd been running facial recognition for Wendy and our mystery man in the greater Parker and Dallas counties.

"I think we found your guy," he said.

I walked up to the screen and peered at the pictures. Maxwell stood right beside me, smelling delicious. *Nope. Can't think like that.*

"Who is he?" she asked.

"His name is Robert Roman."

Turning around, I said. "So Mr. R. is a Roman." It shouldn't have surprised me, having considered the possibility, but I'd hoped, for Wendy's sake, it wouldn't be true.

"He's Richard's nephew," my father answered. "And by all accounts, he's spoiled rotten and has caused more than his fair share of trouble."

"Legal, I presume, but what kind?" Maxwell asked.

"He's had run-ins with the law for everything from petty theft to drunk driving, but nothing stuck," Jamie answered. "He currently works for his uncle."

"Where's Blake?" I asked.

"She's safe. Eric's bringing her here now," Dad answered.

"And AJ?" Maxwell asked.

"Dean's already en route to replace him, so he'll be back soon," Dad added. *Smart move.* He couldn't risk the company's reputation if AJ went all protective ape and left a client unprotected. AJ was reliable and responsible, but he was also prone to losing his mind if he thought Blake was in danger.

No, that wasn't true. He'd compartmentalized his feelings earlier this year when we had to trade Blake for Meg. And he'd shown remarkable restraint when he gave Roman's goon, who was holding a gun to Blake's head, a chance to surrender.

"Once I had a name, I found out everything I could about his recent whereabouts." Doug clicked on a picture and enlarged it. "That's when I found this."

It was a picture of Robert and Wendy leaving Maison Beaumont, a high-end restaurant where you had to know someone to get a reservation. Wendy was dressed to the nines, and wearing the same chandelier necklace we saw in the photo from the party.

Maxwell stared at the photo for a good minute before saying, "She doesn't look happy." She turned to Doug. "Do you have a date on this?"

"The Saturday before her father noticed she was missing," he answered.

She was alive Saturday night, but the look on her face and the tension in her body made me nervous. What happened? Why hadn't she come home?

"Anything more recent, of either of them?"

"Nothing." Doug answered Maxwell.

"What's your gut telling you?" Dad asked her.

"Something happened that night." She paused. "A place like this has to have cameras. Did you get any footage?"

"No, they hung up on us when we called and asked," Jamie said.

Just then, Jack walked in. "Blake's downstairs with Meg. Door's locked and Eric's with them." I think he said the last part for his benefit, not ours. Jack was still freaked out about

Roman's, Richard not Robert, goons taking Meg, forcing us to exchange Blake for her. I couldn't blame him; they'd found out she was pregnant a week before it happened.

Jamie looked down at his phone, his shoulders relaxing as he read. "Sammie will be here any minute with Emily," he said. Emily wasn't threatened last time, but Roman would use any means necessary to get to us once he learned we were investigating him.

No one was safe until we put that fucker behind bars.

*Or six feet under.*

I looked at Dad. "And Ma?"

He laughed. "She refused to leave the shop, reminding me she's locked and loaded. So is Beth." He shared a look with Doug. "I called the chief and asked him to park a cruiser outside. And Chase is currently living the dream at WPD." That kid loved police officers and would tell anyone who'd listen he wanted to 'be the police,' when he grew up.

"No doubt talking the ear off anyone who'll listen," Doug said. He kept his voice calm, but the tension in his body showed how worried he was for his fiancée and soon to be son.

Everyone we loved was accounted for. The only other person Roman could threaten to get to us was Jamie's twin, Madi, but she was currently living on a Navy base in Louisiana.

"I'll make some calls," Maxwell said, already pulling out her phone and stepping into the hall. When she came back, she said, "I should have the footage in a few hours at the latest."

Having friends in the FBI was helpful when we needed to do things the right way. Or when we got stone walled. No doubt Doug could hack the restaurant's surveillance cameras, but the evidence wouldn't be admissible in court.

"We need to a make game plan," Jamie said. "I wrapped up my case today, and don't have anything I can't shuffle around for the week."

"I should be free by tomorrow afternoon," Jack added.

"I can help before and after my protection detail tomorrow and Friday," Doug added.

"I'm yours for whatever you need. I've asked Meg not to schedule anything else for the rest of the week," Dad said.

# Chapter 21

## Cate

"Sheppard and I have to go back to the cleaners tomorrow." *I should probably resort to calling him Jaden when in a room full of Sheppards.* But I wanted to keep him at an emotionally safe distance. "They had an 'equipment malfunction' after hearing him beg me to go to Wynd Star."

"Adam mentioned they have a friendly, low stakes game in the area. He seemed eager to invite me," Jaden added.

"As you know, we're posing as a married couple." I paused long enough for everyone to laugh.

While I waited, I realized I was still wearing my wedding band.

*No, my fake wedding band.*

I glanced over. *So is Jaden.*

We took them off and shoved them in our pockets, much to everyone's amusement.

When they quieted down, I filled them in on the recent developments.

I left out the kiss, praying Jaden wouldn't feel the need to mention it.

When Jaden added in his two cents, he left it out. *Thank God.*

I don't know why he didn't take advantage of the opportunity to embarrass me, but I was grateful. I really didn't need another team looking at me like I was the type of woman who slept her way to the top.

"I'll update my timeline and get the information to everyone," I said.

"Do we know where Richard Roman is, or what he's doing?" Jaden asked.

"No, he's been lying low since we…" John paused. "Rescued Blake."

Roman going underground wouldn't help us. We needed to know where he was and what he was doing.

I was about to leave when John said, "I want everyone checking in every hour when you're not here. We've poked this hornet's nest before and know how far he'll go."

"Yes, sir," we answered together.

"Sir?" Jaden asked. I could only imagine what stupid shit would come out of his mouth.

"What is it?" John asked, humor and exasperation mixing in his voice.

"What about while we're sleeping?" Jaden asked.

"Unless you're sleeping. Check in before you go to sleep and after you wake up." He explained it like he was talking to a child.

"Yes, sir. Thank you, sir." Jaden saluted, making everyone laugh.

John pointed at the door. "Get out of here."

Jaden was two steps past the door when John called out, "Be careful."

"Copy that," Jaden said without breaking stride.

Jaden was being a wiseass, but there was no tension between him and his father while they teased one another.

We greeted everyone in the lobby when we reached the bottom of the stairs. Meg was sitting in the lounge with Blake and Emily, laughing. Sammie and Eric, two of our three part-timers, were standing nearby. John would keep at least one of them on duty, to watch over the girls, until their husbands could take them home.

In some ways, I envied them. I only had one close friend, Charlie, but she lived in Arizona, so the only way we could hang out was via video chat or by taking a vacation.

*It's better this way.* Even though I knew in my soul the people at SSI weren't like the men I'd had the misfortune of working with at the FBI, I wasn't ready to let them in.

Back in our office, Jaden and I updated the timeline, organized our notes, and emailed the team.

We heard AJ before we saw him run into the lobby. You'd think Blake was dying the way he called out for her.

"I'm right here. No need to yell," she said. Not at all bothered by his obsessive need to protect her. I'd misjudged her, I think we all did, when her father first brought her here. She acted like a bratty, spoiled rich kid, but in reality, she was just scared.

Blake's short body all but disappeared when AJ wrapped his arms around her. Meg and Emily shook their heads in amusement.

A few minutes later, AJ knocked on our door. "What do I need to know? And what do you need me to do?" No greeting, no small talk, just down to business. I'd wonder what was wrong with him, being the jokester of the team, but I knew his behavior had everything to do with the woman he loved being in danger.

I briefed AJ and sent him to work with Doug. AJ wasn't as savvy as Doug with tech things, but there was a lot of footage to go through and the second set of eyes would help.

"I emailed everyone, and messaged Darling asking if we can meet tomorrow," Jaden said.

I appreciated mission-mode Jaden; he was focused and a team player. Skills he would've needed as a Raider, but rarely showed at SSI unless shit got real.

But I still had a bone to pick with him.

Knowing someone could be outside the door, I chose my words carefully. "We need to get a few things straight. First, never pull another stunt like you did earlier."

He grinned. "Unless I have to protect our cover."

"No. Never. Find another way." I didn't trust my body to remain faithful to my heart and brain if he kissed me like that again.

And just like that, mission-focused Jaden was replaced by his normal irritating, sarcastic self. "Afraid you'll fall in love with me?" The mischievous glint in his eye told me he was teasing, but it still hit too close to home.

I rolled my eyes. "Obviously. Because there couldn't possibly be another reason a woman wouldn't want to be kissed by you."

"No one's ever complained before."

Did he just puff up his chest? *Typical playboy, he thinks no one can resist him.*

"There's a first time for everything." I shrugged and turned my attention back to my monitor.

"Admit it, you liked it."

"I didn't." *Liar, liar, pants on fire.*

"Sure." He drew out the 'u' far longer than necessary.

"What, your ego can't handle being turned down?"

"My ego is just fine, thank you."

"It's inflated."

"It's earned."

*I bet it is.* My eyes roamed down his torso to his… Damn, now my mind was thinking of changing sides.

"Whatever, Sheppard."

"Whatever, Mrs. Bishop," he said, reminding me we were going undercover again.

I took a calming breath. "Just don't do it again."

He laughed. "Fine. I'll let our cover get blown."

*Lord, give me patience.*

He flipped a switch and asked, "Can we plan now?"

Gotta love spec ops guys, they could switch off and on a dime.

"Our cover isn't strong enough to withstand any kind of search, so we need to go in with our eyes open." That was the problem with on the fly cover stories; they didn't stand up to scrutiny.

"Do you think they'll piece it together that quickly?"

"Hard to say. Richard Roman isn't an in-the-trenches guy, so it isn't likely we'll run into him at the Quick Wash." Possible, but not likely. So far, we'd only dealt with Adam, but I wasn't worried about him. He was just a recruiter. And Robert Roman had been MIA for days. "We need to stay the course at the Quick Wash for now. It's our only solid connection to Wendy."

"There is no greater danger than underestimating your opponent." Jaden impressed me by quoting Lao Tzu.

"We won't. Adam's a recruiter, so he just wants to bring you into the game and collect his cut. And just because he suggests it, doesn't mean you'll get an invitation."

"I wonder if one of the Romans will interviewed by one of the Romans?"

"Let's hope not." Lucky for us, men like Richard usually stuck to the shadows and had their lackeys do the work. "I have a feeling Richard's memorized every face from SSI." And he'd want revenge for the destruction we caused. "The sooner we get this over, the better." Knowing our adversary was Richard Roman meant the clock for solving this case was ticking faster than normal. And Wendy's wasn't the only life on the line.

"We should talk to Dad about taking the who's who page down," he said, more to himself than to me.

"It'd be a good idea, given recent activity," I said. If SSI was entering the undercover game, we needed to keep our faces off the internet as much as possible. "Can you shoot him an email?"

Jaden and I decided we'd go to Fort Worth before lunch to pick up our laundry and ask Adam when the next game would be. We agreed I'd act hesitant and Jaden would sway me. In an effort to lure Adam to my side, I'd try to get a moment alone with him. I wanted to play up the concerned, this has happened before with a bad outcome, wife role.

The only sound was the clacking of our fingers on the keyboards until Jaden asked, "What was the second thing?"

"What?"

"You said, first, when you told me to never," he looked at the door, "do the thing again."

Oh, *for fuck's sake.* Was he like this with his teammates? If he was, how the hell was he still alive?

"I don't remember."

"Right." He lingered on the i.

"I'll tell you when it pops back into my head, but right now, I'm busy. You should be, too."

"Aye aye, Captain." He saluted.

Refusing to let him upset me, I played along. "That's lieutenant to you."

"Aye aye, Lieutenant." He exaggerated his salute.

"And stop fucking saluting."

"Aye aye-"

"For the love of God, will you please let me get back to work?"

He grinned and winked, but didn't say another word. And damn if that wink didn't stir up a few butterflies.

When I finished my research, I asked Jaden what he'd found.

His search on Bill turned up nothing, so we chalked his presence up to coincidence and crossed the boyfriend off the suspect list.

"Adam's history is clean, too. Not squeaky, but nothing suspicious popped up."

"He's just a foot soldier," Jaden said. "Or in this case, the gatekeeper."

"I'd feel a lot better prepared if I knew who was in the office with him earlier today."

Jaden agreed.

A shadow filled the doorway a second before a knock sounded.

"We're taking the girls to our place," Jack said. "You're welcome to join us and work from there."

Jaden accepted. I declined.

"You sure? Meg's making her famous bacon mac and cheese." Jack tempted me.

That sounded a lot better than eating at my desk again. My hesitation gave Jaden an opening.

"Come on, Maxwell, it won't kill you to relax for a few minutes," Jaden teased.

"Thank you, Jack. It sounds delicious. If you're sure I won't be intruding, I'd love to come."

"Christ, even your acceptance is stiff and formal." Jaden said, rolling his eyes.

I ignored him. Having manners didn't make me stiff or formal.

Jack ignored him, too. "Of course you're not intruding. We're happy to have you. And you're in for a real treat. Meg's bacon mac and cheese is to die for."

"Thanks. Can I bring anything?" I asked.

He nodded towards my desk. "Just you and your case files." He turned to Jaden and pointed. "You can grab some beer."

"I figured as much," Jaden laughed. Watching them, I saw a hint of the brotherly banter I often witnessed between Jamie and Jack.

The kind Jaden wanted but pretended he didn't.

Jack was right, Meg's bacon mac and cheese was to die for. The cheese, seven kinds according to her, was so rich and creamy I thought I'd died and gone to heaven. It was a good thing I didn't eat like that at every meal or I'd have to go to the gym twice as much. I allowed myself one beer with dinner, more to keep Jaden off my back than anything else. Dinner was lively, with people crowded around the table, talking and laughing. I observed more than I interacted.

More than once, I felt Jaden's eyes on me.

More than once, I looked up and made eye contact.

More than once, I ignored the questions I saw reflected in his gorgeous amber eyes.

After dinner, I offered to help Meg clean, but she ushered me and the rest of the team away. Emily and Blake backed her up.

"You guys go save Wendy. We got this," Emily said.

I loved how everyone in the group supported each other. I knew from experience the guys wouldn't hesitate to clear the table or wash the dishes, so it wasn't a big deal to let the girls do it today.

We took over the living room, using every surface we could find to work. Doug came over after dropping Beth and Chase off at John's. He said they were happy to spend time with Mary and John, who'd be watching over them.

"Leave it to Dad to slack while we're all slaving away," Jack joked.

AJ pretended to fold a note and put it in his pocket. "I'll just pack that away for the next time I fuck up."

"Dude, you'd throw me under the bus like that?" Jack asked.

"To save my own ass, hell yeah," AJ answered.

I laughed with everyone else. SSI reminded me of the Marines. Having no siblings, and being a military brat, the sense of brotherhood quickly became one of my favorite things about serving. Another thing Gavin took from me, my ability to trust my teammates on a personal level.

"Let's focus," Jaden said.

"Damn, I expect that from your big brother…" AJ trailed off.

"Fuck you, Andrew," Jaden said with a shit-eating grin.

The room went quiet. AJ glared at Jaden. Jaden smirked at AJ.

Jack broke the tension. "Let's not poke the bear, shall we? Ma'll kill us if we let AJ kill you."

Jaden displayed the trademark Sheppard grin, the left side lifting a smidge more than the right, while holding eye contact with AJ. "He could try."

AJ laughed, diffusing the tension.

"Can we get back to work?" I asked. "Please."

"Back, we haven't started," Jamie said, with a hint of humor. "What do you need from us?"

We worked late into the night until Jamie insisted it was time for everyone to get some rest.

# Chapter 22

## Jay

"I'll drive," Maxwell said. We'd just finished the Thursday morning meeting with the team and agreed on our plan of attack for the day.

"No, I'll drive," I argued.

"What's your problem?"

"I don't have a problem."

"You have a problem with women driving," Maxwell huffed.

It wasn't that I had a problem with women driving; I didn't like giving up the control.

But I wouldn't tell her that. "You know what they say about women drivers." I shrugged it off like I hadn't just insulted her and her gender.

"Fine, but only because I don't feel like arguing," she grabbed her phone and shoved it into the back pocket of her jeans.

Jeans that fit her perfectly round ass. *I bet I could bounce a quarter off that ass.*

"Sheppard!"

"What?" I yelled back, pretending it was a conscious choice to ignore her.

"Did you hear a word I just said?" she asked.

"Of course." One look at her exasperated expression warned me I should fess up. "Fine, I didn't hear you. Happy now?"

"No. I need to know I can trust you."

That stung. I might be a smart ass, but she could trust me.

I couldn't tell her what I was thinking about, so I forced the image from my mind and focused.

"You can trust me. I'm sorry I got distracted."

She nodded. "When we get there, we should leave our phones, IDs, credit cards, and personal items in the glove box. Just in case."

"You think they'll frisk us?"

"No, but it's easier to lie if we're telling the truth. I'll feign forgetting my purse. You can come to the rescue with cash."

"You don't think they'll question us both forgetting our wallets?"

"You'll have yours, just not your ID or credit cards," she said. "They won't know what isn't in your wallet unless they look over your shoulder."

I pulled out my wallet and removed my military ID and bank card, putting them in my desk. Images flashed across my mind at the sight of my picture. My team was in the thick of things when I renewed, so I looked ragged and sloppy in my photo.

*I bet Maxwell looks picture perfect in every ID photo she's ever taken.* I wonder if she has curls or waves. Does she straighten her thick red hair? I'd only seen it out of her trademark tight bun twice, and it was pulled back in a bouncy ponytail after being in a tight bun for hours.

"Let's go."

I felt naked without my military ID. Instinctively, I reached for my dog tags, but they no longer hung around my neck. Five months out and I still reflexively reached for them in times of stress.

"How long did it take you to get used to not wearing your tags?"

"I'll let you know when it happens," I said, leaving my usual levity behind. I'd only taken them off three weeks ago. *I wonder how long it took her?* I didn't ask, and she didn't offer.

"I imagine it takes longer to adjust for Special Forces guys."

I shrugged it off. "Maybe." I didn't want to talk about the customized dog tags I had to wear behind enemy lines. The ones that were the only personal item we carried with us. The ones that were the only way to identify one of us if we got killed. The ones we clung to when we prayed.

Maxwell must have sensed I'd gone somewhere dark, because she lightened the mood by saying, "Come on, Henry. Let's see if we can get you into a poker game."

Shutting the memories down, I said, "Right behind you, Babe." And blew her a kiss.

"This assignment will be the death of me," she whispered. But not low enough.

"What was that, Snookems?"

"I just remembered the second thing."

"What's that, Sweetie Pie?"

"No pet names."

I hung my head and frowned. Looking back up, I gave her my best puppy dog eyes, and said, "But…"

"Fine." She conceded. "I'll tolerate Babe, but nothing else."

"Copy that. Babe." I laughed. Ruffling Maxwell's feathers was even more fun when she played along.

Maxwell went to the cleaners while I ran to the store to grab a coke. She wanted a couple of minutes alone with Adam, to feel him out. And, armed with our new intel, I wanted to see what I could see.

When I joined her, she introduced me to the manager. Robert Roman.

He carried himself like a guy who knew he could get away with murder.

*I guess having a criminal mastermind as an uncle does that to a guy.*

"It's nice to meet you, Mr. Roman." I stuck out my hand to shake his and then fought the impulse to wipe my hands on my jeans.

"Honey, I was in such a rush that I forgot my purse. Can you pay for our laundry?"

I laughed, "You'd forget your head if it wasn't attached." I turned my attention back to Roman, who was smirking. "What do we owe you?"

Roman explained Adam wasn't authorized to give us a discount, and made sure we knew how generous he was being by honoring it. Roman carefully counted back my change then went to the back to get our clothes.

The hair on the back of my neck stood up. *This is taking too long.*

Maxwell sat on an old plastic chair feigning boredom, but her tapping fingers gave away her anxiety.

*Shit, she feels it too.*

"Mr. Bishop, can I call you Henry?" Roman asked as he set our bag of clothes on the floor at my feet, his eyes never leaving my face.

"Of course." I smiled.

"Adam made a note on your account that you're interested in joining our poker game."

I smiled and poured on the charm, "I am, if it's not a problem."

Maxwell stood and cleared her throat.

Glancing her way, I added, "But only if my wife says it's okay."

"Wouldn't want to piss off the old ball and chain," he joked.

She feigned a laugh, and said, "I don't know, we can't really afford it."

"What if I let you set my limit?" I begged, "Please, I've been on a roll. And we could use my winnings to replace the washer."

"Maybe, but only if you stick to your budget. I don't want you losing more than we can afford again." She'd set the trap.

"No worries there, Mrs. Bishop. We run a small, friendly game with low stakes," Roman said. Something about the way he said her name made the hair on the back of my neck stand up.

Resisting the urge to scan for the threat, I begged, "Please, Babe?"

"Fine, but no complaining about your limit. And you have to take me to the Chinese restaurant. I really like their Kung Pao Chicken and I'm too tired to cook."

"I can live with that." I winked. "Thanks, Babe."

"Got you on a tight leash, huh?" Roman only half whispered.

"I don't mind, it's worth it." I pretend whispered.

"If you give me your number, I'll text the details," Roman said.

I gave the number to the burner phone, now registered to Henry Bishop. We said our goodbyes, put the clothes in the back seat of my truck, and walked to the restaurant.

"Something's going on," I said after we ordered.

"I felt it too. That's why I suggested coming here."

I wasn't sure I followed her logic, so I swallowed my pride and asked.

"I wanted to give him time to text, thinking we can check the address before we leave."

"You think he will?"

"Hard to say. I think they're suspicious. When I asked about Adam, Robert spared no detail while explaining why he had to cover the desk today. It made the hair on the back of my neck stand up." She rubbed her arms as if the memory gave her goosebumps.

"I had the same reaction." *More than once.* We were running out of time.

Our server brought our drinks. We thanked him when he said our meals wouldn't be long.

"You think they'll try something in broad daylight?" I asked.

"It'd make more sense for them to grab you at the poker game. We'll have someone run intel on the location, once we have it," she said. "We'll put backup in position, too."

I didn't like the sound of being alone with Roman and his goons, even if I had back up in the area, but it was too late to turn back now. If the game led us to Wendy, it was worth the risk.

We'd left our personal phones in the truck, so we couldn't do any research at the restaurant.

"We need to be careful," she said.

I nodded. The humming birds tap dancing in my gut wouldn't let me forget.

Being careful was useless if I couldn't see the enemy before they fired on us.

"Come on, Babe, two hundred isn't enough for the night," I argued as our server dropped off our food.

"Maybe if you won more, I'd trust you with more money," she replied without missing a beat.

I had to admit, Maxwell and I worked well together. When we weren't biting each other's heads off.

We kept the conversation to small talk while we ate.

We were almost done when my vision blurred.

*Fuck.*

I looked at Maxwell as she leaned back in her seat rubbing her eyes. "I think they drugged uth," she slurred the last word.

They couldn't have.

Unless…

Unless Roman owned the restaurant too. *Or he's blackmailing them like he did Davenport.*

I tried to stand up but my balance was off. Falling back into my seat, I checked on Maxwell again. Her hands were gripping the edge of the table as she fought to stay conscious.

"Don't bother trying to fight it." The voice sounded muffled, like it was coming from underwater.

I looked up to see Richard Roman approaching our table. His too big smile making my stomach turn.

"Sheppard. Maxwell." Our cover was blown. "I'd say it's a pleasure to meet you, but we both know that's a lie."

I opened my mouth to say something but Maxwell's unconscious body slumping against me ripped my attention back to her. *Fuck.*

The room spun as I turned back to ask Roman, "What'd you…"

# Chapter 23

## Cate

I woke with a pounding headache and cottonmouth. As I struggled to open my eyes, I tried lifting a hand to rub them, but couldn't. They were tied behind my back, and my head felt heavy and sluggish.

*Shit. Where's Jaden?* I did a quick assessment using my other senses.

The seat felt soft and I could hear a motor running, so a car. I sensed someone beside me.

"I know you're awake, Miss Maxwell. You can open your eyes."

*Who the hell is that?* And opening my eyes was easier said than done. They felt like I'd rubbed them with sandpaper.

The first thing I saw when I forced my eyes open was a blurry Jaden sitting across from me, his chin on his chest. *Unconscious.* I blinked rapidly, clearing my vision as I slowly turned my head.

And looked right into the creepy-as-fuck smiling face of Richard Roman.

"Hello Catelyn, can I call you Cate?"

I grumbled low in my throat.

"I'll take that as a no. Maxwell then?"

"What'd you give us?" I croaked out. I needed to know what was in my system and how long it'd take to wear off.

He shrugged. "It'll wear off soon enough."

Jaden stirred. He didn't wake up quietly and observe the situation. No, he woke up thrashing. Until he made eye contact with me.

"No use fighting, Mr. Sheppard. Can I call you Jaden?"

Roman laughed when Jaden growled. "Aren't you two a testy pair? Sheppard, it is then."

"What do you want?" Jaden demanded.

"I want you to look out the window." The window to my left, Jaden's right, rolled down right on cue.

Jaden and I turned our heads just in time to see his truck go up in flames. Jaden pulled against his ties and tried to stand up, swearing the entire time. "What the fuck!"

The big guy sitting next to him shoved him back down.

"Mr. Sheppard, if you don't sit still, we'll drug you again." Roman's calm voice was far scarier than if he'd been angry.

Calm, collected, calculated. A lethal combination in an enemy.

Jaden calmed down, but didn't stop glaring at Roman.

"Thank you. Your wallets, burner phone, and all your jewelry are in your truck. I'd say I hope you have good insurance…" He looked down at his phone and smiled. "But it doesn't really matter."

Jaden and I made eye contact. Roman's death threat was thinly veiled. For a brief moment, we saw each other's fear. The tinted window dimmed the sunlight as it rolled back up. On Roman's order, the limo pulled away.

"Where are we?" Jaden asked.

"Does it matter?" Roman answered.

I didn't recognize the surrounding area. It looked like a deserted field lined with trees. Which meant one, the truck wouldn't be found right away, and two, when it was, it wouldn't lead SSI to our location.

My headache faded as we drove on. Because of the tinted windows, I couldn't see outside to get my bearings.

"How long were we out?"

"Long enough for us to be far from where we were," Roman said with a snicker.

He was good at not answering our questions. *He's enjoying this. Never a good sign.*

Jaden and I held eye contact while we tested our bindings, which I now realized were handcuffs. My vision was clear enough to watch Roman and his goon in my peripheral vision. The goon kept his face neutral, but Roman smiled as he watched us.

"Where are my manners?" Roman asked. "Would either of you like a drink?"

"No, thanks," I said. Jaden's reply was less polite.

We had different approaches to dealing with our captor. Not that I would've expected anything less.

"What happened to Wendy?" Jaden barked.

"Poor Wendy met with a sad end."

I glared at Jaden, willing him to keep his mouth shut. He didn't. "What'd you do to her?"

"Me?" He sounded shocked to be accused. "I didn't do anything. It was that reckless nephew of mine."

*Robert.*

"He's always getting himself into trouble. That's why my sister sent him here. I'm supposed to straighten him out," he said, acting like we were old friends sharing our stresses over a beer.

"He's gotten into trouble before?" I asked.

"You have no idea. He thinks because he has the Roman name, I'll always bail him out."

"Did you?" I asked. "Bail him out?"

"Of course, he's family," Roman answered like it was a given.

"What happened to Wendy?" Jaden asked. He played the bad cop to my good cop, though I hadn't wanted him to. We wouldn't get anywhere with Roman being rude, instead we'd have to play his game and stroke his ego.

"So impatient. You really should learn some manners."

Roman nodded, and the goon punched Jaden, causing his head to whip to the side.

Jaden stretched his neck before glaring at the goon.

"As I was saying. Young Robert attracts trouble like a magnet."

Roman told us how Robert and Wendy met at the cleaners, and how Robert wined and dined her. Emphasizing how eager Wendy was for his attention.

"She threw herself at him, and he liked the power dynamic of dating the daughter of someone who owed us money. His words, not mine. I'd never stoop so low." His voice thick with disgusted at Robert's actions. "He told Wendy she had to keep their relationship a secret, that way her father wouldn't figure it out. Poor man."

"So Robert runs the gambling ring?" I asked.

"Oh no, he gets a cut of my winnings for each person he brings in. He's barely more than an errand boy."

Like his uncle, Robert like to play games, but I had a feeling he didn't have half his uncle's patience or control when dealing with people.

"Do people ever win in your game?" I asked.

"The house rarely loses," he answered with a wink. "And Mr. Darling was no different."

Of course not. Roman was good at putting people in debt with his gambling ring.

"So your nephew was using Wendy?"

"Oh, he liked her well enough, but she started asking for more than he was willing to give."

*Money? Relationship?* More what?

"I see your wheels turning. Wendy was blinded by Robert's charm. He's chip off the old block." He chuckled at his self compliment. So did his goon.

"So what happened?"

He studied me.

"There's no harm in telling them now, eh, Franks?"

"No, sir. They won't be telling anyone," Franks, the goon, answered. His voice sounded a lot like a hammer driving a nail into my coffin.

Roman told us Wendy wanted them to hang out with her friends more, and introduce him to her father. He didn't want to, and they got into a fight at dinner. Which explained why Wendy didn't look happy in the video footage. When they got back to Robert's place, Wendy made the mistake of challenging his manhood during the argument.

We listened without expression. Without questions. It was better to let Roman tell us everything. If we escaped, we could relay the information.

"When Robert slapped Wendy, she fell and slammed her head on the corner of the table." He shook his head back and forth, sounding genuinely remorseful. "She never woke up."

Robert killed her. She was dead before her father knew she was missing. *He'll be devastated.*

"If it makes you feel any better, her death was instant," he said.

"It doesn't," Jaden barked. When Franks reached out to punch him, Jaden moved.

"He's a quick study," Franks said with a laugh before throwing another punch.

Roman's confidence that we'd never have the opportunity to tell anyone what happened was alarming.

His full, detailed confession hammered home his intent to kill us.

*And there's no way for SSI to track us.* They'd have to get creative, but it'd take longer and I had a feeling time wasn't on our side.

However, they knew everything right up to the time we were drugged. We'd checked in when we sat down to eat. How long ago was that? Had we missed a check in yet?

They'd spare no expense and tear the world apart looking for us. *I pray they find us in time.*

"You have no idea how excited I was when I reviewed the tape to see who Adam invited to the game. Imagine my surprise when I realized it was two PIs from Sheppard & Sons." His smile sent shivers up my spine. "You two saved me a lot of legwork by walking into my humble establishment. Now, I'll have the opportunity to exact my revenge sooner rather than later."

My eyes locked on Jaden's. This was all my fault; the instant I knew Richard Roman was involved, I should've changed tactics.

We had to hope Roman didn't intend to kill us right away. *Or maybe it'll be better if he does.*

# Chapter 24

## Jay

"What'd we do to you?" I asked. I wanted to gauge his emotional reaction. If Roman was calm, he'd probably take things slow. We'd be in for a world of hurt, but it'd give SSI time to find us. I didn't want to think about what would happen if he was emotional.

He tsked. "They say the youngest is always the dumbest."

I glared at him, ignoring Maxwell's silent plea to keep my mouth shut.

"Perhaps he wasn't there," Franks said with a laugh.

I was there, not in the house but in my sniper's nest, and I'd added a few tallies to my kill sheet. Keeping a tally was a sniper thing; all the special operation team snipers did it. Not that I took pleasure in killing people, but some people deserved it. Like the idiots Roman hired to kidnap my sister-in-law and Blake.

Roman looked at Maxwell before looking back at me. "Oh, he was there when SSI killed twenty-three of my men and robbed me of the hundreds of thousands Davenport owes me."

*Owes? He still plans to collect?* Not for the first time in my life, I wished telepathy was real. We needed to tell the team what happened to Wendy, and that Roman still wanted to collect Davenport's debt.

"Blake's an innocent," Maxwell said.

"She is," he agreed. "But paying her father's debts, and the accruing interest, is the least she can do after all the trouble you caused me."

Roman's phone pinged, distracting him for a moment while he replied to a text.

"Surely, Mr. Sheppard," he annunciated my name, "you can see why I'll take great pleasure exacting my revenge against one of the sons of Sheppard & Sons."

"You've got it all wrong. I'm not one of them." I was a son, but not one of the sons from the business title. "Much like your nephew, I'm the family fuck up."

I shouldn't have glanced over to see Maxwell's reaction. Seeing her eyes widen and then fill with sympathy wasn't helpful.

"Maybe, but I'm sure they'll still be sad when I start sending you back in pieces."

The goon, Franks, snickered.

Roman looked at Maxwell and added, "Don't worry, Maxwell, I won't leave you out of the fun."

She paled as he laughed.

I'd lost track of time, but figured we'd been driving at least a half an hour when the limo came to a stop and the driver cut the engine. Not that it mattered. We could have been driving in circles for all I could see.

Roman typed out a message on his phone while waiting for someone to open his door. Before he got out of the car, he ordered, "Blindfold them."

"Yes, sir," another goon said before getting in the car and carrying out the order.

With no way to see where we were, I counted fourteen steps before they led us through a door. The lack of echo told me the rooms we walked through were furnished. I listened for voices or movement but didn't hear any.

*Is he hiding the number of goons on site?* Or was he confident he didn't need more?

A door creaked open before someone said, "Watch your step." Holding my arm, he led me down rickety stairs, the wood bowing under our weight. Judging from the footsteps behind me, Maxwell was also being led down.

*A basement.* The door clicked shut behind us.

The first thing I noticed was the cold.

The second was the light. Even with a blindfold, I could tell it was blinking fast. *A strobe?*

Fuck. They wouldn't just beat us, they'd deploy psychological torture.

I brushed against a cold bar as I was pushed forward. A few seconds later, Maxwell bumped into me.

Metal scraped against concrete. Steel crashed into steel. A lock clicked into place. A death knell if I'd ever heard one.

"Stand still," someone said after they forced me to turn around. I could only assume Maxwell was getting the same treatment.

When I felt a hand on the back of my head, I shut my eyes. I didn't want to shock them with the bright blinking light.

*God, I fucking hate strobe lights.*

"Close your eyes." I took a chance and warned Maxwell, earning a punch in the kidney.

When I grunted, someone said, "Shut up."

I'd said all I needed to say.

When I turned my head, it was forcibly turned back, so I faced forward.

"We have four guys with rifles aimed at your heads. If you turn around before we give you permission…" He laughed. "It'll be the last thing you ever do."

*Copy that.*

Someone removed my blindfold and handcuffs before removing Maxwell's.

As I stood still, facing a wall, waiting, I rubbed my wrists to get the blood flowing again. Fuckers put the cuffs on too tight.

Metal scraped against the concrete floor; the sound worse than nails on a chalkboard. I gritted my teeth, rolled my shoulders, and cracked my neck to the right and left. But I didn't turn around.

This time, I flinched when I heard the click of the lock sliding into place; it sounded far worse the second time around.

I didn't turn around.

I listened carefully as footsteps sounded, counting at least five people walking away. The sound of boots on the wood stairs echoed through the cold room.

Still, I didn't turn around.

The door opened, the light lessening the effects of the strobe. Eerie shadows danced across the wall as those exiting blocked the ray of light.

"You can move now," someone said two seconds before the door slammed shut. I waited for the telltale sign of a door locking and wasn't disappointed.

I turned to Maxwell, asking, "You hurt?"

"No," she said, using one hand to shield her eyes. "You?"

"Just my ego." My laugh felt out of place as it echoed back at me. "And I'm not loving the mood lighting here."

"Ha! Be sure to mention it in your review."

I didn't like the fear in her voice, so I egged her on. "Did you just crack a joke?"

The subtle shake of her head in the strobe looked weird.

"We should check out the accommodations," I said.

Neither of us had turned yet, but I'd used my peripheral vision to notice the blacked-out windows.

No doubt Maxwell had too.

I walked to the bars first and tested their strength.

I crouched. Every bar of the cage was anchored in the cement.

Imagines of old time prison breaks filled my mind. *We won't be using a spoon to dig our way out.*

I walked to the blacked-out window. The only reason I knew it was a window was because of the bars covering it. I tested them; just as solid as the others.

"They've been doing this for a while," Maxwell said.

"You think?" I hadn't intended on sounding snarky, but that's how it came out. When I turned, I noticed the second cage.

Thankfully, it was empty.

The fucking strobe was making it hard to gauge anything with our eyes.

Walking from the wall to the dividing bars, I estimated our cell to be ten feet. The depth was about the same. "Ten by ten. And look, a pisspot."

"Yeah, I saw that." She sounded as thrilled about it as I felt.

I leaned against the back wall, with my eyes closed to shut out the strobe, while Maxwell paced in the cell.

Her mumbling did nothing for my already foul mood.

Tired of the bullshit she was spewing, I opened my eyes so I could watch her reaction when I asked, "What the fuck, Maxwell? How is this my fault?"

She lost her balance when she turned to face me.

"If it's anyone's fault, it's yours. You're the one who overreacted and blew our cover," I spat at her.

"Don't you dare blame me," she yelled. "That wouldn't have happened if you hadn't kissed me without warning."

"Well, forgive me for trying to make sure our cover didn't get blown."

From what Roman said, it was luck—good for him, but bad for us—that he'd ID'd us on the video feed after Adam mentioned my interest in gambling. Neither of us was at fault, but we blamed each other anyway.

*It's easier to be angry than afraid.*

"You can blame me all you want, but it won't help us get out of this mess."

"What do you think I've been doing?" I huffed out.

"Holding up the wall," she said, taking a step forward.

I pushed myself off said wall and took one step forward.

"You're wrong. I was thinking of ways to break out while conserving my energy."

"What do you think I'm doing?"

"Wasting your energy by pacing. We could be here a while and the strobes will give you a headache if you don't give your eyes a break."

My helpful advice came out sounding like a reprimand, but I didn't care as long as she listened.

*We'll need every ounce of energy we have to get through this.*

# Chapter 25

## Cate

He was right, of course. And while I didn't appreciate his snarky attitude, something in his resigned tone hinted at knowledge from experience.

We could be here a while and conserving energy was a good idea. I leaned against the side wall, keeping my distance from Jaden, and slid down to a seated position. The cold from the cement seeped through my jeans in no time.

I closed my eyes and prayed for courage. Roman wanted revenge, which meant he'd make this as unpleasant as possible.

Choosing not to continue the argument, I said. "There's no way we can break out. We'll have to find a clever solution."

"Obviously."

I could hear him rolling his eyes. I took a deep breath in and held it, steadying my nerves and calming my irritation. We'd never get out of this if we couldn't work together.

"I'm sorry. I didn't mean to imply you didn't know."

"Thank you."

I opened my eyes, the strobe making me regret instantly it, when Jaden landed on the floor with a thud, stretching his long legs out in front of him.

"So, any ideas?" he asked.

"Not yet." We hadn't even been here an hour. "You see any cameras?"

"No, but it's safe to assume they're watching," Jaden said. "And listening."

Which would make it hard for us to plan. I spoke fluent Spanish and passable Arabic, but didn't know if Jaden spoke any other languages. Besides, they'd be easy enough to translate. Speaking in code might work, but we didn't have one and creating one on the fly would create confusion.

I nodded, which was stupid; his eyes were probably closed. "It's safe to assume so."

"How long do you think he'll leave us here before-"

The strobes cut off, and a horn blasted, startling us both, a second before the door opened. We stood, walked to the center of our cell, and faced the stairs, waiting. Three men stomped down; Roman and two men with rifles in their hands.

Jaden laughed.

"Knock it off!" I hissed. The last thing we needed to do was piss Roman off and make things worse for ourselves.

"We're literally locked in a cage, and they're still afraid of us."

"Hardly, but I'm not taking any chances," Roman said.

If he had armed goons every time he came down, we had no hope of surviving an escape attempt.

When Jaden walked towards the front of the cell, I followed.

"I'm giving you a onetime offer. Tell me everything you have on me and my nephew, and how I can find Ms. Davenport, and I'll make your deaths relatively quick and painless," Roman said.

*Relatively quick and painless?* I doubted either Jaden or I would think it was quick or painless.

I said, "We didn't get very far." At the same time, Jaden said, "Go to hell."

Roman wouldn't get anything out of us.

"Suit yourselves." Roman shrugged before making eye contact with Jaden, then me, and slowly turning his back.

The two guys with rifles followed him, walking backwards until they reached the staircase. Roman sauntered up the stairs like he didn't have a care in the world.

Like he hadn't just promised to kill us, slow and painful.

Unable to suppress the trembling in my hands, I clenched my fists.

He hadn't actually said it, but his implication was loud and clear.

After the two guys left the basement, Roman called down, "You have no idea who you're fucking with."

*I have a feeling we were about to find out.*

The door slammed shut.

The lights cut out.

A piercing alarm split the silence, making me jump.

I covered my ears and turned to Jaden. This was his fault. I wanted to get Roman talking, buy us some time. But no. He had to piss him off.

"What the fuck was that?" I shouted over the incessant blaring of the alarm.

"We don't negotiate with terrorists," Jaden yelled, his hands covering his ears to dampen the sound.

"Are you fucking kidding me?" I understood his sentiment. What I wanted to know was why he insisted on poking the bear.

I could barely stand hearing my alarm go off in the morning. *This will drive me certifiably insane long before Roman kills me.*

Which was why they did it; to torture us and break us down physically and mentally.

"We're not telling him shit."

"No, but there are better ways to handle the situation."

"I got my point across."

"You're going to get us killed," I yelled.

He pointed to the door. "That fucker torched my truck!"

"Are you fucking serious right now?" *That's what he's worried about?*

"As a heart attack!" Anger rolled off him in waves.

I took the bait. "That's why you have insurance. You do have insurance, don't you?" I asked. Not that it would matter if we died here.

*Will this fucking alarm ever stop?*

"Of course I have insurance. I'm not a complete idiot."

"From where I'm standing, you're the idiot who wants to piss off the guy who gets to decide if we live or die." My voice sounded hoarse from the strain. *I should probably stop arguing.*

"He plans on killing us no matter what we do. Or were you not paying attention?" His sarcasm was thicker than molasses.

I returned his glare. "I was, but I'd rather not rush to the scaffold, if it's all the same to you."

"He has a plan; our actions are irrelevant," Jaden shouted as he turned and walked to the back wall. He slid down to the floor and rested his elbows on his knees, his hands still blocking out the sound.

"Your actions will piss him off and we'll die sooner because of it."

"You think playing nice will save you?"

"No." Maybe. Hopefully. "But it could buy us some time." Time for SSI to find us and save us.

"Maybe, but we may not want to buy ourselves too much time." Resignation replaced his sarcasm.

Once again, I had a feeling he was speaking from experience. I wanted to ask him about it, but discussing anything in a calm, rational manner was near impossible with the alarm blaring non-stop.

"So, what? You're just giving up?" I pulled my hands away from my ears to put my hands on my hips and instantly regretted it. The alarm seemed loud with my ears plugged, but it was nothing compared to the eardrum-rupturing level when they weren't.

The sliver of light coming from under the door was just enough for me to see him shake his head back and forth. "I didn't say that."

Good. We'd need to work as a team if we had any chance of survival.

I went back to the side wall and sat. Plugging my ears as best I could and waited it out. It may have lasted minutes or hours, but it was hard to tell.

When the alarm finally stopped, the silence sounded foreign.

*Finally, I can hear myself think again.*

"Thank God." Jaden said, as he stood and stretched his neck.

Given how my mind raced with a thousand and one ways this could end, all of them badly, it wasn't much of an improvement.

My brain had conjured up images of everything from Jaden and I slowly starving to death in the cell while being psychologically tortured, to being physically tortured, clinging desperately to life until our broken bodies gave up the fight.

There wasn't a single scenario among them I wanted to experience.

"You okay?" Jaden asked.

I wasn't. But Roman was probably watching, so I refused to admit it or show any sign of weakness.

"I'm okay. Pissed off, but okay. You?"

"Same."

We sat in dark silence, for who knows how long, as time lost all meaning. I'd just dozed off when the strobe lights came back on.

"What the fuck?" Jaden yelled, jumping to his feet and looking around like he'd forgotten where we were. *He must have fallen asleep, too.*

"You don't happen to know how long we've been here, do you?" I asked, hoping he could judge time better than I could.

"No." I was afraid he'd say that. "Fucking strobe and alarm. Audio and visual torture are designed to distort our perception of time and reality." I didn't call him out for telling me what I already knew, knowing it'd start another fight.

I doubted we'd been here more than a few hours, but it already felt like the longest day of my life.

My bladder complained, so I asked Jaden to look away while I used the pail. It was humiliating having to empty my bladder with him nearby, but I didn't have a choice. *Thank God he can't see me.* The strobe fucked with my balance as I hovered.

"Thanks," I muttered as I walked back to the wall. The snap shots of his head nodding would have been comical under different circumstances.

Luckily, it was easier blocking the light than the alarm, so I relaxed for a few minutes.

But it was too quiet, and I didn't like being left alone with my fear-driven, morbid thoughts.

*Will I ever see my father again? Will I see Charlie say I do in the fall?*

Then my brain remembered all those romance books I'd read where two people think they're going to die and decide to have sex before they do. Only to survive and regret it. *At least at first, they almost always fall in love…*

I looked at Jaden, his arms resting on his legs, his head resting on his ink-covered, corded forearms.

*Not happening.*

"Jaden?"

"Yeah?"

"Can I ask you a question?" I wanted to know what he'd experienced.

"You just did." His forced laugh echoed in the space. "Go for it."

"Have you ever gone through something like this before?" I asked, intentionally keeping the question broad.

Silence filled the space as the light flashed off and on.

He lifted his head and answered, "Yes." His voice was barely above a whisper.

Just one word, but it spoke volumes. As a Marine Raider, it was safe to assume he'd seen a lot of shit and probably suffered through some shit.

"How long?"

Another long pause.

"Five days," he said. "But it felt like a hell of a lot longer." He rested his head against the back wall and hung an arm over his eyes to block out the light.

"Were you alone?" I should have let it go, but something in me needed to know.

*If he survived it once, maybe he can do it again.*

The pause was long enough that I didn't think he'd answer. Figuring it was bringing up memories he didn't want to revisit, I apologized.

"It's okay." He turned towards me in what I assume was an attempt to make eye contact. "To answer your question, no, I wasn't alone. I was with my team buddy. It took the rest of our team five days to find us."

I was still debating whether it'd be rude to ask what happened when he said, "I can practically hear you wondering if it's okay to ask." His laugh sounded hollow and sad. "It's fine. They chained us to a wall in an unfinished basement that felt more like a fucking cave." His voice was thick with emotion. "They released us for random beatings, but otherwise we shared five square feet of space to eat, shit, and sleep."

I couldn't imagine how horrific that must have been. At least they hadn't chained us, and we had room to walk if we wanted to.

"Though we didn't eat much. We didn't dare to. On the plus side, it meant we didn't shit much either." He ran both hands through his hair. "The fucking lights and noise made it impossible to sleep."

Five days, chained to a wall, with little to no food or water, subjected to psychological torture and random beatings. An icy chill swept over my body that had nothing to do with the temperature of the hard floor I sat on.

I squinted at Jaden, trying to read his expression. His voice sounded flat, but there was no way the experience hadn't left a lasting impact.

He lifted his head off the wall and said, "We needed two months to recover enough for them to let us operate again, but we both made it back."

# Chapter 26

## Jay

I didn't like talking about it. Didn't like thinking about it. Henderson, that girlfriend stealing jerkoff, and I spent a week with metal shackles around our wrists, and after trying to kick anyone who came too close, our ankles.

I shivered, the cold in the basement reminding me of the cold in the 'resort' as we called it. We'd been on patrol when the enemy ambushed us, separating us from the rest of the team. We fought for as long as we could, but in the end, they surrounded us. Because we were hyper focused on the firefight in front of us, we didn't hear them sneak up behind us.

But the muzzle of a gun, as it pressed into the back of my neck, got my attention.

My hand twitched in the dark basement at the memory of taking my finger off the trigger before turning to see if

Henderson was still with me. He was, and he had company too.

Our only option was to surrender and hope our team found us before it was too late.

"Jaden?" Maxwell's voice pulled me back to the present.

"Yeah?"

"Are you okay?"

"Yeah."

"Want to talk about it?"

I didn't. Talking about it would prolong the memory, and I didn't want to scare Maxwell with tales of thirst and hunger so intense it made eating rats sound tempting, or the daily beatings, which included old school electric shock torture.

*It might be old school, but it's effective at wearing a person down.*

We endured it all without giving up a single piece of information beyond our names, ranks, and serial numbers.

"What level SERE training did you have?" I deflected the question to a relevant one of my own. Maxwell would need everything she learned in the Marine's Survival, Evasion, Resistance, and Escape training if she wanted to get through this with her mind intact. As an officer, she may have had level B if she was stationed near the front lines.

I'd been through it twice. Level A, which all Marine's are required to take, and Level C, which all Raiders are required to take.

The first was a cakewalk. The second kicked my ass.

*That training is the reason I'm still alive and of sound mind.*

"Level A."

I was afraid she'd say that.

The strobe cut out, leaving us in the pitch black. The only speck of light was from the bottom of the door at the top of the stairs.

"The alarm will probably come on again," I warned.

"Thank-" the alarm cut her off. We did our best to block the noise by stuffing our fingers in our ears.

I recited the Marine Raider creed to keep my mind occupied.

*My title is Marine Raider. I will never forget the tremendous legacy and sacrifice of those who came before me. At all times my fires will be accurate. With cunning, speed, surprise, and violence of action, I will hunt the enemies of my country and bring chaos to their doorstep.*

The alarm cut out after what felt like forever but was probably only about ten minutes, given I'd recited the creed twenty- three times.

*I wonder what Maxwell thought about.*

A foghorn sounded before the door opened, and light flooded the space. We stood and walked towards the front of our cage. I instinctively moved closer to Maxwell, wanting to protect her for as long as I could.

The last guy in closed the door behind him, throwing us back into darkness until two weapon mounted lights shined in our faces.

Rifles pointed at our heads. *Duly noted.*

Nice tactic, using the lights to blind us. Not that they planned on letting us live to identify them.

Roman wasn't with them this time. But I recognized Franks, the fucker who punched me in the limo.

"Mr. Roman thought you might be hungry," he said. "Walk to the back and face the wall." The sound of paper rustling filled the air. "If you behave, I'll give you food and water."

"What'd you lace it with?" I asked as I walked backwards to the wall.

"Nothing, we want you fully conscious for what's coming," he answered with a smile that made my hair stand on end. "Now turn around."

Turning my back on an armed enemy was not at the top of my list of things I was comfortable with, but I didn't have a choice. And we needed water.

*If it's safe to drink.*

I complied. I didn't trust him, but there were ways to check the water.

He didn't open the cage door, but I heard two paper sacks hit the floor before footsteps sounded again.

He called out, "Bon appétit!" and slammed the door.

I clenched and unclenched my fists as I forced myself to take a few breaths and calm myself down. Holding back the desire to choke the life out of Franks, Roman, and his goons, had my heart racing and my eye twitching.

Paper crinkled as Maxwell picked up a bag and felt inside. "A bottle of water, a sandwich, chips, and a cookie." She pulled out the water. "If we squeeze it, we'll know if they tampered with it," she said.

"Exactly what I was thinking." I grabbed the other bag and tested the water bottle. No leaks. "I think it's safe to drink."

The test was good but not foolproof, so I said, "Take tiny sips and wait between drinks."

"I'll go first." Maxwell opened her bottle and sniffed. "No odor. Here goes nothing." She took a small sip. "Tastes clean."

I took a sip and rolled the water around in my mouth, verifying what she'd said before swallowing. Not that I didn't trust her; I wanted a second opinion.

"You think we can eat the chips since they're sealed?" she asked.

My stomach rumbled at the thought. My last meal was the spiked Chinese food, so of course I was starving.

"Probably, but they'll make you more thirsty. Might be a ploy to get us to drink more water."

"That's what I thought, but was hoping for a different answer." Her stomach grumbled, rather loudly, at being denied food.

"Doesn't mean we can't eat them. We just need to do it with our open eyes." I took out the bag and squeezed it to see if there were any air leaks. None.

"You going to eat them?"

"I'm debating," I answered. "I'm starving, so my stomach is screaming at me to eat. But my brain knows it's a bad idea."

"We'll need the energy, so that's a tick in the eat them box," she said.

"But if they drugged the water or chips before they were sealed, we'd be helping them by eating. Tick in the don't eat box."

"Franks said they want us conscious for what's coming." Despite her attempts to sound nonchalant, I could hear her fear. "Whatever that might be."

"I think we can assume it'll be unpleasant," I said, making the understatement of the year. "And there are lots of drugs that would render us immobile, but leave us conscious."

"I know." Her voice fell flat.

I dropped the chips in the bag and tossed it out the bars, removing all temptation.

"Better safe than sorry." I'd never suffered through being conscious while unable to move, but heard it was the worst form of hell.

That'd be a hard pass from me.

"Better safe than sorry." Maxwell's bag followed mine out of the cage. "I could stand to lose a few pounds, anyway." She chuckled.

I disagreed, but now wasn't the time to pick a fight about how perfect her body was.

"Cheers," I said, holding my bottle up before realizing how stupid it was. "Nevermind."

"Is it just me or is the temperature dropping?" she asked.

"It's dropping." We could expect the strobe or alarm to come back on again soon.

Or maybe we'd get a special treat, and they'd both come on.

We sat back down. This time, Maxwell joined me along the back wall.

In what could only be considered a blessing, the basement stayed dark and quiet long enough for us both to fall asleep. And to dream.

I expected nightmares. Instead, I dreamed of Maxwell curled up next to me.

Because of the fucking alarm, I woke with a start. So did Maxwell. She pulled away quickly, but not before it registered that she'd been leaning against me, her head resting on my shoulder.

I didn't mind, but I'd never tell her that.

The alarm shut off as abruptly as it started.

"Guess they don't want us to sleep."

"Guess not," she said. "I'm surprised they even let us fall asleep."

I wasn't. Roman would take great pleasure in letting us fall asleep, only to scare us awake.

"Me too. Wish they'd let me have a little more," I said. "I was having a delightful dream."

"I wish mine was. Tell me about yours. It'll take my mind off mine."

"I was on a warm sandy beach with a beautiful blond serving me a tropical drink with a pink umbrella in it," I lied.

But it worked, making Maxwell laugh. "Of course you were."

"The strobe and alarm will probably start again soon. How'd you manage the last time?"

"I was okay with the strobe, but the alarm made me feel like I was going crazy."

"Can I offer a suggestion?"

"Please," she practically begged.

"I recited the Raider Creed in my head. Is there something that brings you pride or joy that you could recite, maybe a song?"

"Does it work?" she sounded skeptical.

"It worked for me. Worst case it doesn't; but you're no worse off."

"True. I wonder if I remember the Marine's Hymn?" she mumbled.

"Of course you do." I sang, "From the Halls of Montezuma."

"To the shores of Tripoli." She joined in, surprising me with her soft soprano singing voice.

We kept our voices low while we sang. We didn't get to the end before the alarm started. I went back to reciting the creed. When the strobes started, I could see Maxwell's lips moving as she sang to herself.

*I hope it helps.*

I lost track of how many times I repeated the creed before the noise stopped and the room was dark again. Slumping against the wall, I asked, "How'd it work?"

"I feel less crazy."

"Good."

# Chapter 27

## Jay

A foghorn blaring snapped me awake. I was on my feet before the upstairs door opened, once again flooding the basement with light.

It's *a warning*. Every time the foghorn blasted, the door opened, and we had visitors.

Maxwell stood, and we walked to the front of our cell, just like last time.

Four riflemen flanked Roman. When he saw the bags on the floor he tsked. "I see you failed to appreciate my generosity." He kicked the bags out of his way. "Did you not like the selection, or is it because you don't trust me?"

"What do you think?" I asked, crossing my arms as I stood near the cage door. I moved in front of Maxwell, but she shifted beside me.

He laughed. "I suppose I can't blame you, but you really should've eaten your breakfast when you had the chance." He nodded to Franks. "You'll need your strength for the day's activities."

*Breakfast?* Was it morning already?

Franks stepped forward, pointed at the far corner, and ordered, "Stand in the corner."

*Fuck.* I figured they were here for one of us, but hoped they'd take me first. I took my time, glaring as I walked backwards, following his orders.

He stared back at me the entire time. His sick smirk did nothing to calm my already frayed nerves. When I was where he wanted me to be, he said, "Put your hands on your head."

Having no other choice, I laced my fingers and put my hands on the top of my head.

"Move, and we shoot your partner."

I had zero doubt he was bluffing, so I bit my tongue and stood perfectly still. Every cell in my body wanted to say something, to test my limits. But knowing Maxwell would pay the price forced me to be on my best behavior.

He pointed at Maxwell. "Face the back wall and put your hands behind your back."

She complied, her jaw clenched and her hands fisted.

"Remember, if either of you move, we'll shoot your partner."

"Sir, yes, sir," I barked. Maxwell didn't answer.

I expected him to tell me to turn around, but then again, Roman would enjoy forcing me to watch Franks cuff Maxwell. She stood stock still while he did it. When he grabbed her arm and pulled, she didn't move, saying, "You told me not to move."

*That a girl, show them how well Marines obey orders.*

He shoved her, almost knocking her off balance, then continued pushing her until she was outside the cage. There was no point in trying to fight.

Too many guys with guns.

*Is that a fucking cattle prod?*

I prayed for Maxwell.

# Chapter 28

## Cate

The zing of an electric current behind my right arm made my hair stand on end. I turned just enough to identify what made the sound.

A cattle prod. Not strong enough to harm a cow, but I was a lot smaller than a cow. Knowing it wouldn't kill me was little comfort.

"Be a good girl, and Franks won't have to use it," Roman said.

I prayed for strength to get through whatever was coming as Roman and his men escorted me up the wooden stairs, down a hall, and into a small room.

"Sit." Franks ordered.

The sun was rising outside the window. *I'm facing east.* Not that it mattered, I thought, as Franks tied me to the small wooden chair.

"Now, Catelyn, can I call you Cate?"

"It's Maxwell." My plan was to rely on my Marine and FBI training, which meant saying as little as possible. And suffering the consequences as bravely as I could.

"Alright, Maxwell, tell me what Sheppard & Sons knows about my nephew."

"Nothing." I braced for the expected hit.

"Now Cate, excuse me, Maxwell, you must know something if you ended up at his store."

I stared at the cattle prod Franks held in his right hand and bounced against his left, while leaning casually against the edge of Roman's desk. If I weren't an expert at reading body language, I would've thought he looked bored. He wasn't. If the look in his eyes was any indication, he was eagerly anticipating the opportunity to zap me. Of course, Roman's enforcer was a sadist. I made a mental note to warn Jaden.

Franks stood when Roman said, "I don't enjoy waiting."

"It was a coincidence." I shrugged.

"And I really don't like liars." His nod signaled Franks.

When he tapped the prod on my thigh, all thoughts left my mind as my muscles seized. It only lasted a few seconds, but the feeling lingered.

"I don't like having to do that," Roman said.

The shock sparked my sarcasm. "Who's the liar now?"

When my body relaxed after the longer shock, I recognized my mistake. But I didn't regret my choice.

"How'd you link Robert to Wendy?"

"Facial recognition." My non-answer answer brought Roman to his feet.

"I must say, I expected better from you, Ms. Maxwell. This is the sort of behavior I expected from Mr. Sheppard."

"Sorry." I made sure it sounded as insincere as I felt.

Roman stood in front of me, staring.

I stared back, pretending my heart wasn't racing a mile a minute.

He moved faster than I'd anticipated, barely giving me time to brace before backhanding me.

His hit split my lip, filling my mouth with the copper tang of blood.

"Your lack of cooperation will only make what time you have left on this planet miserable," he said, cleaning his hands with sanitizer before wiping them on the towel one of his guys handed to him.

*He doesn't like getting his hands dirty*. I added it to the list of things to share with Jaden.

Roman asked more questions. I gave more half and non-answers. Franks enjoyed deploying the cattle prod.

When Roman asked about Blake, I said, through gritted teeth, "Leave. Her. The. Fuck. Alone."

His sadistic smile sent shivers down my spine. "You're in no position to give orders." He nodded and Franks punched me, making me see stars.

My teeth hurt from clenching them. My muscles ached from seizing over and over and over again. My head pounded from the hits doled out between shocks.

When Roman was done and they finally untied me, I was too weak to stand.

"Help her downstairs," Roman ordered. "If she's faking it, shoot Sheppard in the kneecap." That last part was for my benefit, but he didn't need to worry. I didn't have the energy to respond, let alone fight.

My hands were still cuffed behind my back so Franks supporting me was awkward. His lack of compassion and gentleness meant it was also painful.

Because of the light flooding the basement as Franks half-dragged me down the stairs, I saw Jaden's reaction.

He looked downright murderous. I wouldn't want to be Franks if Jaden got his hands on him.

"What'd you do to her?" he yelled.

"Back in your corner," Franks ordered instead of answering.

"Do it," I said, doing my best to sound okay.

Thankfully, he complied, but his eyes never left mine.

Jaden was a statue until the cage lock clicked into place. Then he ran, catching me as my knees gave out. How I'd managed to remain standing without help for as long as I had was a mystery.

"What'd they do?" he asked, far more gentle than when he'd asked Franks.

"Cattle prod. I'll be okay once it wears off." He'd seen my face, which had to be covered with bruises and red welts, so I didn't feel the need to tell him about the hits.

He helped me to the back wall, eased me to the ground in front of him, and pulled me back into his warm, hard chest.

"It's morning," my voice shaky as I updated him. "And it's a lot warmer upstairs."

"Relax." His breath tickled my ear.

I sat up. "There's something else I have to tell you, but I can't remember."

"It's okay, we've got time. Just lean back and relax. I've got you." Jaden's deep, soothing voice comforted me as he gently pulled me back to his chest.

The pain and weakness subsided slowly, allowing me to doze off as I relaxed in Jaden's arms.

I don't know how long I napped before I snapped awake with a hypnotic jerk and panicked. It only took a second to remember where I was—the cold, dark room a harsh reminder.

"Are you okay?" Jaden asked, his arms still wrapped around me.

*Why are his arms around me?* When I tried to move away, my body screamed. *The cattle prod.* Every muscle felt overworked.

"Sore, but otherwise okay." I pulled away, immediately missing his warmth. "How long was I out?"

"Maybe thirty minutes."

I braced my hands on his knees and stood. His hands hovered nearby, ready to support me if needed. "Thanks."

"You're welcome." He stood behind me. When I started to stretch, he said, "Start slow."

"I don't think that's an option." My laugh sounded more like a whimper.

He handed me a bottle of water. Remembering my fear of drugs, I sipped slowly, despite my thirst.

"Thank you for everything," I said as I handed him the bottle. I was seeing a new side of Jaden. *He's a good guy when he's not trying to prove he's not 'less than' his brothers.* Not that I'd say it out loud, at least not here.

"No problem." He shrugged it off.

Remembering what I wanted to tell him, I whispered, "Franks is a sadist and Roman doesn't like to get his hands dirty."

"That doesn't surprise me. He hides behind a lot of shell corporations and lets his enforcers do the work."

"No, I mean literally. He backhanded me and immediately reached for sanitizer."

"Interesting. How can we use it?"

"Not sure. I doubt he'll be hands on often." He had Franks and his other goons for that.

"Feeling better?" he asked.

I wished I could see his expressions. Not that I doubted his sincerity, I could hear that, but I wanted to give him the answer he needed. There was no guarantee they'd question him before taking another go at me, and I didn't want him more pissed off than he already was.

"I am." It wasn't a total lie. "I just need to move a little." Walking the perimeter of our cage, I trailed my right hand along the wall and bars for added support.

We talked about what they'd asked, my answers, and their methods for extracting information. Jaden's low growls didn't go unnoticed when I told him about the hits and zaps.

"It could have been worse," I played it off.

"You're one tough cookie, Maxwell."

"Was that a compliment, Sheppard?"

He laughed. "Don't let it go to your head."

When the foghorn blasted, I jumped, making me wince.

The door opened, and three guys stomped down the stairs. One of them tossed two paper bags through the bars before they all stomped back up the stairs.

"Breakfast is served." Shockingly, Jaden's snarky sense of humor helped me stay calm.

"Bon appétit." I quoted Franks.

The meal was the same. A sandwich, chips, a cookie, and a bottle of water.

We tested the water bottles and ignored the food, making our stomachs grumble in protest. At some point, we'd have to risk eating something if we wanted to keep our strength up, but we weren't there yet.

*And as long as we have water, we have six to eight weeks before starvation kills us.*

Not true, we'd succumb sooner. The cold, physical abuse, and torture induced lack of sleep would weaken us significantly and shorten our life spans.

A shiver that had nothing to do with the chill in the basement ran down my spine. I prayed SSI found us before it was too late.

When the alarm started blaring, I blocked my ears as best I could and tried to remember the lyrics to my favorite song, hoping the concentration needed would keep my mind off the noise.

When the strobe started, I squeezed my eyes shut and prayed.

# Chapter 29

## Jay

It felt like days, but probably wasn't more than an hour or two, before they shut the alarm and strobe off. I gave up reciting the creed and took a walk down memory lane, remembering the extensive training I'd taken to become a Raider instead. It served as a reminder I could get through this.

Hell, I'd already survived hell like this once. And these guys had nothing on our enemies in the Middle East. Though I figured it was only a matter of time before they upped the ante and got more creative with the torture.

I didn't know how long it was before the foghorn sounded, Franks and two riflemen came down the stairs, and two more bags landed in our cell. Once again, we tested the bottles and ignored the food. Tossing the bags out of the cage to remove temptation was harder this time around.

They left us alone in cold, dark silence for a few blissful hours, giving us time to talk.

We were getting along, but I was about to disrupt that. Not that I wanted to upset her, but I didn't want Roman thinking we were friends and could be used against each other.

*Too late.* My mind reminded me I'd held her in my arms and comforted her when they'd brought her back. *At least I can get to know her and kill some time.*

"Let's play a game," I suggested.

"You know it's dark, right?"

"Yup. You don't need light to play twenty questions."

"I'm not in the mood."

*She sounds tired.* Not that it surprised me; she'd been through a lot.

"And here I thought you were tough." I tsked.

"Fine. Ask."

"First the rules. You have to answer the question you ask after you hear my answer, same for me. What's your favorite color?" Starting with simple questions would help us relax.

"I don't really have one."

"Lame answer, Maxwell. Pick one."

"Fine." After a pause she said, "You know the color of the first daffodils in spring? I think that's my favorite color."

Interesting, a color tied to a flower and a season. "I never would have pegged you for a flower girl."

"Most women like flowers, even the ones who don't talk about it."

"That's what Meg says. My favorite color is green."

She laughed, "Figures. OD?"

After years of wearing the military shade of green, olive drab wasn't even in my top ten. "Is that your question?"

"No, it's clarification. Besides, I already answered the question."

"My game, my rules, and I say it counts as your question. And my answer is, no, not OD. I like the dark shades, though I can't name them." I didn't give her time to respond before asking my next question. "What's your favorite food? It can be general."

"That's easy. Pasta." She laughed.

"Good choice. Have you tried Meg's bacon mac and cheese or my mom's lasagna?" I asked before remembering she'd tried Meg's signature dish the night before Roman kidnapped us.

"That's cheating," she huffed.

"Right, my answer is there isn't a food I won't try, but my favorite is steak."

She laughed. "That specific, huh?" Before I answered, she said, "I retract the question."

"I'll allow it." We kept our voices low and the questions light and fun, learning about each other while killing time.

I asked, "Why, in your professional opinion, won't Roman or Franks come down without at least two riflemen?" I wanted her to tell me they were afraid we'd find a way out, but she didn't.

"To remind us they're in charge," she said. I'd explored the cage while she was upstairs, but hadn't found a weak point. And while physically I could overpower one goon, I couldn't take them all, even if they didn't have rifles. Under the circumstances, trying would be a poor life choice.

The foghorn blasted, letting us know we had company. We stood and walked to the middle.

*Like Pavlov's fucking dogs.*

Roman paid us a visit, flanked by his rifle-carrying friends. I didn't care what Maxwell said; we scared him. Which was amusing, considering we were locked in a cage.

"I do wish you'd speak up when you talk to each other. I'd love to hear what's making you laugh," he said, confirming our suspicion.

"Go to hell," I said.

"Such bad manners," Roman said. His fixation on manners wasn't lost on me. "I think it's time I taught you a lesson, son."

Oh, hell no. This man wasn't a fraction of the man my father was. "Don't call me that," I growled. "My father is a thousand times the man you are."

"Too bad you'll never see him again." His laugh made the hair on the back of my neck stand up. He ordered, "Take him."

Grateful they weren't taking Maxwell again, I complied with their instructions like a good soldier.

They followed the same protocol as they had for Maxwell. Cuffing and escorting me upstairs.

The first thing I noticed was how much warmer it was. I'd gotten used to the cold and had all but forgotten about it.

I looked around, but the wall of men surrounding me made it hard to see anything. The one thing I could see; the sun was setting. We'd been here twenty-four long-ass hours.

I prayed Roman was wrong, and I'd get to see my dad, and my family, again.

Franks left my wrists cuffed behind my back. Warning me they'd shoot Maxwell's kneecap if I fought back, as they tied my ankles to the chair, guaranteed my compliance. Making the thick, scratchy rope they wrapped around my chest tight enough to dig into my skin, unnecessary.

*Not that they'd trust me.* Even with the threat, I might involuntarily lash out in self-defense if the abuse was severe enough.

I looked around. It wouldn't do me any good to fight; I was outnumbered and outgunned.

*And that cattle prod doesn't look like much fun.* I saw what it did to Maxwell; it'd take longer to have the same effect on me, but it would still suck. I doubted Franks would hesitate to deploy it as often as needed to make sure I suffered.

Roman waited a good five minutes after they tied me up to talk. "Will it make a difference if I tell you this will be easier if you cooperate?"

"Probably not." I grinned. "Where are we?" I asked. I could see a yard behind him, but there was nothing that hinted at our location.

"Does it matter?" He grinned back.

"Nah, just curious." The tight rough ropes scratch my arms when I shrugged.

Careful to keep a safe distance from the tip of the cattle prod, Roman walked around his desk and leaned against the front. He crossed one ankle over the other, looking relaxed and casual. His hands gripping the edge of the desk were the only sign he wasn't.

"Jaden."

"That's Mr. Sheppard to you, Mr. Roman, or can I call you Dick?"

The look on his face was worth the resulting punch and bloody lip. Remembering what Maxwell said, I spit towards his shoes before saying, "I'll take that as a no."

"You have terrible manners. I'd like to think your parents raised you better." He wandered back to his seat. "I have to wonder if your brothers would be as rude if they were in your shoes."

He struck a raw nerve. I clenched my back teeth and held back a smartass response. He didn't need to know I felt inferior to my brothers in every way.

He asked me the same questions he asked Maxwell. I gave him the same half and non-answers.

When he asked me about Blake, I said, "She's protected. Go after her again and it'll be the last thing you ever do." It wasn't an exaggeration, AJ's intense protectiveness gave new meaning to the phrase, "Touch her and die".

If Roman gives me the chance, I'll teach him what it means.

"We'll see." He paused. "But you won't." His calm response caused my blood to run cold. I prayed for Blake's safety, and that I'd live to see AJ rip Richard Roman from limb to limb. *And if I'm lucky, help him.*

Throughout the interrogation, Franks hit me, but didn't apply the cattle prod.

Curious to see how they'd react, I lunged when they told me to stand up. I didn't try getting close to anyone, just provided a sudden movement to gauge their reaction.

They aimed rifles at my head while Franks poked me, shocking me into compliance. Every muscle in my body seized up. I stumbled when he pulled back and my muscles suddenly relaxed.

Unlike Maxwell, I could walk back to the cage without help. I grinned as she watched them remove my cuffs.

As soon as we were alone in the cold and dark, she asked, "Are you okay?"

"Yeah, they only prodded me once." I didn't share why.

"That's good. Did he ask anything new?" She handed me a bottle of water.

"No, and I didn't tell him anything either." I pre-answered the next logical question. "Though I warned him not to go after Blake."

"So did I. Do you think he will?" she asked, fear lacing her voice.

"AJ will protect her."

I walked around the cage until the pain from the shock no longer lingered. When I sat down, Maxwell moved close and asked, "Are you really okay?"

Maxwell's concern and compassion were more than I wanted to deal with. "Yeah. It wasn't so bad." They'd been far more abusive to her. "Let's finish our game."

"Maybe you should rest."

I leaned my head against the hard wall and sighed. "Maxwell, it takes minimal energy to talk." I wasn't in the mood to argue, but I didn't want to sit alone with my thoughts, either.

"Okay. Whose turn is it?"

"I'll let you go."

"Always the gentleman." Her laugh did more to calm me than her concern. I considered making a wiseass remark, but didn't have time.

"Cats or Dogs?" she asked.

"Dogs," I answered without hesitation. I wasn't a cat hater, but I loved dogs. "You?"

"Both, but since I have to choose one. Cats."

"Really? Why? I always pegged you as a dog person."

"That's two questions." I turned my head towards her and made a face. Not that she could see it. She continued, "But I'll consider it one. I like their independence. Why dogs?"

"They're loyal." Bitterness seeped into my voice. "Why-"

"Nope, you had your question. It's my turn again." Maxwell's feisty attitude did weird things to my insides, but I shut that shit down. Now wasn't the time or place to catch feelings. Plus, I'd sworn them off forever.

I reminded myself that under different circumstances, she'd be annoying the fuck out of me.

"Jaden?" Something about her tone hinted she had a serious question.

Wanting to avoid it, I closed my eyes and said, "You know what, you're right. I need to rest."

I felt her arm brush against me as she leaned against the wall. Close enough to touch. But light years away.

# Chapter 30

## Cate

The foghorn ripped me from my fitful sleep. I wasn't the only one. Jaden sprang to his feet in a flash and stalked to the middle of the cage. I was slower to get up, my energy waning as my body tried healing with a calorie deficit.

"How courteous of you to meet me halfway on this sunny afternoon." Roman always brought manners into the conversation.

We didn't respond.

When Roman asked who he should take, Jaden stepped forward. Giving Roman exactly what he wanted. He laughed and said, "Maxwell it is."

*He knows it'll kill Jaden, the typical protective alpha male, to wait in the dark while he questions and beats me.*

The sun was up, which meant it was Friday. We'd been here a day and a half. I prayed to every deity I could think of for John and the rest of SSI to find us sooner rather than later.

There was no doubt in my mind they'd use every resource at their disposal, including my former boss. The FBI had resources SSI didn't, and a former FBI agent gone missing wasn't something they'd take lightly.

*But will they find us in time?*

We followed the same routine: I was bound to the chair; he asked me questions; I refused to answer.

Only this time, his goons hit me harder, and Franks shocked me longer. By the time they finished, I could barely hold my head up.

I didn't want to lean on Franks as he escorted me down the stairs, but I didn't have a choice.

Once again, Jaden stood at the far corner of our cell while they uncuffed me. I stared at him as he stared at the gun pointed at my head, a low, steady growl emanating from him. The cords in his neck standing out as he ground his back teeth together hard enough to turn coal into diamond.

My arms fell to my sides when they removed cuffs. Staring at Jaden, I borrowed his strength to keep myself standing until I heard the basement door close.

As darkness engulfed us, my knees gave out. Whimpering, I sank to the ground. Before my head could hit the concrete, two powerful arms caught me and scooped me up.

Jaden carried me to the back wall and used it to support his back as he slid to the floor, holding me close to his chest. Protecting me.

He smelled awful. The bitter scent of his pain and fear mixing with the metallic scent of my blood.

*I probably smell worse.*

Jaden held me, rocking back and forth in the silence.

I didn't like showing weakness, but there was literally nothing I could do to stop the tears rolling down my cheeks. I was exhausted and everything hurt. Wanting to hold on to anger instead of fear, I focused on Roman's sleazy, snake-like smile.

But it didn't work. My body shook with memories of the cattle prod and the punches to my face and gut. Years of boxing competitively hadn't come close to preparing me for this. Neither had the basic level of SERE training I had as a Marine.

Thankfully, the cold room stayed silent. The hand wiping the tears from my cheeks with a feather-light touch brought me back to the present. Despite his gentleness, I groaned at the touch.

"I'm sorry," Jaden apologized.

"It's okay." Nothing was okay, but what could I say? He wasn't trying to hurt me, and I didn't want him to stop comforting me.

After a few minutes, Jaden started singing, his deep voice soothing as he sang softly.

*Is that Arabic?* I'd learned a little when I was in the Marines, so it sounded vaguely familiar.

"Is that Arabic?"

His chest rumbled when he chuckled. The shaking reminding me just how much my body hurt. "It is."

"Do you speak it or did you just learn the song?"

"I'm almost fluent."

*What?* "I did not know that about you." I wondered what else I didn't know.

"Most people don't."

*Why not?* Before I could ask, he asked me if I spoke it.

"Not really, but I learned a little when I was stationed overseas," I answered.

"I know you speak several languages, but not which ones."

"Spanish and French. You?"

"Some Spanish," he answered. "How are you feeling? Think you can drink some water?"

I felt well enough to drink, but weak as fuck. "I don't think I can stand yet."

"Then we'll sit here until you can." Jaden's low, deep voice was more comforting than his words.

My mind raced with questions while we sat in the cold, dark silence. I couldn't stop thinking about how different Jaden seemed as I sipped my water.

"Jaden?"

"Yeah?"

"Can I ask you a question?"

"Are we back to the game?" he chuckled.

"Sure." I didn't mind playing, but I wouldn't have to answer my next question.

"Why do you hide your intelligence?"

He laughed. "Damn, Maxwell, you're not pulling your punches."

It hurt to laugh with him. The deflection told me he wasn't comfortable with the question. *Duh.* The delay told me he was searching for the right words.

"Because I was never as good in school as Jaime and Madi, or as clever as Jack. When I realized I couldn't compare, I stopped trying. Besides, I was a mistake, so it never really mattered."

I tucked the mistake statement away for later because I needed more time to process it.

"You know none of them think that, right? I haven't been with SSI long-"

"Longer than me."

I ignored his attempt to change the subject. He needed to hear this, in case we died here. When the thought made me shiver, he hugged me close and gently rubbed my arms to warm me up.

*He has no idea what an incredible man he is.*

"I haven't been at SSI long, but your father and brothers have done nothing but praise you, the man you've turned into. They're proud of you."

My heartbeat was the only way to count the passage of time as I waited for him to respond.

"So they keep telling me, but it's hard to believe. I've felt inferior my whole life. That's one reason I wanted to be a firefighter instead of a cop."

Why hadn't he? I could understand wanting to avoid direct comparison, which he'd do by being the only Sheppard male not on the police force. *Well, he would've been if SSI hadn't happened.* I remembered Jack saying he would've joined the local PD but bought into SSI instead.

*So why did Jay join SSI instead of becoming a* firefighter?

Wanting to talk about the more pressing matter, I added it to the list of things to ask him about later. "You know that feeling isn't unique to you. I never felt like I was good enough and I'm an only child." I said, hoping to get through to him.

It shouldn't have mattered to me how he perceived himself or his place in his family, but it did. And I couldn't let him die thinking he was a mistake. Expendable.

"What do you mean, you never felt good enough? You're brilliant."

Ignoring the compliment, I whispered, "I wasn't good enough for my mom to stick around." I rarely talked about her leaving, but it felt right telling Jaden. "She left because my dad couldn't give her what she wanted. She claimed she felt like a single mom, and hated it." *Just say it.* "I wasn't enough for her." The only other person I'd ever shared the details with was my best friend, Charlie.

"Wow." I could hear the shock and disgust in his voice.

"Yeah," I said around a chuckle that hurt my bruised ribs.

"You know that wasn't about you, right?"

Logically I did, but it'd left one hell of a scar. "I do."

"What about your dad?"

"He did the best he could, but he really is married to the Marines. I was raised by an ever changing community of officers' wives." I paused to sip my water. "It could've been worse, but I never felt like I belonged."

"I'm sorry." For the first time, I realized having siblings might not have helped; Jaden grew up in a big family and still felt out of place.

"Because my father was gone so much, I had to take care of the house. It didn't help that he'd be upset if I left a mess and would praise me anytime he came home to a clean house."

"You had to grow up too fast."

I did, and I developed OCD tendencies because of it. The need to be clean, organized, and perfect to feel worthy of love was as much a part of me as my red hair.

Most people thought it was cool that I had so much in common with my father, but it hadn't happened naturally. They didn't know I'd made a lot of my decisions to please him. Boxing, getting an advanced degree, joining the Marines, and becoming an officer.

I forced myself to be like him, so he'd love me. I killed myself to get good grades and excel at everything, so he'd love me. I strived to be perfect, so he'd love me.

I didn't regret my choices; they'd made me the woman I was. *And while there are a few things I wouldn't mind changing, I'm proud of who I am.* It wasn't until I left the Marines that I broke the cycle. Unlike my father, I never wanted to be a lifer. Wanting to use my degree as a profiler instead, I joined the FBI.

Investigating was my favorite part of being in the FBI, which was why it was easy to transition to the private sector when shit went bad.

"I did."

Jaden rubbed my back, offering support, while we sat in silence. When the strobe started again, I curled up in his lap. He tucked me into his chest, using his body to block out most of the light.

The steady rhythm of his breathing, the gentle thumpthump of his heart, and the warmth from his body offered me peace I hadn't experienced since waking up in the limo.

*No, it's been longer than that.*

When the light finally stopped, the alarm started. I blocked my ears the best I could while listing every teacher I'd had since kindergarten. I failed, no longer physically or emotionally strong enough to fight off the intrusive sound.

It lasted forever. *I don't care that Jaden said he only recited the Raider's creed seventeen times.*

When the foghorn blasted, Jaden set me down on the floor and walked to the middle of the cage. Losing his warmth caused me to shiver.

Three men delivered our sack lunches. After they left, Jaden grabbed them and brought them back. "I'll test the chips for air leaks. If there aren't any, I want you to eat."

"What about you?" I asked.

"You first, you've taken the worst of it and need the calories more than I do."

After a few seconds, the sound of the bag opening made my mouth fill with saliva. *God, I'm hungry.*

"Here, eat." He trailed his hand down my arm to find my hand and pressed the bag into it. "Slowly."

"Yes, sir."

His chuckle filled the silence. Two heartbeats later, the crinkle of another bag opening joined my crunching.

"Do you like sour cream and onion?" he asked.

"I do, but if you want them, I don't mind trading." I held my bag out to him.

"Nope, we have the same kind."

Our stomachs rumbled, adding to the sound of the crinkling bags and crunching chips.

"The cookies are sealed, too."

"Gimme," I said before I could censor myself.

He chuckled. "Okay, just give me a sec to check for air leaks."

I'd never wanted a cookie so much in my life, so of course it took forever.

"Here."

I took a bite. "Oatmeal raisin. Yuck." I kept chewing, spitting the raisins into my free hand. "Can you give me one of the bags?"

Jaden said he liked oatmeal raisin and offered to switch if his cookie was different; it wasn't.

The chips and cookies weren't enough to please my empty stomach, but they took the edge off.

*Now we wait.* Eating was a calculated risk, but one worth taking. Our bodies needed the fuel to heal. Especially mine.

When Jaden came back from tossing the bags out of the cage, he sat beside me and said. "My turn."

He asked me why I really left the FBI. *Damn him.*

Like he had done earlier, I took a moment to think about my answer.

I gave him the highlight reel. I'd dated a guy from a different Special Victims Unit team, Gavin. Things were great at first, and while we worked in the same office, we were on different teams, so I didn't feel like I was breaking the unwritten rules about dating a co-worker.

"When we applied for the same position, a promotion, he turned on me. Instead of earning it on his merits, he destroyed my reputation."

Jaden's growl echoed in the dark space.

"I thought I was falling in love with him, but he was only using me. He told everyone who'd listen that I offered to sleep my way to the top."

His growl was longer and louder this time. It felt nice, him not only believing me, but taking my side, especially since it seemed like no one else had. *Except Jones. In hindsight, I think that's why he brought me to Weatherford last year.*

"It wasn't true-"

"Never doubted it."

"But it was enough to ruin my reputation. Initially, I told myself I'd wait it out and look for a position in a different office, but I couldn't handle the never ending snide remarks, leering, or suggestive printouts left on my desk."

"You didn't report him, any of them?"

"No, the FBI is a lot like the military. They'd punish the guilty, but I'd suffer for it." I wanted to believe it wasn't like that in every office, but I'd heard horror stories from other women. "That's how I ended up at SSI."

"Is that why you keep your distance from us?"

It wasn't because I didn't think they were good men, people. *It's because I'm afraid of getting hurt.* When Jaden asked if I remembered any red flags from Gavin, I told him I did.

Sadly, the list was embarrassing long, but the ones that stood out the most were his complete lack of respect for my time, poking fun at my need for order, and his inability to apologize.

*If only I'd seen them sooner.*

"Do you get any from anyone at SSI?"

I thought about it, logically. Clinically.

I didn't. Then again, I wasn't dating any of them. Gavin had damaged my ability to trust anyone, personally or professionally.

"No." Not even with Jaden. He'd pissed me off on many occasions, but it felt more like polar opposites butting heads than red flag behavior.

"I'm sorry I made fun of you for being so organized."

"Thanks." My tone fell flat, not because I wasn't grateful for the apology but because I was preoccupied with wondering why similar behavior hadn't felt like a red flag with Jaden.

"Catelyn," *That's new, he's never used my first name before.* "I mean it. Your neat desk always made me feel messy, and I took it personally." He laughed. "Christ, I was an ass, wasn't I?"

And that was why it never felt like a red flag. Deep down, I understood his motivations.

"A little, yeah. But I forgive you."

# Chapter 31

## Jay

Switching to her first name sounded weird, but it felt right. I no longer needed, or wanted, to keep her at arm's length. She didn't correct me, so I assumed it was okay to keep using it.

The game of twenty questions continued when she asked, "Why do you think you're, and I quote, the expendable Shepherd?"

I barely remembered saying it, but apparently she'd not only heard it, she'd latched onto it.

"I'm a mistake," I whispered.

"Who told you that?" Her voice was well above a whisper.

"My brothers. And my parents admitted it." I lowered my voice, reminding her to keep hers down.

"Did they use those words?" she asked.

"My brothers did." Repeatedly. "My parents said I was unplanned." I used air quotes to emphasize unplanned, not that it mattered; she could barely see me.

"Unplanned doesn't mean unwanted."

It was a simple statement. Similar to the one my parents made the one and only time I asked about it. They'd been emotional, defensive, and wanted to know where I got the idea.

I never told them, knowing my brothers would make my life a living hell. Not that my parents didn't suspect, but they couldn't act on assumptions.

Somehow, my parents' emotional defense hadn't rung as true as Maxwell's blunt statement. Maybe it was because I was six the only time I asked.

"I know." I said, more to get her off my back than anything else.

"But do you believe it?" she asked, refusing to let it go.

*Sort of.* "I've never felt close to my parents." Probably because it seemed like they heaped praise on my siblings and scolded me. "And even less so with my brothers." I knew they loved me, but I never felt like I fit in. "I'm not like any of them. They're all so smart, did well in school, and they stayed out of trouble." I was the rebellious kid who was easily bored and rarely did his homework.

"You know you don't have to be like them, right? Jaime and Jack are different and they get along great. You bring your own unique gifts to your family, to the team, you just have to let others see them."

I took a second to really let her words sink in, before I could respond, she said, "From what I've heard, Jack got in his fair share of trouble and hated being compared to Jamie because he felt like he didn't measure up."

My head snapped up. How the hell did she know that? She'd only been with SSI a few months; I'd been a Sheppard my whole life and had no idea.

"They seemed so close." It felt like Catelyn had opened my eyes, helping me accept what I'd known but refused to see.

With her help, what my parents had been telling me my whole life finally sank in. Not that I hadn't heard them; I just never believed them. I'd convinced myself they expected me to be like my brothers, no matter what they said.

Catelyn made a harrumph noise, sounding a lot like she didn't believe me, but she changed the subject. "I understand you feel like the black sheep, but that doesn't really explain your lack of trust. So tell me, Sheppard, how does a MARSOC team guy become a lone wolf in his family's business?"

Aiming below the belt, she went for the kill shot. Not that she knew it.

I was a team player, and the man I saw in the mirror was nothing like the brat who left for Parris Island. My current 'lone wolf' attitude had very little to do with my family and everything to do with Sara and Henderson.

I didn't want to tell her about Sara, because thinking about her always sent me spiraling into heartbreak, and rage fueled frenzy. But as she asked more questions, no doubt using her fancy psychology degree to break down my walls, I found myself wanting to open up.

So for the first time since it happened, I told someone.

"Did you know I was supposed to backpack around the country before starting at SSI?"

"Yeah, your father mentioned it."

"Well, I was supposed to go with my girlfriend and some guys from my unit. Sara and I had been dating over a year; she was the first woman I ever felt serious about."

"What happened?" she asked after my pause lasted too long.

"A teammate got injured and came home early. Sara lived near base, so I asked her to visit him once in a while so he wouldn't feel lonely. Which she did. A lot." I paused before forcing the words out. "She cheated on me."

"Are you fucking kidding me?" Catelyn asked, much louder than a whisper.

"Just before I returned stateside, she emailed to tell me she'd fallen in love with someone else."

"I'm so sorry, Jaden." She placed a gentle hand on my forearm.

It was the first time she called me Jaden without my brothers around, when it was too confusing to call me Sheppard.

*I like how it sounds.*

"How close were you to your teammate?"

Close enough that his betrayal hurt more than hers.

"It was Henderson." Getting a "Dear John" letter wasn't unusual for deployed Marines, but getting one because your best friend was fucking your girlfriend was.

"The same Henderson you were captured with?" I heard the disbelief in her voice.

"One and the same."

"Damn, I'm so sorry."

"Yeah. He was my team buddy and my best friend. The man who'd watched my six when we were in the deepest pits of hell slept with my girlfriend." Catelyn Maxwell now knew more than any member of my family. Thought I still hadn't told her I'd planned on proposing to Sara during the trip.

"I can see why you have trust issues."

"Yeah." What else could I say?

I could practically hear her gears turning as she processed the information.

"But with your family?" Another sucker punch to the gut.

"To some degree. I'm the mistake, remember?" My laugh lacked humor. I didn't believe it anymore, mostly, but it'd take some time getting used to.

Her weak slap reminded me just how much she'd suffered over the last few days.

*Yet here she is, comforting me when I should be comforting her.*

I felt like a failure all over again.

I should be protecting her. But Roman had devised a way to make sure I couldn't. Forcing me to stand down, helpless and useless, by threatening to shoot Maxwell if I stepped out of line.

"You know they love you, and no one thinks you're expendable." Her statement brought me back to the conversation.

"Logically, I know that, but it feels like nothing's changed. They still think of me as their bratty little brother."

Not that I was doing anything to dispel them of that opinion.

*I'm not behaving like the man I know I am.*

"I won't tell you I know what it's like because I don't. As an only child, there was no one around to tease me. But I know what it feels like to think you don't fit in or you're not good enough."

I still found it hard to believe she'd ever felt that way. She excelled at everything she did.

"I assumed you got along great with your dad."

"We get along, but we're not as close as I'd like. I love and respect him, and I've spent my whole life trying to earn his love and respect. He's the reason I joined the Marines, earned my advanced degree, and became an officer."

"You didn't want to be a Marine?"

"I probably would have done four years and moved on if I hadn't been worried about disappointing him. Don't get me wrong, I don't regret my choices, but I'm not sure I would've made the same ones if I hadn't been trying to win his affection." Her voice had taken on a somber tone.

That sucked. I might feel like the black sheep of my perfect family, but they supported me and my choices.

"I'm sure he's proud of you, everything you've accomplished." How could he not be? Maxwell's resume was impressive. *She's impressive.*

"I'm not so sure. He seemed disappointed when I left the FBI to join the private sector."

"Does he know why you left?"

"Hell, no. No way was I telling him I made a huge mistake by sleeping with the wrong co-worker and got myself chased out with my tail between my legs."

By this time, neither of us was whispering, which explained why the alarm and strobe hadn't come back on. *Roman was probably enjoying the show.*

And taking notes so he could exploit our weaknesses.

"I don't think that's an accurate description," I joked, to lighten the mood. "What made you choose SSI?"

"I was impressed with the team when Jones and I came down to help find Chase."

I'd never met Jones, so I asked her to explain.

"Jones was my supervisor, and the only person I'd talked to about Gavin. When he saw SSI was hiring, he sent me the link. He also wrote me a glowing recommendation."

"But you don't really trust them, do you?"

"Professionally, yes, I trust them to have my back."

"But not personally." I said. She wasn't the only one who could hear what wasn't said.

"No, not on a personal level. I want to, but anytime I think I can, my brain calls up the memories of Gavin and reminds me to be keep my distance. So I'm cautious about what I say, and how close I get."

We weren't so different.

"That's why you seem so uptight." This time I expected the slap, but not her laugh.

"I'm not uptight. I keep a professional distance and I have OCD tendencies. They stem from trying to be perfect to win my father's affection."

Her clinical answer rolled off her tongue, sounding like she'd had to defend herself before. *To assholes like me.*

"I'm sorry. I shouldn't have said anything."

"It's okay. Unlike many people, I understand why I'm the way I am. And I'm not as bad as I used to be, so there's hope for me yet."

I laughed, and before long, she joined in.

The laughter changed from sad to hysterical as we realized why we irritated each other so much.

We were more alike than we'd ever realized.

"We make a hell of a team, don't we? You over-achieve to win your father's approval. And I act like an idiot to meet my family's expectations."

"Yeah. Even when our parents do their best, sometimes they get it wrong and we end up all fucked up because of it."

She'd been sitting on the cold concrete too long, so when she got up to stretch her legs, they barely supported her. Cursing at myself for not putting her back on my lap, I got up and offered her my arm. As I escorted her around the room, I wondered if the cameras had infrared lenses? Given Roman's preparedness, I had to assume they did.

When Roman saw this, he'd use our friendship, if you could call it that, against us.

Not that I'd stop helping her.

As we walked, I formed a plan to make sure they took me the next time they came down.

"You ready to sit?" I asked when her pace lagged.

"Yes, thanks."

When we sat, I pulled her onto my lap. As expected, she resisted, but I convinced her it was to keep us both warm. In reality, it was because I felt compelled to hold and comfort her. And keep her off the cold concrete floor.

Uncomfortable in the silence, I started singing again.

"You're not so bad, Jay." She used the shortened version of my name, bringing us closer still.

"Close your eyes and rest, Cate." It only seemed right to return the favor.

I didn't expect her name to feel so perfect on my lips.

# Chapter 32

## Cate

I tried resisting when Jay pulled me onto his lap, but I had neither the physical nor mental energy to argue. Besides, his warm lap was a lot more comfortable than the cold concrete floor.

Initially, it annoyed me when he asked to play twenty questions, but because of the game we'd gotten to know, and understand, each other. And maybe even become friends.

*Roman will use that against us.*

Jay singing softly with his beautiful deep voice lulled me to sleep for the second time. But it wasn't restful.

When I awoke with a start, the first thought I had was that I didn't want to die without apologizing to Jay for punching him.

"You okay?" he asked.

"Yeah, no." I yawned. "I'm sorry I punched you." My whole body felt stiff and sore. *Even my hair hurts.*

He laughed. "Forgiven. I'm curious, though, what specifically set you off?"

"Gavin told everyone to call me Catie Cat, because I liked to scratch. He and his friends thought it'd be funny to make sure everyone knew it. They all made scratching motions anytime they called me that."

"He's an ass."

"Yes, he is."

"I'm sorry I called you that."

"It's okay, you didn't know." It seemed like it'd been forever since the strobe or alarm had tortured us, though I wasn't sure just how long.

"How long has it been quiet?" I asked.

"Longer than usual, but other than that, I don't have an answer."

Jay helped me up, and we walked around the cage to loosen our sore, stiff limbs. It had to be worse for him, because he'd used his body to keep me off the cold floor.

We'd finally started talking to each other like friends instead of enemies. No doubt our tenuous friendship existed because neither of us thought we'd make it out alive.

As we walked, we continued our game of twenty questions, though we'd passed that number long ago. We asked each other about the good memories from our childhoods and our accomplishments. Keeping it light and not lingering too long on any one subject.

When we got tired, we sat back down on the cold, hard concrete, with our back against the cold, hard wall.

Time dragged on and we eventually fell silent—too cold, hungry, and tired to keep talking. It seemed to me we'd been left alone in the dark and silence for hours, and that scared me.

*It's always calmest before the storm.*

When the foghorn next sounded, Jay had to help me stand. The physical abuse combined with the lack of food was making me weaker by the hour. Sitting for too long in the cold wasn't helping either.

"Happy Saturday, my caged birds. It's time for you to sing." Roman's cheerful voice sent chills down my spine.

Had he heard Jay singing to me? Or did he have a plan to make us talk?

"Happy suck-my-dick-Saturday, Dick," Jay said, spitting out the name.

Two thoughts slammed through my head at once, making it hard to think.

What the fuck was he thinking, talking to Roman like that? He'd get himself killed.

And Saturday? I thought it was still Friday. *Holy shit, we've been here for over* three *days.* It was hard to keep track of time with no change of light.

"I thought we'd moved past that, son." Roman's voice dripped with sarcasm. I couldn't see his face because the only light in the basement was behind him, casting him in a creepy silhouette.

*Dramatic much?*

Jay stepped forward, looking every bit like he wanted to challenge Roman. He hadn't taken two steps before rifles lifted to shoulders and muzzles pointed at our heads.

"I wouldn't do that if I were you," Roman said. Though it wasn't necessary; Jay had stopped the instant the rifles moved. "Now go stand in the corner like a good boy while we cuff your girlfriend."

Girlfriend? *Fuck.* This was going to get so much worse now that he thought he could use us against each other.

Jay clenched his fists and back teeth, growling as he walked to the far corner. After cuffing me, they took me upstairs and tied me to one of the two chairs in front of Roman's desk.

Two chairs?

I could feel Franks and Roman staring at me while I stared at the empty chair.

"Bring Sheppard up," Roman said, bringing my attention fully back to him.

*He'll use me to make Jay talk.* Not that there was much to share. Most of what we knew came from Roman himself. Everything before that was speculation.

Jay stayed quiet while they escorted him in and tied him to his chair. They took the extra measure of wrapping a thick rope across his chest, making sure he couldn't move more than an inch off the back.

When we made eye contact, I pleaded with him to stay strong. *How do you tell someone 'I can take it' with only your eyes?* I didn't know, but I tried to relay the message anyway.

They started slow. Slapping me anytime either of us didn't answer Roman questions about his nephew or Blake.

"Why don't you pick on someone your own size?" Jay growled.

"We don't have to pick on anyone," Roman smirked. "Answer my questions, and it'll all stop."

I yelled, "Don't you dare!"

The resulting slap caused more blood to coat my tongue as my lip split again. I spat on the floor in defiance.

"We can't tell you anything you don't already know," Jay said, playing nice.

"That remains to be seen," Roman said before walking behind me and yanking my hair to force my head back. "It's a shame we have to damage such a pretty face."

*Have to?* They'd already made it puffy, black and blue.

I pulled against him, but he yanked harder, causing me to grunt in pain.

"How much do you do you think she can take?" Roman asked.

Roman's question scared me, but it was nothing compared to the overwhelming fear induced from hearing Franks laugh at the question. I broke eye contact with Roman and looked at Franks.

My head throbbed from having a fistful of hair almost yanked out, but I forgot all about the pain when I saw the sadistic glee on Franks's face. I broke out in a cold sweat and couldn't stop my hands from trembling.

"I don't know, but I'll bet fifty he breaks before she does," Franks answered.

"Make it a hundred, and I'll take it," Roman said.

They ignored Jay when he asked if he could get in on the bet. I prayed that was his way of telling me he'd stay strong, no matter how bad it got.

Every time Jay refused to answer a question, they hit me. Blood spilled from my lips and my left eye was swollen shut. The backhands weren't as strong as the punches, so my right eye wasn't as swollen, but he'd torn my cheek to shreds with the rings on his fingers. And the punches to my gut winded me every time.

Jay's resolve waned as Franks hit me harder and harder.

"How do I get to Blake?" Roman asked again. I didn't understand his tunnel-vision focus on getting money from Blake. He didn't need it, and he had to realize it wasn't worth the risk.

"You keep asking the same question, and I keep giving you the same answer. Are you hard of hearing, or just stupid?"

Jay let out a pained oof when a nameless goon kicked him in the ribs hard enough to tip his chair back. Luckily, a different nameless goon caught him and set the chair back on all four legs because there was nothing Jay could've done to prevent his head from slamming against the floor.

More questions. More non-answers. More hits.

They hurt like hell and I was pretty sure Franks had broken, or at least cracked, one of my ribs by the time he stopped.

*At least they didn't use the cattle prod.*

Roman ordered his men to take us downstairs after getting a text. Whatever the message said was bad news, because his face turned red and he looked like he was about to explode.

We'd held out. *This time.*

They brought me down first. When the guy holding me upright let go, I crumpled into a heap. Using nothing but determination, I sat up. I didn't want Jay to worry any more than he already was.

After they locked the cage door, they threw in two bags. Food and water.

Jay picked up the bags and handed them to me before gently picking me up and carrying me to the back. He used a little of the water to wet a strip of his t-shirt and carefully washed my face.

I tried not to wince, but it was impossible. My face now knew what a punching bag felt like.

When Jay handed me water, I ignored the copper taste mixing in and drank it. When he gave me a cookie, I ignored the pain caused by chewing and ate it. Raisins and all.

The salt made it hurt too much to eat the chips, so Jay gave me his cookie and ate my chips.

"I'm sorry," he whispered as he rubbed my back. "You're so fucking strong and I know you can take it, but I still wish there was something I could do."

I wanted to smile at the compliment and the sentiment, but my swollen lips refused to comply. He wouldn't see it anyway. "Thanks," I mumbled.

Jay held me on his lap and sang me to sleep.

When the foghorn blasted, it scared the shit out of me, causing me to jump awake. Pain speared my left side, reminding me of the abuse my ribs had taken. The resulting grunts of pain caused my face to hurt.

"Let me help," Jay said, lifting me off his lap before standing next to me. "I'm sorry, Cate, but I won't let them do this to you again. I'll tell them whatever they want to hear," he spoke close to my ear as footsteps echoed down the stairs.

"You can't. The minute you do, they'll kill us," I begged.

"Cate." He whispered, resting his forehead on mine. "I don't think I can do it. You're so much stronger than I am."

"No, I'm not. You have the harder job." It was true. I didn't need a psych degree to know it was a million times harder for him to watch me get hit without retaliating. It might be easier physically, but not emotionally.

Light flooded the basement as Roman and his men stormed down the stairs. He didn't bother with a polite greeting, or any greeting at all—just ordered us to opposite corners. I moved slower than Jay and hadn't made it to my corner before a goon grabbed me and yanked my hands behind my back, making my ribs scream.

*Something happened.* I made eye contact with Jay; he'd picked up on it, too. Roman was pissed off, and no longer playing his game.

They took us together, trusting Jay not to risk my life by fighting. *There's no reason to worry about me.* Even uncuffed, I couldn't have put up a fight.

Everything in the office looked the same as the last time, except the plastic sheet covering the floor.

Fuck. Roman wanted to protect his precious rug from our blood. Not that I hadn't bled on the floor before. But it'd never been a lot.

*We're going to die here.* I couldn't have held back my shiver if I'd been fully healthy.

Once again tied to our chairs, Roman walked to the back of his desk, sat down, and leaned forward with his hands clasped.

"I was hoping you'd cooperate and I could get some answers." He shook his head, as if realizing the error of his ways. "But now I have somewhere else I need to be, so we're going to speed things along," Roman said.

My heart beat against my ribs and I had to force myself to take steady breaths, so I didn't hyperventilate and pass out. *He's going to kill us.*

"Franks, don't you think Cate here is pretty?"

"I sure do." He answered, licking his lips while his eyes trailed down my body.

*Fuck.* They'll threaten rape to force Jay to talk. I turned to see Jay's reaction, never doubting he understood their intent.

He strained against his ropes, his teeth clenched so tightly I could see every vein in his neck and forehead.

*Fuck.* "Sheppard, don't." I ordered.

Ignoring me, he growled, "If you touch her, I will kill you."

"How noble. But how do you plan to do that?" Roman smiled his sick, snake-like smile.

Jay leaned back. "I'll tell you everything you want to know." His nostrils flared as he spoke. *He needs to calm down before he gets us both killed.*

"Pay up." Franks held his hand out. Roman handed him a hundred-dollar bill.

Turns out he didn't have any more questions. Roman told us they arrested his nephew for the murder of Wendy. That was the text he got that ended the last session. *That's why he's in a hurry.* He needed to get out of dodge before the cops came looking for him.

He let his henchmen take turns beating Jay, this time just for fun. Franks held my head and forced me to watch. Roman wanted to make sure our last moments on Earth were as emotionally, mentally, and physically painful as possible.

When it was my turn, Roman made them stop hitting Jay. One of them held his head, forcing him to watch through swollen eyes as Franks took out his frustrations.

Roman stood behind his desk and watched, a smug smile on his face.

*He thinks he'll get away with it.*

# Chapter 33

## Jay

Being forced to watch Franks attack Cate was enough to make my blood boil, but there was literally nothing I could do. I struggled against the ropes binding me, but it was no use. *Doesn't mean I'll stop trying.*

A commotion outside the house brought everything to a standstill.

*Please, God, let it by my* dad.

Roman's eyes rounded as he realized he'd waited too long to leave. He grabbed a gun from his desk and ordered Franks to kill us before running out of the room with his henchmen on his tail.

The door banging sounded like a coffin slamming shut.

*Please hurry.* Don't let us die here.

Franks knelt in front of Cate. "I think I'll have a little fun before I kill you." He turned to me and said, "You get to watch me with your girl before you die."

251

I prayed they'd get here in time..

*I won't sit around and wait to be saved.*

Finding a reserve of adrenaline fueled strength, I fought against the ties. The rope cut into my skin, causing blood to mix with sweat and drip down my arms. The metal cuffs cut into my wrists.

Franks grabbed Cate's chin, forcing her to look at him. When he leaned in, she spat, covering his face in blood drenched spit.

*That's my girl.*

He backhanded her before wiping his face.

I fought harder, jumping up and down in the chair, trying to break it against the floor.

"Your boyfriend doesn't like watching, does he?" He ran his hand down her thigh as he spoke.

I wanted to kill this guy, and if I could break free, I'd happily do it with my bare hands.

"Untie me, you fucking coward, and I'll show you how much I don't like it." My bruised and bloodied lips made the threat less menacing than I would've liked.

Franks laughed as he reached down and ripped Cate's shirt. When he leaned in close, she head-butted him.

I loved her for refusing to give up. He might kill her, but she'd go down fighting.

Franks saw blood on his hand after wiping it under his nose. "Fuck this," he said before punching her. He got up and grabbed a syringe from the desk. Cate's eyes widened as she saw it in his hand.

So did mine. I doubled my efforts to break free.

He made quick work of finding a vein in her arm and sliding the needle in. "This will make you more cooperative." His laugh turned my blood cold.

*Fuck! Fuck! Fuck!*

I screamed and struggled against my ties, this time standing and slamming the chair onto the floor. No way in hell was I letting him do this.

Franks walked to the desk and picked up another syringe. "Your turn." He punched me in the sternum, knocking the wind out of me. I struggled as he held my arm still, easily finding my vein and shoving the needle into it.

"You suck at this." All my straining against the ropes had created just enough wiggle room for me to yank my arm away, causing the needle to tear my skin. Unfortunately, the rope around my chest prevented me from head-butting him like Cate had.

The drug acted fast in my undernourished body, rendering me mostly immobile. I tried yelling, but my words sounded like gobbled garbage as Franks spun my chair, forcing me to witness his assault on Cate.

Gunfire sounded from down the hall. *They're getting closer.* I prayed we could hold on long enough for my father to find us.

Would they find us before Franks shot us?

*Please hurry.*

He yanked Cate's hair back and slammed his mouth over hers while grabbing a breast and squeezing. She didn't cry out. Didn't flinch.

She couldn't.

Unable to control her muscles, her eyes stayed open. Which meant I saw her pupils widen as tears rolled down her cheek. He'd drugged the fight out of her, and she had to watch as he closed the distance again.

Rage and fury burned through my veins, but I was helpless to stop him.

Footsteps in the hall made Franks stop. Stepping back, he said, "Time's up."

*No, no, no.*

There was nothing I could do as he drew his gun, aimed it at me, and fired. I barely had time to register that he'd missed before the door crashed open.

Franks didn't bother checking to see if he'd hit me, instead aiming at Cate and firing again. She wasn't as lucky; her body jolted before blood stained her shirt.

*Cate!* I fought against the drugs in my system, which were already wearing off thanks to the needle tearing out of my vein before the syringe was empty.

More shots sounded before Franks hit the floor and the team rushed in.

I couldn't see who'd entered, but knew they'd clear the room before helping us. Precious seconds ticked by as blood continued to flow from Cate's wound and her head drooped forward.

Jack sank to his knees in front of me and asked, "Are you hit?"

I tried to answer, but my tongue felt like it was three times too big for my mouth and made of lead, so all that came out were grunts and squeaks. He searched my eyes, looking for answers, so I blinked and turned them to Cate.

"I got you, little brother."

A half a second later, AJ slung his rifle and dropped to his knees in front of Cate.

Jack needed to leave me and help Cate, but my mouth refused to work, so all I could do was plead silently for him to get the message.

AJ applied pressure to the upper right side of her chest. *The bullet missed her heart, but did it puncture her lung?* AJ said, "She's hit."

Hearing that, Jack checked me for bullet wounds before helping AJ.

I tried to move, but couldn't. Fear and frustration consumed me as I sat there helpless to help them help her.

Jack cut the ties binding Cate while AJ continued applying pressure.

"I need a chest seal," AJ said.

Jack leaned her forward and checked her back. "We need two."

*Please don't die.* I didn't realize I was crying until the salt from my tears made the cuts on my face sting. *Please don't die.*

As soon as they had her on the floor, AJ pushed her torn shirt to the side and applied the first seal. They carefully rolled her over so he could apply the second one.

The sound of more people entering the room wasn't enough to pull my attention from Cate's body. She was unconscious, but her chest was rising just enough for me to know she was still breathing. Still alive.

I tried to move again. "Cate?" I cried out. It sounded more like a long, hard 'A' than a word.

"Jaden?" My father's voice caught my attention. Shifting my focus made me dizzy, so I waited for him to step in front of me.

He kneeled down in front of me, held my face in his hands, and stared into my eyes.

Relief flooded my system as I struggled to breathe through my fear. Under normal circumstances, I'd use combat breathing to control my heart rate and calm my racing thoughts, but I didn't have that much control over my muscles.

I opened my mouth, but all that came out was a garbled mess.

"It's okay, Jay. We'll get you out of here."

I shifted my focus to Cate and watched helplessly as Jack and AJ helped her.

"She'll be okay. The ambulance is on the way." As if summoned by his words, sirens sounded in the distance.

I tried to lean forward, but the rope still held me to the chair.

"Help me cut him free," Dad said a few seconds before the ties holding me up fell away, causing me to collapse forward in his arms.

"I've got you," he said as he helped me to the ground. Someone must have asked because he wasn't talking to me when he said, "He's banged up, and they've drugged him, but he should be okay."

The sound of sirens grew louder while I sat on the floor, held up by my father, as Doug conducted a head to toe check for injuries. I gave up trying to speak.

All I could do was watch and wait.

*I've never felt so helpless in my life.*

"Hold on, Max, help is coming," Jack said as he assessed her for other wounds.

*We made it this far. Don't you dare die on me now.* With what little control I had, I leaned towards Cate. "Help me," I grunted, the words nothing more than noise.

But my father understood; he and Doug shifted me closer to Cate.

It took every ounce of energy I had to reach out and touch her hand.

Her lashes fluttered. The vacant look when her eyes opened briefly scared the hell out of me. The drug in my system might have rendered most of my muscles useless, but not my heart. It was beating a mile a minute as precious seconds ticked by.

*Please, God, let her come back to me. Don't let her die.* I begged. I pleaded. I prayed.

I don't know how long it was before my father pulled me away, saying, "The paramedics are here. Let them help her." My focus never left Cate as my dad and Jack sat me back in the chair.

I watched and listened as they checked her wounds. They were about to start an IV when Doug interrupted, handing the small female paramedic a syringe. "Got it, thanks," she said.

Before long, more people arrived. I assumed paramedics and police officers, though I didn't take my eyes off Cate to verify.

After handing my care over to the new paramedics on scene, my father told Doug to stay with me while he talked to the LEO in charge of the scene.

Cate remained unconscious while the paramedics rolled her onto a board, lifted her to a gurney, and strapped her in.

When I tried to get up, to go with Cate, I fell into a paramedic.

"You need to sit still so we can treat you," he said, his stern voice meant to stop me.

It didn't work. *She shouldn't be alone.* I needed to go with Cate. *If only I could make my tongue work better.*

"Give us a minute." After the paramedic stepped away, my father said, "Jay, I know you want to be with her, but there's nothing you can do right now."

I grunted out, "I need–"

"I know. I know." He turned my head, so I had no choice but to look at him. "But you need help, too. You'll be at the same hospital and we'll make sure she's okay."

It wasn't enough. And if my stupid body worked properly, I would've fought to stay by her side.

# Chapter 34

## Jay

Dad rode with me in the ambulance, leaving Jamie behind to finish with the local law enforcement.

As the paramedics rolled my gurney outside, I noticed the sun hadn't set yet; *it's still Saturday.* They'd held us hostage for three days.

I'd regained a tiny bit of control over my limbs, including my tongue, by the time we arrived at the Fort Worth Hospital. Not that I could move or talk easily. And since it hurt like hell to do either; I did neither.

As my adrenaline wore off, the pain worsened, making it hurt to breathe.

When I tried to convince the nurse that I didn't need an X-ray, she said, "Doctor's orders."

Apparently, the bruising on my mid-section made him think I might have a broken rib or two.

*Might?* I could tell from the pain I did. But they'd heal in time, with little to no medical intervention.

Not like Cate. She needed a lot of help.

*Please be okay.* I prayed.

"You scared the shit out of us," Dad admitted when we were finally alone.

It hurt, but I turned towards him. "Cate?" I croaked out, sounding like a carton a day smoker on a weeklong drinking binge.

"She's in surgery."

"How bad?" Being eloquent or wordy wasn't an option.

He held my look for a heartbeat, then another, before answering.

"It was a through and through, but the bullet may have nicked her right lung."

I sucked in a sharp breath. Forcing myself to ignore the pain, I asked, "When know if-"

Anticipating what I was trying to ask, he cut me off. "The doctor will let us know as soon as she's out of surgery."

The nurse arrived, preventing further discussion. Dad asked her if she could give me anything for the pain.

"Not yet." She stepped up to the side of the bed and addressed me. "We can't give you anything until we know what was in the syringe." I nodded, wanting to wait until Cate was out of surgery. "We're working as fast as we can."

I nodded again.

"Can you lift your arm for me?" she asked.

Gritting my teeth, I lifted my right arm. Sweat broke out on my brow. My arm only made it about six inches before falling back onto the bed.

"More than last time," she said. "Let's get you cleaned up."

"That's my cue to leave," Dad said as he stood. "I'll be right outside if you need me."

I nodded.

I was beat up, had three cracked ribs, and was dehydrated—nothing I couldn't cure with an IV and some downtime. When I used that as my argument against being admitted, the doctor ignored me. Turns out three days without food and very little water gives civilian doctors cause for concern. My father sided with the doctor, so I resigned myself to my fate.

*At least I'm close to Cate.*

A half an hour later, they brought me to a room. Thankfully, no one occupied the second bed.

When my father noticed me squinting, he turned down the lights. When I shivered, he added an extra blanket. Sensing I wasn't in the mood to talk, he offered quiet support.

*I need to see Cate.* The thought repeated in my head. It wouldn't stop until I knew she'd be okay.

Before long, even the steady pain wasn't enough to keep me from dozing off.

I awoke to my brothers whispering with my dad.

"Cate?" My tongue was nearly back to normal, and even though talking was still tough, I at least sounded mostly human.

"She's still in surgery," Jamie said. He looked me up and down, a pained expression on his face.

I waited until he finished looking me over before answering. "Thanks."

He cleared his throat and nodded.

"You scared the fuck out of us," Jack said, sounding like he was choking back tears.

Not knowing what else to say, I defaulted to, "Sorry."

"You okay?" Jamie asked.

When I said yes, he was the first one to hug me. "We thought we'd lost you," Jamie said as he crushed me in a bear hug. When I grunted, he released his hold. I went through the same thing with Jack.

"I'm still here." Wanting to sit up, I reached for the bed's control. My muscles still lacked coordination, so Dad helped me. When I reached for the cup, he helped me with that, too. The water soothed my strained throat, but the fact that he had to hold the cup for me bruised my ego.

Forcing the embarrassment from my mind, I thanked him after pushing the straw away.

"You sound better," Dad said. He looked at the door before asking, "Do you want to fill us in on what happened before your mother gets here?"

When I paused, he said, "You don't have to." He searched my face for clues. "And if you want to talk about anything else, I'm here. No judgment."

"Thanks," I answered. I figured I could fill in a few details. "You obviously know about Wendy." He nodded. Using brief, broken sentences, I explained how we got caught, what happened to my truck, and then apologized for fucking up.

"Did he… did you just apologize for getting kidnapped?" Jack asked.

"Shoulda seen it coming," I mumbled.

"No, Son, you shouldn't have," Dad said.

"I saw the basement," Jamie said, his voice thick with emotion.

"Yeah." I told them about the cage, leaving out the personal details but emphasizing how strong Cate was.

My father tried not to show it, but his anger was visible. His neutral facial expression was a mask, but his clenched jaw gave him away. My brothers didn't hide their emotions, letting their anger come out in huffs and puffs when I summed up the last session in the office.

I'd always felt like I didn't belong, *the expendable Sheppard*, but I could see how hard it'd been for them when they thought I might be dead.

*I'm an idiot. Instead of building my relationship with my brothers, I pushed them away.*

"I'm okay. Worse for Cate."

And I didn't just mean the gunshot. Cate was as tough as they come, but she didn't have the extensive training or experience I had, and they'd treated her far worse.

"Cate, huh?" Jack asked, smiling for the first time.

Somewhere, during our time in hell, we'd become Cate and Jay instead of Maxwell and Sheppard.

*I need to see her.* The only thing that mattered was making sure she was okay. Something I wouldn't believe until I saw her with my own two eyes.

"Is she-"

"I'll check with the doctor," Dad said, before standing and leaving.

"What happened between you and Maxwell?" Jamie asked.

I leaned back against the soft pillows and closed my eyes, hoping to avoid the conversation I didn't want to have. Not here. Not now.

*Not without talking to Cate first.*

"Jay?"

"What?" I barked without bothering to open my eyes.

"Don't bite my head off. If you don't want to talk about it, just say so."

"I don't want to talk about it." I sounded madder than I felt.

"Then I'll wait until you're ready," Jamie said. Jack stood with his arms crossed over his chest, his stare boring into my soul like he could see everything I felt.

"Thanks." I'd expected them to hound me, and was grateful they hadn't.

I lifted my head and opened my eyes when the door opened.

"Maxwell's in recovery. Doc says the bullet missed her lung."

A collective sigh of relief filled the room. Mine rattled my ribs, while tears of gratitude filled my eyes.

"The doctor expects her to make a full recovery, but it'll take time."

"Thank God." I could live with that. "When can I see her?"

"He'll let us know when she's cleared for visitors."

It wouldn't be soon enough for me. "Thank you."

While we waited, Dad fussed over me, not the same way Ma would when she got here, but in his own way.

"Ma will be here in thirty," Jamie said. "She was scared silly about you."

"And you weren't?" Jack asked.

"I was scared stupid," Jamie admitted, giving me a grin.

"I didn't realize there was a difference." Jack laughed. "My bad."

"Of course there is," Jamie fired back. "How scared were you?"

"In keeping with the alliteration. Shitless," Jack answered.

For the first time in four days, I laughed. It felt wrong, given the circumstances, but it was exactly what I needed.

Only it hurt.

"You told Ma I'm okay, right?" I asked.

"Yes, but you know how she is. She won't believe me until she sees you," Dad answered.

"That won't help convince her," I said with a half laugh. One look at my face, and she'd freak out. I didn't need a mirror to know I resembled a human punching bag. *Because I had been.* I could feel the cuts and bruises, and would bet there wasn't more than an inch on my face that wasn't black and blue, or scabbed over.

"Probably not," Jack agreed.

I must have dozed off, because I awoke to my heart punching against my ribs as visions of Cate slumping forward, blood spilling from her body, ran through my mind.

*I almost lost her.*

"Jay, are you alright?" Dad asked, as my brothers stepped closer to my bed.

"Yeah," I paused, "I am." *At least I think I am.*

"Your heart is racing and you look like you've seen a ghost," Jamie said, shifting his focus to my EKG monitor.

With a shaky laugh, I said, "I'm fine." I had just enough time to take a few steadying breaths before someone knocked.

When I nodded, Jamie let them in.

My mom rushed to my side and pulled me into a bone-crushing hug.

When I grunted, she apologized.

She pulled back and wiped tears from her bloodshot eyes. "I'm sorry." She held my face in her hands. "I'm just so grateful you're alive."

"What made you think I wouldn't be?"

"You were gone for four days, and your truck was burned to a crisp."

I groaned. My truck. *Not what's important.*

"As you can see, I'm fine." *Thank God, I can talk again.* "Don't let the cuts and bruises scare you."

Ma sat on the edge of the bed and held my hand. Poor Ma. She hadn't had a break since high school, when she fell in love with my dad, a Marine. He hadn't chosen safe careers; the Marines, law enforcement, PI. And neither had their kids.

As a corpsman in the Navy, Madi's career was the safest, but it wasn't without risks.

I couldn't imagine how hard it'd be, sitting at home, waiting helplessly, when someone you loved was in danger.

Yes, I could. It was how I'd felt waiting to hear if Cate had made it out of surgery. I squeezed my mom's hand. "I'm okay. I promise."

Everyone seemed to know I wasn't in the mood for small talk, so the room was quiet except for the beeping of my machines.

When Dad left to check on Cate, I didn't let him fully reenter the room before asking, "How is she? Can I see her?"

"She's doing well. The nurses are moving her to her room shortly."

The breath I'd been holding rushed out. *She'll be okay.*

"When can I see her?" I asked.

"Maybe tomorrow."

That wasn't good enough. I needed to see her. I sat up, ignoring the protest from my ribs.

"Jay, you shouldn't get out of bed," my mom said, gently pushing me back against the pillows.

I didn't care if she was awake or not, I couldn't relax until I verified she was okay. "I need to see Cate," I barked.

"Jaden." My father corrected my behavior with nothing more than my name.

"Sorry, Ma, but I need to see her." Desperation filled my voice.

"You can't see her in a hospital gown that barely closes, and the clothes you had on when we found you are, to be perfectly blunt, offensive," Jack said, half joking to lighten the mood.

*He's right.* There was no way in hell I could put on what I'd been wearing. The clothes I'd worn for four days stank of blood, sweat, pain, and fear. The only thing I'd be doing was burning them.

"Do either of you have any extra clothes?" I asked. I was taller than Jamie and broader than both, so their clothes wouldn't fit well, but I was too desperate to care.

My father shared a look with Jamie before saying, "Jamie will bring clothes when he comes back tomorrow."

A knock on the door prevented me from arguing.

"Dinner," the nurse said, carrying in a tray.

My stomach growled at the mention of food. "You know you're hungry when hospital food sounds good," I said.

"You say that," the nurse joked, "but the doctor has you on a bland diet for your first few meals." He set up the table over my bed.

"Dude, that sucks," Jack said, grinning.

"Not helping, asshole," I said, causing the nurse to laugh.

"Boys." Dad corrected us.

"Oh, for Christ's sake, John. Just let them swear." She sounded exhausted. "It's not like I haven't heard it before." She pointed at Jack before turning to me. "But don't get used to it."

"Yes, Ma," we answered together. I shouldn't have looked at Jack, but I did. He made a stupid face, crossing his eyes and making me laugh. Not wanting to upset my mother, I tried holding in my laughter, which made me cough. Reminding me of the abuse my ribs had suffered.

I groaned as I looked at the small chicken breast and side of mashed potatoes. "Thanks."

"Sorry, man, doctor's orders."

I read his name tag so I could appeal to him, dude to dude.

"Paul, could you do me a solid and at least get me some more salt and pepper?" I practically begged.

"I'll see what I can do." He laughed as he left the room.

"Thanks, man."

As soon as he was out the door, I turned to Jack, interrupting his text conversation. "Any chance you can get me a steak?"

He chuckled, "On it." A few seconds later he said, "AJ said he'll run to the cafeteria." I don't think I'd ever loved my brother more than I did right then.

"You're the best," I said.

"Just don't tell Jamie," Jack fake-whispered.

"I'm the one bringing your clothes," Jamie reminded me.

"Steak trumps clothes," I teased.

He didn't miss a beat. "Unless I forget them."

Ma cut our banter short. "Do you think it's a good idea? There's a reason the doctor ordered this food for you."

Her fear was unfounded. I hadn't had an actual meal in four days. There was no reason I shouldn't enjoy a nice, juicy, tender steak.

"Mary, let the boy eat," Dad said.

*Thanks, Dad.*

"I'm starving, not sick." I comforted her as I tore the top off the green jello and sucked the sweet, jiggly glob out of the plastic cup.

My brothers laughed and Dad pretended he didn't see it while Mom reminded me she'd raised me better.

When Paul returned with more salt and pepper, I thanked him and sent him on his way. "Anyone want some bland as fu- some bland chicken?" I asked, shoving a spoonful of the potatoes in my mouth.

Even Ma said no. Ten minutes later, AJ snuck in with my steak.

"You're a lifesaver," I said as I opened the to-go container—the rich scent of beef invaded my nose, making me drool. "Now that smells like food."

I cut the steak into tiny bites and forced myself to eat slowly, savoring every bite.

I should take Cate out for steak when this was over. *If she'll let me.*

After eating half my steak, and most of the toppings on the loaded baked potato he'd gotten as a side, I dozed off. Much to my irritation, I was told I couldn't see Cate when I woke up.

Visiting hours were over. A fickle rule, since my visitors were still here.

"I checked on her while you were sleeping. She's stable," Dad assured me. "You can see her in the morning."

I huffed and dropped back onto my pillow.

# Chapter 35

## Cate

Beep. Beep. Beep. *They changed the alarm.*

I wanted to block out the incessant beeping noise stabbing into my brain like an ice pick, but I couldn't move.

Franks must have given me another drug, because I couldn't feel anything, not like when yanked my head back and slammed his mouth over mine.

*I can't hear Jay.* Panic set in.

What'd they do to him? What was in the syringe? Had Franks already killed him?

I wanted to open my eyes and check, but my muscles ignored the command. Maybe unconscious was better, so Jaden wouldn't have to watch Franks rape me.

Beep.Beep.Beep. *If I die, at least I'll never have to hear another alarm.*

A crash sounded. Suddenly, everything happened in slow motion.

Franks shooting Jay. I couldn't move to save him.

Franks shooting me. I couldn't move to save myself.

Franks falling.

My last thought, before my mind got fuzzy and my head rolled forward was, SSI is here but they're too late.

BeepBeepBeep. Faster and faster and faster.

*Do dead people hear beeping noises?*

Peace washed over my mind, erasing my fears.

# Chapter 36

## Jay

I expected to sleep like the dead. But the dark, quiet room and warm, comfortable bed weren't enough to keep the nightmares away. I jerked awake whenever the door opened, the light and sound triggering memories of Roman's basement. My mind, half-asleep and fuzzy from painkillers, would brace for what was coming.

My parents, who'd convinced the staff to let them stay overnight, would gently bring me back to the present each time.

None of us had a restful night's sleep.

When Jamie and Jack came back, with Emily and Meg in tow, my parents went to the cafeteria for breakfast. *And a much needed break.*

Waking up to your panicked screaming child, even an adult child, couldn't be easy.

Emily's hug was gentle, but heartfelt. "I'm glad you're home safe."

Meg tried to crush me to death. When she pulled away, she slapped my leg.

"What was that for?" I asked, sounding hoarse from holding back my grunts of pain. *And my emotions.*

"For scaring me half to death." Meg sounded a lot like my mom when she let her Mama Bear show. "Don't you ever do that again." She wiped away a tear.

I hated causing my sisters-in-law's stress or worry, so I defaulted to humor and saluted when I answered, "Ma'am. Yes, ma'am."

Jamie and Jack stood back and watched, matching grins on their faces. My grin would match if my lips weren't swollen.

Meg snuck me a blueberry muffin and coffee from Grannie's. "I know how much hospital food sucks."

I drank half the lukewarm coffee in one long pull before thanking her. "You are my new favorite person," I said before eating the sweet, perfectly baked muffin in three bites.

"Dude, slow down before you choke yourself," Jack said.

I let my middle finger answer as I enjoyed the rest of my coffee.

My parents returned to a room full of adults, who looked more like kids who'd just put the lid back on the cookie jar.

"How was breakfast?" I asked, brushing crumbs off my blanket.

"Their muffins aren't as good as ours," Ma said, "and the eggs were runny."

Dad's focus shifted to the garbage can behind Meg. His left eyebrow rose in question when he saw the Grannie's sleeve on the cup. "We brought you some coffee. It won't be as good as your mother's," he winked from behind Ma's back, "but it'll hold you over until breakfast comes."

When Jamie finally handed me a backpack, he asked, "Who's your favorite brother now?"

"The one holding my clean clothes." I grinned. Getting out of the stupid hospital gown was at the top of my to-do list, just below getting discharged and seeing Cate. "Thank you."

"We can't have you walking around with your ass hanging out," Jamie joked, echoing the thoughts rolling through my head.

"The nurse said you can see Cate after breakfast," Dad said.

"I can't wait that long. As soon as I'm dressed, I'm going." A herd of wild horses couldn't keep me away.

I made a face before glaring at Jamie after pulling out a robe. "Seriously?"

Ma put her hand on Dad's arm and said, "I'll go talk to the nurse and ask if we can sneak you in now."

Dad was great at intimidating people, but in a hospital, that wouldn't work. Ma would use sweet talk and empathy. I had no doubt the nurse would let me see Cate after my mom got done.

While she was gone, I dragged myself out of bed, with Jack's help, and put on the robe. "Real clothes would have been better," I grumbled.

"Beggars can't be choosers," Jamie said, a look of guilt flashing in his eyes. I had a feeling Dad put him up to it. If they didn't think I'd walk out of here in nothing but a robe, they were sadly mistaken.

Ma convinced the nurse to let me have five minutes with Cate. I wanted more, but I'd take it.

Dad pushed my wheelchair while Ma followed close behind with my IV stand. The wheelchair was humiliating, but it was the only way the nurse would let me leave my room. When I tried to argue, my father cleared his throat. That was all it took for me to stand down. *I hope someday I'm half the father my dad is.* Images of kids, a blend of Cate and me, flashed through my mind. Dismissing them, I willed my father to push faster.

Refusing to be wheeled into Cate's room, I stood and took the IV stand.

I thought I was prepared for what I'd see, but I wasn't. I gripped the door frame as the air left my lungs. The sight of Cate, who'd been so strong, so brave, so larger than life, looking pale and fragile in her hospital bed, brought tears to my eyes. Tubes and wires stuck out of her like a fucking science experiment gone wrong. They were helping her breath, feeding her, and sounding off her slow, steady heartbeat.

Relief wasn't the only emotion coursing through my body. Fear she could still die. Anger at the assholes who did this. Guilt she'd suffered so much.

*I'm so sorry, Cate.* My whimper had nothing to do with my pain as I walked to the edge of her bed. Holding her hand, I sang softly, hoping she'd hear me and know she wasn't alone.

Back in my room, Dad asked, "You ready to tell us what happened between the two of you in the cage?"

*I can't believe he brought up the cage.* Did he tell my mom about it? "We had time to talk."

Not wasting any time, Ma cut to the chase and asked, "Are you in love with her?"

I didn't have to look at my brothers to know they had identical smirks on their faces.

"No."

"Liar," Jamie coughed around the word at the same time Jack coughed out, "Bullshit."

"Don't you have somewhere else to be?" I asked.

"No." They said together. Jamie glanced at his phone. "Dean's here to replace Eric. I'll be right back."

Why was Dean replacing Eric? Why was Eric here? Where was he?

"Is there something I need to know?" I asked, the beeping on my monitor picking up speed. Dad told me they'd killed most of the men at the house, including Roman, who'd taken a shot at Doug and paid the ultimate price for his mistake. *So why do we need security?*

"No, it's just a precaution," Dad answered.

During breakfast, I asked my father if he'd talked to Mr. Darling and apologized for not thinking of it sooner.

"I did. He's taking it hard and blaming himself." None of this was his fault, but I doubted he'd be able to hear that.

As soon as I finished the scrambled eggs and toast, I got dressed and checked myself out. My mom thought I should stay longer, but I didn't care. I couldn't stay, knowing Cate was alone.

The doctor wanted to keep me another day, but I refused, signing myself out against medical advice. All I needed was rest and Grunt Candy, or ibuprofen as my mom called it. But for now, the painkillers in my system would be enough.

After hugging most of my family goodbye, I walked to Cate's room. My parents insisted on going with me. I didn't say it, but I was grateful they'd stayed.

Bracing myself for what I'd see, I took a deep breath before opening the door. It still wasn't easy seeing her lying there, but at least I didn't lose it in the doorway. I grabbed a hard plastic chair, moved it to the side of her bed, and got as comfortable as I could. Cate looked less pale than she had earlier, which I took as a good sign.

Dad got an update from the nurse while my mom grabbed a blanket from the empty bed and draped it over my shoulders.

I grabbed her hand to show my gratitude.

"The doctor said they'll remove the breathing tube later today," Dad attempted to comfort me, putting his hand on my shoulder. "It'll take some time, but she should make a full recovery."

"Should isn't good enough," I said.

I slipped my hand under Cate's and gently laced our fingers together. I'd be there, by her side, making sure she wasn't alone. *No matter how long it takes.*

"You don't have to stay," I said to my dad, who'd moved two chairs near the door.

"We know," he replied, making no attempt to move. Ma just smiled and settled into her chair.

"Thank you." I turned and blinked away the tears forming in my eyes.

I prayed Cate would wake up.

I begged her, silently, to come back to me.

I bargained with God.

When my brothers showed up at lunch with burgers, I inhaled them.

After lunch, Ma kissed me goodbye and left with my brothers. I told Dad he could leave, but he said, "I'll stay."

I dozed off with my head resting on Cate's bed, my hand holding hers. The sound of Dad's voice woke me, saving me from a memory-induced nightmare.

He was on his phone.

"General Maxwell, I'm glad you've landed safely. I trust you found your drive?."

*Her father's here, which means my time with her is limited.* It was a selfish thought, but I didn't care.

"I'm with her now; she's unconscious, but stable."

I willed him to put the phone on speaker, but he didn't.

I felt a tug at my hand and snapped my attention back to Cate. Her eyelids fluttered, and she mumbled, but she didn't wake up.

"I'm here," I whispered. "You're safe."

"Yes, sir. I understand." Hearing my father call someone else sir sounded foreign.

"Jaden and I will stay with her until you get here."
A brief pause.
"Yes sir, we'll see you then." He hung up and pocketed his phone.
"When will he get here?" I asked.
"About an hour," he answered. "Is everything okay?"
"Yeah, she moved her hand and tried opening her eyes."
*That has to be a good sign, right?*
Assuming I'd have to leave when Maxwell's dad arrived, I selfishly hoped she'd wake up before then. I wanted to be the first person she saw, the first person she talked to, the first person to reassure her she'd be okay and promise to help her every step of the way.

The one thing I wouldn't do was tell her how I felt. Not here, not like this. She deserved to be drug free and fully healed when I confessed my love.

Not knowing what else to do, I sang, so she'd know she wasn't alone.

# Chapter 37

## Cate

My eyelids felt like lead and my thoughts swam in an ocean of mud. The annoying beeping set my nerves on edge, but I couldn't remember why.

Opening my eyes was impossible, so I listened. Nothing.

Wait. *Is that Jay?* I wanted to turn my head towards the sound, but it weighed a thousand pounds.

*It is, and he's singing.* I dozed off to the familiar, soothing sound of Jay's deep singing voice.

When I regained consciousness, the only sound was the never-ending alarm. No, not an alarm, an EKG machine.

*I'm in the hospital. I survived.* The beeping sped up.

"Come back to me, Cate. Don't you dare die on me."

After a pause, Jay whispered, "Please Cate, I love you and I can't lose you."

The beeping picked up speed as his words overwhelmed me.

"That's my girl. I see your eyelids fluttering. Keep trying."

Wanting to see him, I tried again. *And failed.* But I turned my head a fraction of an inch. The beeping noise speeding up was my reward.

That, and Jay's soothing voice while he squeezed my hand. "Shh, it's okay. Rest. I'll be right here when you wake up."

The sounds faded as fog blanketed my mind. Two large warm hands surrounding mine were the last thing I noticed before sleep took over.

The next time I woke up, the loud, steady, annoying beep brought it all back. Being kidnapped, the alarm and strobe lights, the beatings, the shocks.

Beep.Beep.Beep. Louder and faster.

"It's okay, Cate. You're safe."

*I got shot. I can't move or open my eyes. He drugged me so I can't fight back.* BeepBeepBeep. *But I have to. I have to fight back. I won't die here.*

"Cate, you're in the hospital. You're safe." Jay's voice cut through the haze and fear. "The beeping is your heart monitor. Shh, it's okay. You're safe."

Hospital. Jaden. Safe. I repeated the words in my mind as a large hand gently stroked my arm. The beeping slowed down as I continued repeating: Hospital. Jaden. Safe.

This time, when warmth enveloped my hand, I squeezed to let him know I'd heard him. Squeeze was probably an exaggeration, so I wasn't sure he'd even felt it until I heard him say, "I got you, Cate."

# Chapter 38

## Jay

Luck wasn't on my side, and Cate was still unconscious when General Maxwell, one seriously imposing human being, arrived. He marched, not walked, into Cate's room, his presence filling the space.

"John Sheppard, I presume." He greeted my father, who'd been sitting near the door with a brisk handshake before walking to the other side of the bed. "How is she?"

When I stood to answer him, I had to fight the urge to salute. "Still unconscious." My wince when I stood hadn't gone unnoticed, nor had the bruises covering most of my face.

"Jaden Sheppard?" he asked.

"Yes, sir." I reached over the bed and shook his hand.

He eyed me up and down before saying, "You were with her."

It wasn't a question, or at least it didn't sound like one, but I answered anyway. "Yes, sir."

He looked at Cate, the machines, then back to me. The accusation in his eyes was hard to miss.

I hadn't protected his daughter. My face looked like Ali had spent hours practicing on it, but Cate looked worse. And she'd been shot.

I stood tall, despite wanting to hang my head in shame, but didn't defend myself. How could I? I'd failed her and was still beating myself up over it.

After looking us both over, he said, "They used her to get to you."

"Yes, sir, they did." I let pride fill my voice when I said, "But she was strong as fuck." I lifted my eyes to his and apologized.

He smiled, "I'm a Marine. I've heard worse."

And with that, the tension in the room relaxed.

"She fought right up to the end," I said. "You should be proud of her."

"I am." My dad had moved a chair over so General Maxwell could sit.

His expression softening as he looked at Cate. I took advantage of the moment to look at him. His brown eyes were nothing like Cate's blue ones. But even with a high and tight, and sprinkled with greys, it was obvious where Cate got her red hair. And her freckles. Cate only had a few on her nose, but her father had them all over his face.

"We'll leave you with your daughter." Dad's voice interrupted my thoughts. "If you need anything, please don't hesitate to call." It killed me to leave, but I wouldn't deny General Maxwell time with his daughter.

I silently promised to return the next day.

"Thank you."

"One of our guys, Dean, is outside the door."

"Is Catelyn still in danger?" The General asked, standing.

"No, but she's part of the SSI family and we don't abandon our own," Dad spoke a language Maxwell would understand.

"Spoken like a true Marine." Her father's expression changed from concerned to respectful.

"Oorah," I whispered, in agreement.

# Chapter 39

## Cate

I jerked awake, fighting against the ties holding me down. "Jay?" My voice sounded more frog than human.

The bright light filling the warm room blinded me.

"Shh, Catelyn, it's okay."

Pain and fear flooded my system as I remembered getting shot.

The beeping picked up speed, along with my heartbeat.

*Dear God, make it stop.*

"You're in the hospital and you're safe."

Hospital.

"Jaden?" I asked, my voice low and gritty. "Where's Jay?"

"He's fine. He went home."

Thank God he was okay. Wait. He went home? When? I swore I heard him talking to me earlier. I leaned back and tried blocking out the noise so I could think.

*Holy shit!* "Dad?" I asked, sitting up too fast and immediately regretting it.

"Has it been so long you don't recognize me?" His laugh sounded forced.

"No, sorry, I just. I…"

"It's okay. Waking up to me is probably a bit of a shock."

It was, and yet, it wasn't. We weren't close, but my father had been there for every major milestone in my life. Of course, he'd rushed to my side when he heard I got shot. The shock was how quickly he'd gotten here.

"I'm glad you're here." The words didn't adequately express what I felt, but everything hurt and my mind felt like mush, so forming complex sentences was beyond my ability. When I asked him what day it was, he said Sunday.

I'd lost a full day.

I yawned, just as someone knocked on the door.

A nurse walked in, asking, "How are you feeling?"

*How am I feeling?* What kind of question was that? I'd been beaten within an inch of my life, starved, drugged, and shot.

I felt like shit.

My face must have given me away because she said, "Your face just answered me, so no point in lying."

Guilty. I would've lied so my father didn't worry.

"What are you giving me?" I asked, as she used a syringe to add something to my IV line.

"Morphine. Your body took a lot of abuse and you'll heal faster if you aren't in pain," she answered.

That made sense. She kicked my father out of the room to change my bandages. My eyelids felt like lead weights, so I closed them and drifted back to painless, nightmare-free sleep before she was done.

I woke to the sound of two voices. My father and John Sheppard.

Grateful my mind felt semi-normal and I could think clearly, I pretended to be asleep and listened.

It wasn't hard for me to imagine the guarded expression on my father's stoic face as John filled him in.

"Thank you for not holding back," my father said, his voice strained. It sounded like he clapped John on the shoulder.

"You're welcome, sir." It was the first time I'd heard John defer to anyone. But then, John was a marine and my father was a three-star general, so it shouldn't have been surprising.

"How's your son?"

"Recovering, thanks for asking."

"Catelyn asked for him when she woke up last night." There was a pause, making me wish I could see them. "Is there something between them I should know about?"

"Not that I know of, but you should probably ask Cate," John said, surprising me by not only using my first name, but the less formal version of it.

"Seems to me you know more than you're letting on." He accused John.

"What I suspect and what I know are two very different things, sir." John laid the sarcasm on thick. "And it's not mine to share, regardless."

My boss talking back to my father, after showing deference only a moment before, almost made me laugh.

John ruled the office, and his family, with nothing more than a firm tone of voice. But that wouldn't work on my father, a man accustomed to having his orders followed before he finished giving them.

Neither man was easily intimidated, and while John would show my father every respect, he wouldn't back down when it came to his family.

I squinted to watch their body language, but my eyes felt like I'd rubbed them with sandpaper—blurring everything and preventing me from seeing the nuances I needed to assess the energy between them. The last thing I wanted was for my father and my boss to butt heads.

My father's nod, as he dismissed John, was big enough for me to see.

John's acknowledging nod was just as big. "We're right outside if you need us, Cate."

Again using my first name. *He's never called me Cate.*

Duh, he couldn't call me Maxwell when there were two of us in the room.

Shit. *He knows I'm awake.* My eyes snapped up to meet John's.

"Thank you, sir," I croaked out just above a whisper.

I hated sounding so weak, but nothing in my body was working as well as it should.

My father turned around, so he didn't see John wink before he left.

"Hi, Dad," I said.

"How much did you hear?" He asked, as he hurried to my side.

Reaching for his hand, I said, "I'm glad you're here." Lacking the physical or mental strength to sound stoic, my voice hitched with emotion as tears threatened to spill over.

Never comfortable with feelings, he changed the subject. "You seem more alert. How are you feeling?"

"Not painful, but weak." Moving too much or too fast reminded me of my wounds, so I mostly laid still.

He chuckled at my awkward sentence. "The doctor said you'll heal faster if you're not in pain, so they've had you on a steady dose of morphine."

When I tried to talk but coughed instead, he picked up a cup of water and held the straw to my lips, bringing back memories of the rare times he'd comforted me when I was sick or hurt as a little girl. Reminding me that his distance wasn't because he didn't care, but because of his duty to the Corps.

The water soothed my parched throat as I sucked it down like a man possessed.

He pulled the straw away, causing me to drool on my chin. "Slow down."

I nodded, but wanting more, I reached for the cup. Dad forced me to drink slowly, so it took a while, but I finished every last drop. Sadly, the water did nothing to ease the hunger that made itself known with a loud rumble.

"I'll page the nurse and ask her to bring you something to eat."

While he did that, I wondered how long it'd be until Jay came back. I had to make sure he was okay. Was he shot, too?

The vivid memory of Franks firing at Jay sucked the air from my lungs.

"She'll bring you something in a few minutes." Dad's voice cut into my thoughts. "What's wrong?"

"Nothing, just awful memories." I focused on my breathing to bring my heart-rate back to normal, which slowed down the infernal beeping.

"I'm here if you want or need to talk."

"Thanks." Then, despite not wanting to hear the answer, in case it was only a few hours, I asked, "How long are you staying?"

"I took three days leave, with the option of extending it if needed."

Wow. I assumed he'd need to go back to work sooner rather than later.

He looked me over. "And from the look of things, it's needed."

"John didn't tell you about my injuries when he called?" I assumed it was John who called him.

"He said you were hurt and in surgery. I was already on a plane when he called to tell me you were out of surgery and expected to make a full recovery." He paused and collected himself before continuing, "I just now learned the extent of the hell you went through prior to being shot."

Knowing I was the reason for the fear, anger, and pain in his eyes was more than I could handle, so I looked away. The gunshot wound was bad, no denying that, but the sleep deprivation, starvation, abuse, and drugs did the most damage to my body. I was half-grateful John had filled him in, so I didn't have to. I also half wished he hadn't, so I had the choice of never telling him.

When the nurse brought my lunch, Dad asked if the doctor had an ETA for when I could leave. The nurse didn't know, but said she'd send the doctor in to talk to us.

The chicken noodle soup was more broth than chicken and the dry roll was bland, but it was the first meal I'd had in days. Which meant it tasted like heaven.

The doctor came in as I was sipping the last of my broth.

"Miss Maxwell, it's good to see you awake. How's the pain level?" she asked.

"Please, call me Cate," I said. "And I'm too drugged up to feel much, so good."

She chuckled. "We can cut back the dosage tomorrow, as long as the pain is manageable."

"Thanks. When do you think I can leave?"

"I'd like to keep you one more night."

My protests were useless; my father sided with the doctor.

"It's for your own good, Catelyn."

Did they tell Jay the same thing? If they had, how come he went home? *I'll ask him when he gets here.* Turning my attention back to the doctor, I nodded my consent.

"If things look good tomorrow, we'll send you home. As long as you have someone who can stay with you."

"I'll be with her," my father said. "Just tell me what I need to do."

"Good," the doctor said. "We'll provide all the details at discharge."

I yawned, and then tried to shake my head to wake myself up, making me dizzy.

"Don't fight the urge to sleep. Your body needs it." The doctor sounded more like she was issuing an order than giving a suggestion.

*I want to stay awake so I can see Jay.* They said he was okay, but I wanted, needed, to see it for myself.

*And I want to thank him.* I couldn't have gotten through the ordeal without him.

My big, loud yawn irritated my bruised split lips; I wouldn't be awake much longer.

"Get some rest. I'll be here when you wake up." My father's words were the last thing I heard before sleep claimed me.

The nurse, checking my vitals a few hours later, woke me up. When I looked around, I couldn't see my dad. *Did he get called back to DC?* My heart raced as I looked around the room. Surely he wouldn't have left without saying goodbye.

"He went to grab a coffee. He'll be right back," the nurse assured me. "Let's get you cleaned up and change your gown before he does."

*Good idea.* The quick sponge bath was painful despite the nurse's attempt to be gentle. She apologized, but it wasn't her fault. Cuts and bruises covered my face and torso. I had several cracked ribs and two holes from the bullet.

A soft knock signaled my father's return. *Or maybe it's Jay.*

"I'll let him in," the nurse said, grabbing the wash pan and my dirty gown.

"Thank you."

It wasn't Jay. *Why hasn't he come back?*

"Are you feeling better after your nap?" Dad asked, returning to my side.

"I am, and very well rested." I chuckled. I'd slept more than I'd been awake. "Overly rested."

"You need the rest to heal," he said with a sad smile. "Especially if you want to go home tomorrow."

Considering myself gently chastised, I answered, "Yes, sir." I added, "If you want, I can have John give you the keys to my apartment so you can stay there tonight."

"That won't be necessary."

"There's no reason for you to pay for a hotel."

"Catelyn, it's unnecessary because I'm staying here." His voice didn't give away his fear, but his eyes did, showing more emotion than I'd ever seen. *Because I've never given him a reason to worry, not like this.*

Knowing better than to argue, I said okay. Besides, it did my heart and soul good to know he wanted to stay.

"Did Jay ever come?" I asked.

"I haven't seen him." He didn't offer more.

I turned to hide my disappointment. Maybe something happened and he couldn't come back. *Is he okay?* Maybe my drug addled brain made it up. Maybe Jay hadn't said he'd come back.

"Catelyn? Everything okay?"

"Yeah." I forced myself to smile as I turned to him. *I'm sure he's okay. He just got delayed.* If I repeated it enough, I'd eventually believe it. I gave my father my full attention.

We talked off and on through the night. Sleep must have eluded him too, because he was alert anytime I woke up. He told me about the current happenings in DC, as much as he could, and how much he hated the political games that came with being stationed at the Pentagon.

It wasn't the first time he'd mentioned hating the political aspect, though he rarely went into much detail. When he said he was considering retiring, I had to ask him to repeat himself.

My father loved the Marines. He always had, and I assumed he always would. When I said as much, he assured me he loved the Marines, but hated DC.

"I'm considering an instructor position," he said.

I could see him as drill sergeant at Parris Island, whipping recruits into shape. I didn't envy anyone with the good fortune of learning from him. Being in his recruit training unit would be hard, but they'd be better Marines for it.

"You'll scare away all the recruits." I laughed.

"I'll whip their sorry asses into shape."

My mind thought back to Jay and how gentle he'd been after I got my ass beat. Suggesting I sing to help keep from going crazy, when the alarm rang non-stop, was the first step of our new relationship.

Friendship, I corrected myself. I doubted Jay wanted more.

I didn't realize I'd started humming The Marine Hymn until my father joined in. Comforted by his deep tones, I soon fell back to sleep.

# Chapter 40

## Jay

"How'd it go at the PD?" My father skipped the pleasantries when Ma and I arrived in the waiting room on Cate's wing Monday morning.

It was tough giving a detailed play-by-play, but I'd gotten through it. They'd given me a signed report for my insurance claim, plus anything else that needed to be replaced. "Fine," I said.

I wasn't about to rehash the ordeal in front of my mom.

Not because I thought she was soft or fragile; she wasn't. She was tough as fuck, especially when her Mama Bear instincts kicked in. But she didn't need to hear the details, not when I could still see the fear and stress in her eyes.

She hugged my father, who kissed the top of her head before pulling back and tipping her face up. "How are you holding up?"

"Shouldn't you be asking our son that?" she corrected him with her question.

"I asked you, but if it'll make you feel better, Jay, how are you holding up?"

"I'm fine, Dad. How's Cate?" I wasn't in the mood for games. "Can I see her?"

"She's awake, and doing well. Her father's with her. I think it's best if you give them more time."

Not what I wanted to hear. *I need to see her. Talk to her.* Ignoring my father's suggestion, I headed towards the door. Before I could knock, he grabbed my arm. "Son, that's not a good idea. They need time together and you barging in there will complicate things."

"What the fuck does that mean?" I huffed at him. Shockingly, my mom didn't correct my choice of words when she put her hand on my arm to offer comfort.

"It means now isn't the time to tell her how you feel," he answered. His voice was calm, but his expression made it clear he was issuing an order.

Dumping my feelings wasn't on the agenda. I'd already done that when she was unconscious, like a fucking coward. I didn't plan on doing it again, especially in front of her father.

I lowered my voice, practically begging, "I need to see her, Dad." Now that she was awake, I needed to hear her say she was okay. The image of blood staining her shirt refused to leave my mind.

"I promise you, she's okay," he offered.

It wasn't enough. I opened my mouth to argue, but one look at my father and I knew there was nothing I could say to change his mind. The devil on my shoulder told me to fight. The angel told me to choose my battles carefully.

I listened to the angel. Gripping the back of my neck, I said, "Fine. I'll come back after lunch."

Sympathy radiated off my mom as my father shook his head. "Give them today."

*Why?* Had her father told mine to keep me away?

He added, "I'll call General Maxwell and figure out a good time for you to visit. Tomorrow."

So the General was calling the shots. *Does he blame me? Is that why he won't let me see Cate?* Not that I could blame him; I should have done more to protect her.

Which explained why I was so desperate to see her. If she could tell me she was okay, maybe I could let go of some of the guilt.

Going against the need I felt in every cell of my body, I nodded.

"Let's grab some lunch," my dad offered.

During lunch, Ma told me everyone was coming over for a family dinner. Her less-than-subtle hint that she expected me to be there was unnecessary.

"I planned a video chat with Madi; she's worried about you," Ma added.

"Why?" I found it hard to believe anyone would've told her I was missing in action.

"Why?" she asked, incredulously. "Because your big sister loves you and you were missing for four days." Her voice went up an octave or two.

I was wrong. "You told her?" I asked, knowing it was a stupid question since she obviously had. Not wanting to start an argument, I joked, "What, didn't you trust Dad to find me?" I laughed as I reached across the table and squeezed her hand.

Dad's eyes sparkled, the only hint at his humor.

"I. He." She laughed, "Don't turn this on me."

"Because I trusted him, one hundred percent." I picked up my water and held it up in salute. "Thanks, Dad."

"Any time, Son. Though I'd prefer not having to do it again."

We clinked glasses. "Noted."

"You look like shit, Little Brother."

"Good to see you, too, Madi," I answered. Ma said Madi was worried, but from her greeting, it was obvious she'd received updates.

It felt weird being on this side of the video. Until a few months ago, I had to video chat from whatever Marine base I was on. Now Madi was the only Sheppard still serving active duty, though she planned on leaving the Navy when her enlistment ended.

"Seriously, though, I'm glad you're okay. Ma said you're in bad shape, but Dad said your injuries aren't too bad, so I didn't know what to expect." As a Navy corpsman, and a soon to be civilian nurse practitioner, Madi wouldn't shy away from the gory details.

Not that I'd share them.

"A lot of bruises and a couple of fractured ribs." I shrugged. "I've had worse."

My mom's sharp intake of breath caused both my brothers to punch me, one on each arm.

"What the hell was that for?"

"For scaring Ma," they said together. Damn it. I hated it when they teamed up on me. Even more so when they were right.

"Sorry, Ma."

Madi laughed, "Can't wait to come home in July and see you guys, even if you are a pain in the ass."

"They started it." I laughed.

Ignoring me, Jamie asked, "You'll definitely be home for my wedding?"

"I wouldn't dream of missing my little brother's wedding." She teased him.

"Twenty-two minutes, Madi," he replied. Their running joke was as old as I could remember. *Probably older.* As the only girl, Madi loved being the oldest child. Even if it was only by twenty-two minutes.

"Meg!" Madi screeched.

"Sorry I'm late. Morning sickness isn't just in the morning." Meg looked a little green around the edges.

"Can I do anything?" Jack asked, pulling her onto his lap.

"You're a good husband, Jack," Madi said, her hands over her heart as she watched Jack fawn over Meg.

"I'm okay now," Meg reassured him. "Did I miss anything good?"

"Just my brothers being shitheads," Madi said with a laugh.

We all grumbled, but she talked over us. "I can't wait to meet my first niece or nephew."

"We're happy you'll be home to stay before he or she is born, so he or she doesn't have to meet you over video chat," Meg said.

"You and me both," Madi agreed. "So, Jay, speaking of love." *We weren't.* "I hear you've got a thing for a former FBI agent?"

"What? No." *Maybe.* "Who told you that?" No way would I have this conversation here, now. *For all I know, Cate will go back to hating me now that the ordeal is over.*

I didn't really believe that, but I didn't think she felt the same way I did. It didn't help I was questioning my own feelings. What if it was some version of Stockholm Syndrome that made me think I was in love with her?

I grinned, thinking Cate would know the correct term.

"I think he doth protest too much," Meg said.

"It's not like that. We suffered through hell together, so it's normal for me to want to make sure she's okay." I sounded lame as I excused my behavior.

Not wanting to see them smirking at me, I refused to look at anyone.

"Whatever you say, but I expect updates from you more often now that you're not hiding away in the dessert."

"I'd hardly call it hiding." I'd gone dark for missions, but I wasn't hiding.

"We didn't know where you were," Madi said.

"No, but The Marine Corps did," I laughed as I answered.

"Fine." She rolled her eyes. "It sucked that we rarely got to talk. I've missed you."

"Missed you, too." I didn't have to fake the emotion behind it. I was closest to Madi growing up because she always stuck up for me. *And she'd never called me a mistake.*

"So, you'll call me when something happens with you and Maxwell?"

Covered snickers filled the room. *Damn it.*

"I wouldn't wait for that, since it isn't likely to happen. I don't want you giving me shi-crap because I waited too long."

I saw the question in her eyes as she tilted her head to the side, her hazel eyes laser-focused as she studied me through the camera.

Every single member of my family saw through my bullshit. But just because I had feelings for Cate didn't mean she had them for me.

Before she could ask any questions, Dad cut in, "Let your mother and I have some time with our daughter."

*Thanks, Dad.* I wasn't ready to have that conversation with anyone. Not even myself.

# Chapter 41

## Cate

I slept through most of Monday. The rest was exactly what I needed, allowing me to feel more like myself when I woke up on Tuesday. Despite feeling better, I was keenly aware of Jay's continued absence.

Any time a knock sounded at the door, I expected to see Jay's tall, strong body strut through it. Expected? I hoped. *Maybe seeing him will help me work through the disconnect between my heart and mind.* And I wanted to make sure he really was okay.

I'd developed feelings for him, but I didn't trust them. I also doubted he felt the same way about me.

When I'd asked, my father said he hadn't heard from Jay, but John had called to check on me.

*Where is Jay?* Why hasn't he come to see me?

I considered calling him, but decided against it. If he didn't want to see me, I'd accept it and move on. I wouldn't call and beg. We'd developed a friendship in the cage, but it could never be more than that. *If it's even that.*

Risking my career for an office romance was stupid; a romance with my boss's son, no less. The idea reminded me of the romcom movie theme of dating the Captain's daughter. *It fits both of us.* I was the General's daughter, and dating me was something no Marine with half a brain dared to do. *Dating?* I wasn't even sure we were friends.

My stomach rumbled, letting me know I was hungry. Starving actually. The only things they'd allowed me to eat were soup, scrambled eggs, bread, and jello. I begged my dad to get a burger and fries so I could steal a bite.

He looked at me, unsure if he should break the rules by letting me eat something the doctor hadn't approved.

"Please, Dad. I need something with flavor." My mouth salivated at the thought of a greasy burger and salty fries.

"Alright. What do I want on my burger?" he asked, fully embracing the idea once he'd agreed.

"Cheese, lettuce, and tomato" I wanted bacon, but didn't think he'd go that far. "And you need fries."

"Do I also need ketchup?"

"Ew, no." I scrunched up my nose. I only dipped my fries in cheese sauce or blue cheese dressing.

"If I do this, you need to eat what they bring you first."

"Deal." I held my hand out, and we shook. "Thanks, Dad."

I practically drooled over the rich smell of ground beef and fried potatoes as I dipped the dry roll in my soup. I forced myself to go slow, so I didn't get sick or fill up too fast.

Nothing would come between me and that cheeseburger.

Dad pretended not to look when I stole his fries and dipped them in the remaining broth. "Drink up," he said.

Like a good soldier, I did as I was told. My reward was the best tasting bite of cheeseburger I'd ever had. I chewed slowly, savoring each layer of flavor.

"So good." I mumbled around my small mouthful.

Then I licked the fat off my fingers.

"You want another bite?"

"I want the whole damn thing, but I don't think I should." My stomach might not handle the sudden onslaught of greasy meat. I reached for the burger. "Maybe one more." After swallowing, I said, "I can't wait until I can eat an actual meal filled with flavor."

"What will you have?" he asked.

Without hesitation, I answered, "A steak and a loaded baked potato."

So far, we'd kept topics light whenever we talked. The only heavy subject was when he told me John had notified Mr. Darling about Wendy's death. He'd squeezed my hand when tears formed in my eyes. Knowing there was nothing we could've done to save Wendy didn't help me feel any better.

I wasn't overly religious, but I prayed for Darling to find peace.

After lunch, I decided it was time for a deeper conversation. If I wanted to reconnect, I had to open up. Be vulnerable.

"Dad, I'm sorry I disappointed you." It was a blanket apology for all the times I'd done so.

"Why do you think you disappointed me?"

I turned and made eye contact before listing off the reasons. "I left the Marines, I left the FBI, I failed again at SSI and got captured-"

He held up his hand to stop me.

"Catelyn, I'm not disappointed in you. And just so we're on the same page, I never expected you to be a lifelong Marine. That's my thing, not yours. And yes, I was proud when you applied for the FBI, but that doesn't mean I was disappointed when you left." He paused. "And I sure as hell don't consider you a failure for getting captured while trying to save a young woman's life."

My jaw fell open. I'd always assumed my choices had disappointed him. Had I misread him?

"But you seemed so upset when I left the FBI."

"I was shocked, not upset or disappointed." He looked out the window before turning back to me. "I apologize if it came across that way."

"Thank you." It sounded lame, but I was too busy processing it all to say much else. *I've had it wrong for so long.* I was so convinced I was a disappointment, I never questioned it. I spent my whole life hyper-focused on trying to be who I thought he wanted me to be, denying him the chance to know the real me.

"It was obvious you loved your work, so I didn't understand why you quit. The reason you gave never sat right."

Because I lied. "I wasn't completely honest with you."

"Are you ready to tell me?"

It wasn't easy, but I ignored my shame and told him about Gavin. His teeth clenched and hands fisted as I talked, but he didn't interrupt.

"I'm sorry you went through that," he paused and leaned forward to take my hand, "and I'm even more sorry you felt like you couldn't come to me for support."

"Thank you." I didn't hide my tears. Ever since I was a kid, I thought I was a disappointment to him. The only time I didn't feel that way was when I earned straight A's, won an award or a boxing match, or followed in his footsteps.

Despite all my psychology training, I never thought to question my assumptions as an adult. They'd been with me for so long, I accepted them as the truth.

"I know I wasn't the most attentive father, and I've never been good at expressing my emotions, but I'd like to change that."

I blinked back more tears. "I'd like that, too."

"Luckily, we have a week to lay a solid foundation."

"A week."

"Well, five days, but I'm all yours for every minute of them."

I nodded. My father and I would heal our relationship while my body healed my wounds. I wasn't glad I went through hell, but I was glad for the opportunity to connect with my father and forge the relationship I'd always wanted with him.

"Is that why you kept boxing?" he asked. "To please me?"

"Yes and no," I admitted. "But I grew to love it. I don't compete anymore, but I still train. I found a great coach at my local gym. And I'm taking BJJ. My goal is to beat one of the guys at a monthly training match."

He laughed at that. "That's my girl."

I dozed to as he told me stories about boxing competitively in the Marine Corps.

# Chapter 42

## Cate

"Dad, can you please stop fussing over me?" The doctor released me, after much begging on my part, after I woke up from my nap. Sammie, one of the part-time employees at SSI and a Weatherford cop, had dropped us off at my apartment less than thirty minutes ago and I was already doubting if I could handle having my father around twenty-four-seven for the next four and half days.

He'd done a one-eighty after our talk and was trying to make up for twenty-plus years of 'neglect'. His word, not mine. I loved him for trying, but having him cater to my every whim felt weird.

"I'm going overboard, aren't I?"

"A little. Though I appreciate your effort."

"I wasn't always there for you. My priorities were in the wrong place, and it took almost losing you to make me realize it. I want to be more present in your life."

His confession brought tears to my eyes. Without thinking, I wiped at them, making myself wince. *Damn bruises*.

"Thanks, Dad." I wrapped my good arm around him for a hug, only grunting a little at the pressure my slung arm put on my battered and bruised torso. Getting shot and having several ribs cracked sucked. The bullet had entered high on the right side of my chest, angled down, and exited my back—narrowly missing my lung.

"I love you, too." He hadn't actually said the words, but I read between the lines.

He pulled away. "Can I make you some dinner?"

"Sure. That sounds great." Remembering I hadn't been home in a week, I said, "On second thought, maybe we should order out." Any food in my refrigerator had to be bad by now. "I'll clean the fridge out after we eat." Or maybe after a post dinner nap.

"What do you want? And don't say steak. The doctor recommended lighter meals for the first few days."

I sighed. "Fine. There's a good Thai place that delivers. I'll have Pad Thai with chicken." It would be flavorful and filling without being too heavy, plus the leftovers would be just as good when I warmed them up.

"Egg roll?" he asked.

"Sure."

While we ate, dad asked me about SSI, wanting to know if I liked it and found it fulfilling.

"I love it. I thought I'd miss the FBI and the big city, but I don't. And I'm helping people." *Not Wendy*. But she was dead before her father hired us, so nothing we did would've changed that outcome. I shook off the wave of guilt. "Turns out I like the small town vibe."

"That's good to hear. John sings your praises." He paused. "He seems like a good man, and he genuinely cares about you."

*Damn meds, making me emotional.* I blinked back the extra moisture in my eyes.

"He's a great leader." In my father's eyes, it was one of the highest compliments I could give.

"I sensed that. And the rest of the team?"

Now that he knew about Gavin and his bullshit, I sensed his question was multi-layered.

"Their good men. Honest, reliable, and I trust them."

"Did you trust Gavin?"

I took my time answering. "Yes, and no. I trusted him to have my back and do his job. I let it cloud my judgment when we started dating and ignored the red flags." Red flags I'd been watching for and hadn't seen at SSI.

"Any red flags at SSI?"

I smiled. "No. I went in looking for them, expecting them." Hell, I even tried creating one or two. "But they aren't there."

"And Jaden?"

"What about him?"

He raised his eyebrow. "You called his name more than once while you were out." He said it so casually I did a double take.

"Did I?" I tried to play it off like my heart wasn't racing like a thoroughbred. Like I hadn't asked about him repeatedly while I was awake. I'd tried to act casual, but it was obvious he wasn't buying it.

"You did. And John said Jaden discharged himself against medical advice so he could sit at your side."

"He what?" I almost choked on the water I'd been sipping. He was there. I hadn't imagined hearing his voice. *So why didn't he come see me after I woke up?*

"Cate? Are you okay?"

I was, but a million things raced through my mind. *Deep breaths.* I reminded myself I could control my racing thoughts by focusing on my breath.

"I'm fine. Just surprised, that's all."

He didn't believe me, but at least he had the decency to wait until I was calm again before asking me if I had a thing for Jay.

When I babbled through my no and my excuses, he asked, "Care to tell me the truth?"

Memories of being scolded for lying about not doing my homework flashed through my mind. I'd always hated that feeling, which explained how I'd become an uptight overachiever.

I didn't want to admit I might have fallen for Jay in the cage. Or tell him I wasn't sure how much of what I remembered was true versus wishful thinking. Or admit how much it hurt that Jay hadn't come back to see me.

I pretended to misunderstand him. "I'm fine, Dad."

He leaned forward and asked, "Are you in love with him?"

My eyes shot open like a fucking cartoon at his directness, but at least my jaw didn't hit the floor.

"What makes you say that?" I croaked out. He'll never believe me if I keep sounding like I don't believe me.

"You're not as good at hiding your emotions as you think you are."

"It doesn't matter. If he cared, he would've come back to see me." It was the closest I'd come to admitting it.

"A man doesn't sign himself out AMA if he doesn't care."

"We went through hell together. He probably just wanted to make sure I was okay before leaving." Now that I knew what happened with Sara and Henderson, I doubted Jay would be eager to rush into a relationship. I didn't expect him to go back to hating me, but I didn't expect us to be more than friends either.

"Do you really believe that?"

When I put my head on the table, I had to sit back up because bending over hurt like hell. After regaining my composure, I admitted, "I'm not sure what I believe."

Too many conflicting thoughts. Too many conflicting emotions. Too many painkillers preventing me from sorting through them all.

I explained how Jay and I fought like cats and dogs, but had formed a truce for the investigation. And how a game of twenty questions made us realize we had more in common than either of us could've imagined.

I didn't share Jay's personal stories. They were his to tell. But I shared mine, which included Jay holding and comforting me.

"He cares about you."

"He's a decent human and would've done it for anyone."

"Catelyn, I know your mother and I didn't set a great example of what a healthy relationship looks like, so I'm probably the last person you want advice from, but I'm giving it anyway."

I barely remembered the two of them together, so they hadn't set any example. He paused, as if waiting for permission, so I nodded.

"Don't dismiss him so quickly."

"Why didn't he come back to see me?"

"I don't know, maybe something came up, but don't you think you should give him a chance to explain?"

*Yes. No.* "Maybe." I wasn't sure I wanted to hear the answer. What if I had to leave SSI after hearing what he had to say? I covered my mouth as a huge yawn escaped. All this talking and thinking and feeling was exhausting.

"Why don't we relax in front of the TV?" It wasn't something either of us did often, both preferring to read, but vegging out in front of the TV sounded perfect.

*Maybe I can go to DC with my father for a little while.* I'd ask in the morning, after a good night's sleep.

# Chapter 43

## Jay

Still anxious, Ma hosted a second family dinner Tuesday night and her lasagna was just the comfort food I needed. Filled with ground beef and pork sausage, cheese, and chopped vegetables, it brought back memories of childhood. She started adding the veggies when we were kids, thinking we wouldn't notice if she hid them in our favorite dishes. *She was right.*

It was different now. We were older, and after serving in the military, I'd learned to eat whatever was put in front of me.

*Unless it's in a paper bag and potentially drugged…*

A chill ran up my spine before I forced my mind back to the conversation. Dad raised an eyebrow in question, so I nodded—letting him know I was okay. Ma rubbed my shoulder, offering silent comfort. Just like she had when I was a kid.

My brothers noticed too, but let it go. Which I appreciated; talking about what happened wasn't high on my list.

*I wonder what Cate's doing?* I still hadn't seen her. Before I could leave for the hospital, Dad told me she was going home.

"She'll need time to settle in. You can see her later."

*There's always something.* It'd been three days and the need to see her was eating me alive. Come hell or high water, I'd go see her on Wednesday.

"Have you started picking names?" Emily asked, bringing me back to the present conversation.

*How much did I miss?*

Meg and Jack shared a look; they had.

It hadn't taken me long to fall under Meg's spell. She'd been through hell, but came out on the other side stronger than ever and used her experience to greet everyone who walked through the doors of SSI with compassion.

She and Jack were blissfully happy, even when they argued.

I was happy for them, even if I was a little jealous.

I thought I'd have that, but Sara crushed my heart.

"We're still discussing it," Meg answered. She was about two months along, so they had plenty of time. "I want to keep with the Sheppard tradition, giving boys J names and girls M names, but Jack thinks it'll be a pain in the ass."

We all laughed. Ma would often end up yelling all three of our names anytime she yelled at one of us.

"Maybe start a tradition of your own," Dad offered with a grin. "A less confusing one." He'd had the same problem as Ma.

I laughed, "Jack's right, it was a pain in the ass. I can't tell you how many times my teachers called me Jamie or Jack."

"Like that's a bad thing," Jamie said.

"It is when you want to be your own person, not the youngest Sheppard who can't live up to his brothers' legacies." Shit, I hadn't meant to say that out loud.

"What does that mean?" Jamie asked.

No time like the present to clear the air, and maybe let the past go so I could heal and move on.

"You know I was compared to you and Jack, and don't pretend you don't know I fell short. Every. Single. Time." Not wanting to appear confrontational, I forced my hands to unfist.

"I didn't," Jamie said. "Did you?" he asked Jack.

"No," Jack answered, never taking his eyes off me. "You never said anything."

My chin fell to my chest as I ran my hands through my hair before gripping the back of my neck. "What was the point? I wasn't as good in school as either of you and I couldn't sit still, so I got in trouble a lot. It was one more reminder that I was a mistake."

You could've heard a pin drop in the silence.

"Jaden," Ma's voice cracked with sadness.

"Mary," Dad shook his head back and forth.

Jamie and Jack shared a look before Jamie asked, "Christ, Jay, you didn't really believe that, did you?"

"He obviously did," Jack answered. "I'm sorry, Jay. I was a dumb kid and meant it as a joke. I had no idea how much it hurt you, or that you still carry it with you."

"Thanks," I whispered.

"I'm sorry I didn't realize it either," Jamie added. He looked at me, then at my parents, who wore matching expressions of shock and irritation. "You never told Mom and Dad?"

I swallowed. This part would hurt them more than knowing my brothers teased me relentlessly, calling me a mistake.

"Why would I? I thought it was true." I made eye contact with my mom first, knowing she'd need it. "I don't believe it anymore." I made eye contact with my dad. "I haven't for a long time, but the feeling of not being good enough stuck around."

"Jaden, you were a surprise, not a mistake. We were thrilled to bring another child into the family." Dad stated the facts, this time keeping emotion out of his voice. Somehow, it made it easier for me to hear. For it to sink in.

Which reminded me of Cate, but I didn't have time to linger on the thought.

"We've always loved you and we always will," Ma said. "If you'd told me your brothers were teasing you like that, I would've boxed their ears."

And they would've made my life miserable. *No point in dwelling on it.* I let it go and laughed as I envisioned her putting them in their place. Jamie and Jack brought their hands to their ears, just in case she followed through with the threat.

"Your ears are safe, for now, but never let me hear you talk to anyone like that ever again. Clear?" It was an unnecessary threat; they'd stopped a long time ago.

"Yes, ma'am," they answered, not bothering to keep the shame from their voices as they hung their heads.

"You've apologized, and Jaden accepted it. I say we move on." Dad closed the subject. I had a feeling he'd talk to me later.

"You know we don't think you're a mistake, right?" Jamie asked, ignoring Dad's suggestion.

After a second, I answered, "I do now."

"And we never thought your were stupid," Jack added.

I nodded.

Deciding it'd be fun to shock them in a good way while steering the conversation to safer territory, I asked, "Did you know I speak near-fluent Arabic?"

They gave me exactly the surprised response I was expecting.

"Definitely not stupid," Jamie said after recovering. "Why'd you keep it a secret?"

"I had a pretty big chip on my shoulder when I left for the Marines." *Damn, did I really want to go there?* "I wanted to prove I my worth but was afraid of failing." They opened their mouths to speak, but I held up my hand. "Don't say anything. I was eighteen and still living under your shadows."

Jack got up and grabbed four more beers and the bottle of wine for Ma and Emily. She and Meg sat on the sidelines, letting their expressions do the talking for them.

"I felt stupid. Failing the aptitude test the first time I applied for the Raiders didn't help." I'd never told anyone that. "But I was determined to make it, so I asked what I had to do in order to pass." I chuckled. "I think that was one of the hardest things I've ever done. Anyway, I got a mentor and a tutor, and passed with flying colors the second time."

"You've never been stupid," Ma said with pride.

"No, but I don't learn like Jamie and Jack. And the constant comparison destroyed my self-esteem. It took me getting out of Weatherford, out of their shadows, to finally figure out how I learn best." I sipped my beer. "I have to be moving, doing something. So, I listened to lessons as I ran and learned math by taking cooking classes."

There was a chuckle around the room.

"I'll have to take you up on it the next time you offer to cook," Emily said. I'd offered a few times, but she always said no. Her ex had expected her to do all the cooking and cleaning. Had literally beaten it into her. She was still adjusting to the healthy relationship she had with Jamie.

"When'd you learn Arabic, or maybe I should ask, how?" Jack asked.

"Immersion." Technically, I started with a language app that used games to teach, and then an online class. But it was being in the Middle East and working with our liaison that helped me gain near-fluency. "If I'd been smart about it, rather than learning quietly on my own, I could have gotten certified, but I was afraid of failing."

We talked for another hour, mending the relationship most of them hadn't realized was broken. I'd held on to that fucking chip for far too long, isolating myself from my family and hurting us all. I'd denied them the opportunity to support me, to celebrate with me, and to be there when I needed them. And I'd denied myself their love and support.

I found my family that night and swore I'd never walk away from them again.

When it was time to say goodbye, Jamie hugged me tight and told me he loved me. "Welcome home, Little Brother."

"Thanks, I love you, too."

Jack did the same, and I couldn't help but notice Emily and Meg squeezed a little tighter when they hugged me. Meg got on her tip-toes to kiss my cheek.

"Jack, have you noticed our baby brother is the biggest?" Jamie asked.

"I have," he said. "I guess it's our turn to be in his shadow." He grinned.

"Damn straight," I said, puffing up to my full height. I tried to sound serious, but the move reminded me of my broken ribs, so I ended up grunting.

"That's what you get for showing off," Jack said.

"Be nice," Meg said, slapping his chest.

"Yeah, be nice. I got my ass kicked waiting on you guys." Six sets of eyes shot open in shock. "What?" I laughed. "Too soon?"

"It'll always be too soon," Ma said, but she joined in as we laughed.

Dinner left me drained and emotionally raw, but I'd made the right decision.

After everyone else left, my dad said, "Jay, I trust you believe your mother, and I didn't know your brothers had given you that nickname."

"I know," I answered without making eye contact. I'd been careful not to mention my brothers, or why I thought I was a mistake, the one and only time I'd mentioned it to my parents.

Stepping in front of me, he waited for me to shift my focus from the floor. "We love you. We always have."

"I know, Dad." The emotion in his eyes made me uncomfortable, so I went back to staring at my shoes.

He gripped my shoulder. "You've grown into a good man. I just wish you could see it for yourself," he said, reminding me of what Cate had said. *They're proud of you.*

I renewed the vow I'd made in the cage; to be a better son, a better brother, and a better employee. To be the man I knew I was, not the troubled kid I used to be.

"We've always been proud of you. You didn't have to join the Marines or Special Forces to prove your worth."

I clapped him on the shoulder and smiled. "Actually, I did. I needed to prove it to myself." I wouldn't have changed if I'd stayed here. "The Marines gave me a purpose and helped me find myself."

He nodded and changed the subject. "And just for the record, I knew you spoke Arabic, and Spanish too, if I'm not mistaken?"

"Better than Jamie, but not as good as Isabelle." Spanish was Isabelle's, Jamie's late first wife, native language.

"How'd you find out? You hack the Marine data base?" I joked. Dad used computers, but hacking was out of his wheelhouse, though he'd hired someone who could—and Doug was damn good.

*Good enough to hack the USMC MARSOC records?* Maybe.

"No, I have friends in high places." He winked.

"Damn, Dad. You know that's illegal and unethical." Two words I wouldn't have attached to my father in a million years.

"A father does what he has to when his son refuses to keep him in the loop."

*Shit.* "How much do you know?"

"Enough to know last week wasn't your first time being held in a hellhole."

My head spun to the kitchen where mom was loading the dishwasher.

"Relax, I only told her the good stuff. She's strong enough to hear it, but it doesn't mean she should have to." I'd had the same thought in the hospital.

He confessed he knew broad stroke information because a friend he'd served with was near the top of my chain of command. No legal lines were crossed.

"If you ever want to talk…"

"Thanks. But I think I'll go help Ma." I needed a break from the emotional rollercoaster.

"Good idea."

Once the kitchen was clean, I grabbed a beer. *I have one more secret to reveal.* "Can I talk to you guys?"

"Of course," Ma said, patting my shoulder.

Dad looked at my beer. "Will I need one?"

Need was a strong word. "You might want one. You too, Ma."

With beers in hand, I told them about Sara, making my mom tear up when she realized I'd been ready to propose to a woman she'd never met.

"I'm sorry, Ma. I wasn't in a good head space when it came to the family. And I planned on bringing her home and introducing you to her before I proposed, I promise."

"What happened?"

For the second time in a week, I shared the heartbreak of getting the Dear John letter informing me my girlfriend was sleeping with my best friend.

"That's why you didn't go backpacking?" Ma asked.

"Yup." I popped the p before finishing my beer.

"I'm sorry, Jay. I wish you would've let us help you," she said.

"So do I." I wasn't the only person I'd hurt by keeping my distance. "I'm sorry. For everything." *I have a lot of making up to do.*

"No need to apologize," Ma said.

"Welcome home, Son," Dad said, holding his beer over the coffee table for me to clink.

For the first time in a long time, I truly felt like I was home.

# Chapter 44

## Cate

My father was already up and drinking coffee when I came into the kitchen Wednesday morning. "Good morning."

"Morning. Coffee?" he asked.

"I can get it." Having my right arm in a sling didn't mean I was helpless. And after a week of crazy, I wanted some normalcy. *As normal as things can be.* I poured a cup and added half and half. "How'd you sleep?" My couch wasn't the most comfortable piece of furniture in the world. I looked over; he'd already folder the sheets and blanket and piled them neatly on the table.

"Well enough. I'd ask how you slept, but I heard you crying out."

Which meant my nightmares kept him up, too. "Sorry if I woke you."

"It's okay. Want to talk about it?"

"No, they'll lessen in time," I said. The last thing I wanted was to rehash my time in the cage. "Thanks though."

After we ate the breakfast he made, I asked, "Dad?"

He looked up from his laptop. *He may have taken leave, but he felt compelled to check in.* "Yeah?"

"What do you think about me returning to DC with you?"

"Why?"

*What kind of question is that?*

"I meant, why do you want to come to DC?"

"I need time to heal, and it'd give us more time together." It wasn't a total lie. I needed time away to think. And plan, in case things were too awkward with Jay and I had to leave SSI.

"This have anything to do with Jaden?"

His raised eyebrow told me he saw through my half-truth.

"No… Okay, a little, but only because I need time to think."

"And you can't think here?" he asked, getting up to refill his coffee. When he lifted the pot in question, I nodded. Coffee tasted like a gift from heaven after a week without it.

"I can." Did he not want me in DC? Was he playing the doting father but not serious about mending our relationship? "You don't want me to come?"

"I didn't say that. Listen, I'd buy your ticket right now if I thought you weren't running away from your problems."

*Damn.* I sipped my coffee, savoring the creamy warmth as I thought about it.

"It's not like I can go back to work. Not yet, anyway." I had an appointment with Dr. Greenfield scheduled for the following day and another a week later. Which meant I had almost two weeks before I could even think about returning to work.

Probably longer. John wouldn't let me come back until Doc confirmed I was at least eighty percent. And then he'd put me on light duty.

"No, but that doesn't mean you can't talk to Jaden."

"True, but he hasn't tried to see me or even emailed." I couldn't keep the disappointment out of my voice. "And it's not like he won't be here when I come back."

"I didn't raise you to be a quitter, Catelyn."

*Ouch.*

"I am not quitting." Raising my voice to argue hurt my side. "I just need some time away."

*I'm not quitting, but I'm totally running away.* Delaying the inevitable because I fell for Jay and hearing him say he didn't feel the same way would wreck me.

Time away would give me the space I needed to rebuild the wall around my heart and remind myself why getting involved with a co-worker, my boss's son, was a colossally bad idea.

"Alright, I fly out Monday evening. We'll get you a ticket," I smiled and thanked him, but he cut me off. "But only if the doctor says it's okay."

"Thanks, Dad."

I didn't think Doc Greenfield would have any issues with me flying, so I made a list of things to do before the trip.

At the top of the list, emailing John to let him know. It wouldn't affect the day-to-day of the business since I was on medical leave, but going out of town without telling him felt wrong.

When I got up to clear our breakfast dishes, my father stopped me. "I got this. Go watch TV and relax."

"Dad, I'm perfectly capable of washing a few dishes."

"Please?" he asked.

Damn him; begging was far more effective than arguing.

"Fine." I went to the living room and picked up my laptop. It wasn't easy getting comfortable, but eventually I managed.

"When I'm done in here, I'll change your bandages."

*Thanks for the warning.* It'd hurt like hell when he'd changed them the night before. Not that I'd complain—it wouldn't help anything, and we'd both feel worse.

It was just after eight, so John would be in the office. *I wonder if Jay is working?*

I wrote and re-wrote my email at least four times, bouncing back and forth between being too wordy and not wordy enough. I wanted to tell him I was going to DC with my dad and provide a brief explanation, but didn't want to sound like I was running away.

*Which I am, sort of.*

Having a degree in psychology didn't mean I was good at calling myself on my bullshit, even when I could see it.

In the end, I kept it brief.

Mr. Sheppard,

I'm going to DC with my father. It'll give us some time together while I heal.

Thank you for everything.

Catelyn Maxwell

Focusing on the positive reason for my visit helped me feel better about it.

"Dad, can you take me to the store later so I can replace my phone?"

I didn't love the idea of going into public looking like a human punching bag, but now that I was thinking about it, waiting wasn't an option. I needed a phone and even next-day delivery felt like too long.

"Sure. We can pick up some groceries, too."

"Good idea." Dad had cleaned out all the rotten food in my fridge during the night. Thank God the half and half hadn't been opened. I hated black coffee.

# Chapter 45

## Jay

I still didn't have a car, so I rode with my father to the office on Wednesday morning. Not wanting to go to Cate's too early, I planned on filing my insurance paperwork, ordering a new phone, and grabbing the keys to the SSI sedan my dad said I could use.

Fidgeting with my coffee, I ignored the country music playing softly. Instead, replaying the conversations from last night. Baring my soul and admitting my insecurities hadn't been easy, but it was worth it. Even if thinking about all the time we'd lost because of my stubbornness had kept me up all night.

I almost lost my chance to reconnect with my family. *I won't waste my second chance.*

I applied for my replacement driver's license and credit cards, grateful to live in a time when I could do most of it easily online. The insurance claim was more complex.

It sat unfinished while I stared at Cate's obsessively organized desk and empty chair.

I hadn't seen her since her father arrived. *Not from lack of effort.* I didn't know if it was her father, my father, or the fucking universe, but there was always a reason I couldn't see her.

My leg bounced up and down as I turned towards my monitor and finished my claim. I'd just signed into my cell phone account when a knock on my door pulled my attention away.

"Son, you got a minute?" Dad asked.

"Of course."

"I just got an email from Maxwell–"

"Is she okay?"

"Yes."

"Did she quit?" I stood too fast and had to brace against my desk as blood rushed to my head.

"No." He rubbed his hands through his short hair. "But she's going to DC with her father."

*She's leaving?* After everything we'd been through, I never would've expected her running away without saying a word to me.

If I'd known she'd pull this shit, I would've pushed my way into her hospital room, father or not. The only reason I hadn't was out of respect. The same reason I hadn't rushed to her apartment last night.

*Fuck that.*

"Jaden."

My head snapped up when I heard my name. "What?" I hadn't meant to bark. "Sorry." I slammed my laptop closed and grabbed the car keys off my desk.

"What are you planning?"

*Planning?* I was planning on driving over there and pounding on her door until she opened it and told me to my face what the fuck she was thinking.

"I don't know, but she's not leaving without talking to me."

"You can't just barge in and force her to talk to you." He was right; I needed a new plan. A better, less aggressive plan.

*I'll figure it out on the way.* I needed to see her, and even though I knew she was well enough to go home, I still needed to make sure she was okay, and maybe tell her I fell in love with her. *And probably beg her not to leave.*

It was a simple plan, but not an easy one. *Now to figure out how to say it all without sounding like an idiot.*

"Jay?" My father stopped my runaway train of thought. "Can I give you some fatherly advice?"

*I could use some right about now.* "Sure." My nonchalant answer convinced no one.

"Get your head out of your ass and tell her you love her." My eyes rounded. I hadn't told anyone I loved her. I'd barely admitted it to myself.

"Right, can I borrow your phone? I haven't ordered a new one yet."

"You're new phone will be here later." He said before handing me his phone and some cash.

When I raised an eyebrow—it'd been a long time since I'd taken money from my dad—he said, "You'll need it until your replacement cards come in."

Right, Roman torched my wallet along with my phone and truck.

*Not everything.* I opened my drawer and pulled out my bank card and military ID. "Actually, he didn't burn them all." Handing back the cash, I said, "Thanks."

"Be careful. Your mother will kill me if you get in a car wreck."

I hugged him on my way out, finally understanding just how incredibly lucky I was to have such an amazing family.

I waved my dad's phone toward the reception desk, where Jack was talking to Meg. "I have Dad's phone."

Channeling my inner Nascar driver, I raced to Cate's. During the drive, a million and one questions raced through my mind, turning my fear into anger. What was she thinking, running away? Had our time together, the bond we shared, meant nothing to her? How dare she run away without talking to me?

This bullshit was exactly why I'd sworn off relationships. It was a thousand times better to be alone than with someone I couldn't trust.

*Was that fair to Cate?* Maybe. Maybe not. But leaving without saying goodbye felt like a knife to my heart. And people who stuck knives in your heart couldn't be trusted.

I started doubting my feelings. Were they real or did I have Stockholm Syndrome? Did I think I was in love with her because of the ordeal we suffered through? It wasn't unheard of.

By the time I pulled into the small parking lot at Cate's apartment, I'd worked myself into a confusion-fueled state of anger.

A quick glance was all I needed to know Cate's car wasn't there. Not a big deal, I told myself; her father probably ran out. No reason to freak out.

No one answered when I rang her bell or pounded on her door. My call went straight to voicemail, pissing me off.

*Dumbass.* Roman burned her phone, too.

Where is she? Did she already leave? What the actual fuck? How had she planned it so quickly? I couldn't believe she'd rather run away and hide than talk to me.

The old voice in my head, the one that still believed I was a mistake, told me I meant nothing to her. Locking away my feelings, I cursed myself for letting another woman hurt me.

As I stomped to the sedan, I searched for General Maxwell in my dad's contact list. Before I found it, a car pulling in distracted me.

Cate.

Relief rushed through my system, almost buckling my knees. *She's still here.* I stared the car down as it pulled into a parking spot and the engine cut off. Anger and relief warred for top billing.

Catelyn eased herself out of the passenger side, the effort making her wince. She clutched the door to support herself, her teeth clenched against the pain.

*Why the hell isn't she taking pain medication?* Her father should make her take it. I almost laughed, like anyone could force her to do anything.

"Jaden?"

The anger won as I watched her step slowly towards me. Her face was mottled with shades of blue and purple, and her right arm was in a sling, keeping her shoulder still while her bullet wounds healed. I'd put money on her ribs being wrapped, just like mine. I wanted to kill Roman and Franks, again, for what they'd done.

I wanted to close the distance, wrap her in my arms, and make sure no one ever hurt her again. *But she's leaving.* The pain of that memory added fuel to the flame of my anger.

Fear. Frustration. Pain.

Emotions overwhelmed me. So, I did what I did best and channeled the troubled youth of my past and defaulted to anger.

Directing it all at her, I ignored the vow I'd made to be the man I knew myself to be.

"What the fuck, Cate? After everything we went through, you're leaving? I don't even get a fucking goodbye text?"

This wasn't how I wanted to act, or who I wanted to be. I stepped toward her and reached for the bag she carried, instinctively acting like a gentleman despite my raging emotions.

Her father's voice brought me to a halt when he said, "Watch your tone."

Message received, loud and clear. I nodded without taking my eyes off Cate.

"Are you blind? I obviously didn't leave." A look of pain crossed her face when she raised the bag too fast, but she didn't let the pain stop her. "For your information, I went to get a new phone."

"But you are going to DC?" My fear and frustration bled into the question, which came out far snarkier than I wanted it to. *Why can't I stop?*

"Not for a few more days." She confirmed my worst fear. Taking a step forward, she opened her mouth. But I cut her off.

"Without so much as a goodbye?" I crossed my arms over my chest. Clinging to the anger was easier than feeling the pain.

"What? No, of course not." She held up the bag. "No phone, remember?"

"Maybe we should take this inside," her father said. Standing a few feet off to the side, he was ready, willing, and able to protect Cate.

From me.

He couldn't know I'd suffer a thousand tortures before I'd ever hurt her. How could he? My actions weren't exactly showing my true feelings.

"Did you seriously assume the worst, then march over here to scream at me?" She shook from the effort it took to yell.

"Catelyn," her father said.

She glanced at him but didn't move. Neither did I.

Tension hung in the air, thick as molasses and just as dark.

Cate paled as we faced off in a battle of wills; both too stubborn to back down.

General Maxwell decided he'd had enough and stepped between us, showing me his back. "Cate, go inside before you fall down." After a brief pause, he added, "Please?"

"Fine," she huffed before stepping around us and walking to the door.

Like a coward, I turned to watch her walk away but didn't move. The disappointment I felt towards myself for not being man enough to admit my feelings grew with every step she took.

When I finally took a step to follow, a heavy hand landed on my shoulder and held me in place. It wasn't forceful, but it didn't have to be.

Halfway there, Cate turned. "For the record, Sheppard," she spat out my last name, "I was going to call you as soon as I set up my new phone." She turned on her heels and marched to the door.

She held her head high and her shoulders back despite the pain. *God, she's so fucking strong.* Feeling like the world's biggest asshole, I stared as she walked to the door, wishing I'd been smart enough to apologize the instant I'd fucked up.

Before I could say anything, her father warned, "Do I need to tell you to tread carefully?"

I shook my head, no, and clamped my lips shut. The pain of clenching my jaw and compressing my lips was less than I deserved.

As soon as the door closed behind her, Maxwell's grip on my shoulder tightened, letting me know it was time to turn around and face him. *Now would be a great time for my courage to resurface.*

"Or what I'll do to you if you hurt her?" It didn't feel like an empty threat.

Pretending I wasn't intimidated as he stared directly into my soul, I answered, "No, sir."

I'd left the office with every intention of making sure Cate was okay and telling her how I felt. *When did it all turn to shit?*

When I let the past cloud my judgment.

When I discounted my feelings because I didn't trust them.

When I let my old insecurities take over.

"There's only one thing that can make a man act this stupid."

Did I want to know? Did I already know?

"You're in love with her."

I didn't know what I'd expected to hear, but it wasn't that. "Excuse me?" It was true; at least I'd thought I was until I'd talked myself out of it.

But had I really? No, I just convinced myself I had because I was scared. But how did he know? The same way my father did; I couldn't hide how I felt about her.

"You heard me. Don't bother denying it. I can see it in your eyes. I saw it in the hospital." General Maxwell said. "But that doesn't excuse your behavior."

"No, sir, it doesn't. And I'm sorry."

"I'm not the one you need to apologize to."

He was right. I needed to apologize to Cate, the woman I was terrified of falling in love with. *It's too late. I love her.* My walls fell, my doubt faded, and my panic soared.

*Have I fucked it up beyond repair?*

"Get your head out of your ass and tell her how you feel before it's too late." His fatherly advice sounded a lot like my dad's.

If I wanted to fix this, I needed to clear my head. Cate deserved a proper apology, one presented with a fair amount of humble groveling.

Twisting to look at the door over my shoulder made my ribs scream in pain. I gritted my teeth and ignored them. Turning back around, I ran my hand through my hair.

*Man up, Sheppard.* "Sir, I owe you, both of you an apology. I let my inner demons get the best of me and unleashed them on Cate. She didn't deserve that."

"No, she didn't." He crossed his arms and waited.

Nodding, I said, "I need a minute to fix my head before I talk to her."

He raised his eyebrows at that.

"I need to get it right, because I doubt she'll give me more than one second chance."

His laugh was completely unexpected. "If you act this stupid again, you won't deserve one."

*Damn, the apple doesn't fall far from the tree.* It was easy to see where Cate got her no nonsense attitude.

As if getting schooled by Cate's father wasn't enough, I could hear my father's voice saying the same thing.

"Then I better get it right." *But how?* "I'll be back in an hour."

He held eye contact while he lifted his wrist in front of his face. If I'd blinked, I wouldn't have seen him glance at his watch. He nodded. "I'll see you in an hour."

I relaxed my shoulders while releasing an internal sigh, because sighing in front of a three-star general was not something a good soldier ever did.

"Thank you, sir."

He clapped me on the back. "Roses."

"Sir?" I asked, before realizing he meant I should bring her roses. I remembered her saying her favorite color was daffodil yellow, but daffodils weren't right for the occasion. If I did this right, I'd have plenty of opportunities to shower her with her favorite flower. "Right. Thank you."

"Clock's ticking, Sheppard."

I took off at a sprint, but the pain forced me to slow to a walk.

I had one hour to get my head on straight, so I didn't fuck this up again.

And buy roses.

Maxwell was the type of woman who could scare weak men, but I wasn't a weak man. A stupid one, sometimes. A stubborn one, definitely. But a weak one, never.

And yet, she scared the shit out of me. All because she made me feel everything when I want to feel nothing.

On the drive, I argued with myself. The fear-fueled coward listing all the reasons this was a bad idea, while the warrior in me told me to man up and fight for the woman I loved.

When my brain asked, "Can you trust your emotions?" My heart told it to shut the fuck up.

As I argued with myself, the voices in my head sounded more and more like my parents. My mom telling me to trust my heart. My dad telling me to listen to my mother.

"If I do this, there's no going back," I said to no one. Things would be unbearable in the office if I poured my heart out, and she didn't feel the same.

But it'd be worse if I didn't try.

*What will happen if we think we're in love, but it's not real?*

We'd destroy each other. One of us would have to leave. And while I would willing be the sacrificial lamb, I couldn't imagine a scenario where she'd feel comfortable working for my family.

Once again, my parents' voices filled my head, giving me their opinions. My mom's gentle voice reminding me, love is always worth the risk. My father's matter-of-fact voice telling me to man up.

Making up my mind, I parked and entered the flower shop. I asked for a dozen yellow roses in a vase, and a box of chocolates. When the florist asked me what I wanted on the card, I said, "I'm an idiot."

It was a little embarrassing how quickly those words came to me.

"Excuse me?" she asked.

"Trust me, she'll understand."

She shrugged and wrote the message.

I'd grovel; probably a lot. But before I did, I needed to own up to my mistakes.

Of course, I could only do that if Cate gave me the time of day.

*I half expect her to slam the door in my face when she sees me.*

# Chapter 46

## Cate

*How dare he show up and hurl accusations at me?* And in front of my father. I'd planned on calling him as soon as I set up my new phone, but no, he had to storm in here with his smoldering eyes and broad shoulders and shitty attitude.

Did he really think so little of me?

Because I wanted to be alert when I went shopping, I waited to take my pain pills until we got home. Which meant everything hurt, and tensing my muscles in frustration only made it worse. *I should've listened to my father.*

When I saw Jay in the parking lot, my heart sped up. My mind raced with all the things I'd been forced to wait three days to tell him, to ask him.

More than anything, I wanted him to hold me and tell me he was okay. That I was okay. That we'd be okay.

But no. He had to be an ass and piss me off. I threw my bag on the table.

I expected my father to follow me inside, but he was still outside, talking to Jaden.

*What the hell are they talking about?* Was Jaden arguing with my dad? I almost laughed at that—no one argued with my father.

I didn't love the idea of him fighting my battles, but I half hoped he was. Jaden deserved to be dressed down in a way only a starred general could.

I imagined Jaden standing at attention while my father delivered a tongue lashing to end all tongue lashings.

*Maybe he's telling Jaden to take a long walk off a short pier.*

It was harsh, but I was so pissed steam was probably pouring out of my ears.

I grabbed my pain pills off the counter, swore when I dropped the bottle on the floor, and cried out in pain and frustration when I squatted to pick it up.

By the time I opened the bottle and poured myself a glass of water, I was red faced, panting, and even more angry.

Not wanting to feel loopy, I only took one. I could take the second after talking to my father and setting up my phone.

*How long does it take to tell someone to fuck off?*

I sat at the table and killed time by opening my phone. Which took longer than usual because my right arm was in a sling. Downloading the data from the cloud would take about thirty minutes.

*What is hell is taking him so long?* I drummed my fingers on the table.

When I heard the door close, I stood and asked, "What did you say to him?"

"I told him he needed to calm down."

"Is that all? Because you were out there an awfully long time."

"Did you take your pain pills?" He changed the subject.

"I did. Don't avoid the question."

His eyebrows lifted at my raised voice.

"Sorry. He pissed me off."

"I can see that. Which part pissed you off the most?" he asked as he sat across the table.

Good question. Was it because he didn't care enough to ask how I was doing? Was it because he didn't trust me and accused me of leaving without saying goodbye? Was it because he didn't meet my expectations?

*Or is it because it's obvious he doesn't feel the same way about me as I feel about him?*

Jaden's attitude today reminded me of all the reasons I shouldn't get involved with a colleague. What we shared in the cage was probably nothing more than bonding during a shared traumatic incident. It wasn't real.

*Thank God I didn't have a chance to spill my guts and make a fool of myself.* I had hoped we could work together better, now that we'd gotten to know each other, but after his performance in the parking lot, that hope was fading.

I looked at my dad, who waited for my answer with the patience of a saint.

"After everything that happened, I'd hoped we could at least be friends." Facing the truth hurt more than my cracked ribs. "Obviously I was wrong."

It was probably for the best. Before Jaden became my office mate, I'd been the consummate professional; working hard and never letting my emotions get the better of me.

"Catelyn," my father paused and waited for me to bring my attention back to him, "It's not my place to tell you what to do, but I'd like to offer some free advice."

I tried changing the subject. "You know what they say about free advice?"

"It's worth what you pay for it," he answered. We both chuckled. He continued, "Don't let your emotions cloud your judgment."

My judgment was fine. It was my emotions that got me into this mess. If I hadn't let myself fall for him, I wouldn't be in this situation.

"I learned that lesson the hard way, and I won't repeat my mistake." I didn't like learning things the hard way, so when I did, the lesson stuck. No one needed to know I fell for Jay.

I told myself I could compartmentalize with the best of them and show up every day and do my job.

*But will I be happy?*

The sad look on my father's face seemed out of place. I'd expected him to be proud I'd learned my lesson and happy I wouldn't repeat it.

Before I could ask, my phone came back to life. Alerts buzzed as all the messages I'd missed screamed for attention.

"Sorry," I said, getting up to turn the sound off. The pain meds were kicking in, taking the edge off, so moving was easier.

"No need to apologize."

I nodded as I scanned the messages. Charlie had called and texted. A lot. I opened the text app and scanned her texts, each one more frantic than the last.

"I'm sorry, Dad, I need to call Charlie."

"Go."

I hit the call button as I walked to my bedroom.

"Cate, are you okay? I've been worried sick." Her voice was two octaves higher than normal.

"I, uh, there was an issue at work."

"I know. I called SSI after three days of radio silence."

"What?" I eased myself onto my bed and reclined against my decorative pillows.

"Don't sound so shocked. If my best friend goes missing, I make calls."

Of course she did. Like me, Charlie wasn't a sit at home and twiddle-her-thumbs-nervously kind of girl.

We weren't just Marines; we were warriors, which meant we took action and got shit done.

"How much do you know?" I trusted Charlie with my life, but wouldn't share more than was necessary. No one needed to hear the ugly details.

"That you and Jaden went missing on assignment. Hold on." Footsteps sounded in the background, followed by a door closing. "Sorry, I needed to close my door."

"I can call back if you're busy."

"Hell no. This is more important. Jamie texted me after they found you. He said you were in the hospital and your dad was on his way. Asshole wouldn't tell me anything else."

I laughed at that. Of all the Sheppards, Jamie was the least deserving of being called an asshole.

"He was just protecting my privacy." And following the law.

"I know, but I was scared to death."

"I'm sorry. I'm fine, I promise." *At least I will be in a few weeks.* "I would've called sooner, but my phone got torched to a crisp and I just now got my new one activated." I ignored the fact that I could've emailed because, in all the chaos, I didn't think of it.

"Torched?"

"It's a long story for another time. When we can share a bottle." I told her we'd splurge on a bottle of our favorite high-end wine and I'd tell her what happened and she could tell me about all the ways her future husband drove her crazy while confessing to being madly in love with him.

"How are you really?"

Talking about the physical pain was easier, so I said, "GSW to the right shoulder." I ignored her gasp and continued, "Clean through, a few cracked ribs, and some cuts and bruises on my face."

"Jesus, Cate. What the hell happened?"

"Another time, okay?" I reminded her I wasn't in the mood to talk.

"Yeah, okay. You sure you're alright? Do I need to come kick some ass?"

Laughing made my sides hurt. "No, the team did it for you."

"Are they all dead?"

"You know, I don't actually know." I hadn't thought to ask.

We talked for a few more minutes before she brought up Jaden.

"He's fine." I snapped, my pain and frustration resurfacing.

"Care to try that again?" She called me out on my bullshit.

"No." The pain was too fresh.

"Not good enough, Maxwell. Something happened, and it's eating at you."

I told her about Jay's behavior in the cage, leaving out how I felt, *thought I felt,* about him.

"You fell for him." Sometimes I hated how easily she could read me.

"No. I didn't." I lied to her, just like I'd been lying to myself. "It's normal for two people to bond during a traumatic event."

"Cate, I love you, but you're an idiot."

"Excuse me?"

"Has it ever occurred to you that Jaden gets under your skin so easily because you're drawn to him?"

It had, but not until after we'd had to rely on each other to survive.

"No. He drives me crazy."

"I know he does. That's my point. In all your time working with Gavin, you never talked about him like you do about Jaden. There's a fuck ton of passion between you two, but you're both too stubborn to see it for what it really is."

She had a point, but Jay didn't feel the same. *You don't treat the people you love the way he treated me.*

"You said it pissed him off when he thought you left without saying goodbye. Think about it; maybe he's afraid of losing you."

One perfectly timed question was all it took for me to ask, what if?

"Maybe." But was it worth the risk? Not only to my heart, but to my career? I couldn't afford to lose another job because of interpersonal conflict. "But–"

"No buts, Cate. Talk to him. You owe him that much."

I sighed. She was right. But he owed me, too.

# Chapter 47

## Jay

With ten minutes to spare, I parked in the driveway and did two minutes of box breathing to calm my racing heart. There was too much at stake for me to lose control.

I grabbed the bag of takeout. I was hungry and figured they might be too, and the roses, before walking to the door. Balancing everything in my left hand, I wiped my right palm on my jeans before knocking.

The first thing General Maxwell did after opening the door was look at his watch. He smiled. I'd passed his test by showing up with five minutes to spare. The perfect balance of early, but not obnoxiously so.

The second thing he did was nod in approval at the bouquet.

"Sir," I greeted him with a nod.

"Mr. Sheppard." He returned the formal greeting. "Please, come in." He stepped back, holding the door open.

I couldn't see Cate. "Is this a bad time? Where's Cate?"

"She's on the phone." He tilted his head towards her closed bedroom door. "She won't be long."

"Have you eaten?"

"No, I was just getting ready to make lunch," he answered.

"No need." I lifted the bag. "Can I put it in the kitchen?"

"Well done. What'd you bring?"

"Chicken sandwiches, fries, and salad."

He laughed. "If the roses don't win her over, the food will."

I couldn't speak for Cate, but it'd make sense for her to feel as ravenous as I did.

I remembered feeling like I couldn't get enough food after being rescued the first time, too. Which made sense—my body needed the extra calories to heal. I wasn't in as bad of shape this time, but Cate was. Actually, she was worse.

After putting the food on the counter and setting the bouquet and chocolates in the middle of the table, I wiped my palms on my jeans before running my hands through my hair. I couldn't remember the last time I felt this nervous about talking to a girl. *Because I never have.*

Cate was special, and now that I'd accepted my feelings, the wait was killing me. I paced back and forth, wearing a path in the black-and-white checkered tile on the kitchen floor.

"Sit down, Sheppard. You're making me nervous."

Without thinking, I obeyed. When my ass hit the chair, I laughed.

"What?"

"Nothing." When he raised an eyebrow, I admitted, "I don't know if you meant it as an order, but I obeyed without hesitation."

"You can take the man out of the Marines," he said.

"But you can't take the Marines out of the man," we finished together.

He asked me about my time in the Corps and shared a little of his experience while we waited. Before long, the sound of Cate's door opening interrupted our conversation. *If things go well with Cate, I want to sit down with her father and a six-pack of beer, so I can hear more.*

I stood and waited for Cate.

"Dad, are you ready for…" She turned the corner, her expression quickly turning from shock to stone when she saw me. "Sheppard."

"Hi Cate. Please don't kick me out, at least not until I've apologized."

Her expression softened. "Fine."

I pulled out the chair I'd just vacated. "Here, sit." Not liking that it sounded like an order, I added, "Please."

"What are those?" She pointed at the roses.

"Roses."

"I know that. Why are they here?"

"I'll give you two some privacy," her father said. His knowing grin was subtle, as was the humor in his eyes, but I saw it.

# Chapter 48

## Cate

I didn't miss the look my father gave Jaden. Like they were on the same side. *Traitor*.

"Thank you, sir," Jaden answered. "Please?" he asked again, indicating the chair.

I stared at him, debating whether I should stand and argue or just take the damn seat instead of stirring the pot.

He waited patiently.

"Why are you here?" I asked, staring at the roses as I eased myself onto the chair. The yellow roses, the color of daffodils in the spring, in a gorgeous crystal vase, and the heart-shaped box of chocolates made it rather obvious, but I wanted to hear him say it.

He sat in the chair closest to me, his amber eyes staring into mine.

He broke eye contact first. Taking a deep breath, he looked back at me and said, "I'm sorry I acted like an ass." He paused, giving me a chance to respond.

His heartfelt apology deflated my anger, but didn't erase the pain. His generic apology wasn't enough.

"So why did you?"

"I freaked out."

"Obviously."

He took a deep breath. "I came earlier because I needed to see you, to talk to you."

"You could've visited me in the hospital if the need was that urgent." I'd just told Charlie I'd give him a chance, so why was I acting like a bitch?

He laughed. "I tried, but I got blocked by our fathers."

"What?" Why would they do that? Remembering my father telling me Jay had left the hospital against medical advice so he could sit by my side, I was inclined to believe him. Though I didn't want to believe either of our fathers would've conspired to keep us apart.

"You must not have tried very hard." My tone heavy with pain and doubt.

"Cate." He reached over, running his knuckles down my arm and pulling my hand to the table so he could hold it. My body reacted to his touch, causing me to inhale sharply.

*Traitorous body*. I didn't hold his hand back, but I didn't pull away either.

He took another deep breath and closed his eyes. From the looks of it, he was gathering his courage or preparing to fight.

"Having to leave your side when your father arrived was the hardest thing I've ever had to do."

It was? My heart raced as my professional brain studied his face, his eyes, his body language—he was telling the truth. Thank God, because my heart desperately wanted to believe him.

My hand itched to turn over and lace our fingers together as I forced my breathing to remain steady.

"But it was the right thing to do. He needed to be there for you, and you needed him." He paused and a small smile spread across his lips. "We both needed time with our families." He turned introspective for a moment before saying, "Remind me to tell you about the dinner conversation I had with mine."

I nodded. The effort needed to keep my hand from clutching his made it hard to concentrate.

"Why didn't you come back?" I failed to keep the hurt out of my voice. What I really wanted to know was why the man who'd checked out of the hospital AMA didn't force his way back to my side.

He rubbed small circles on the back of my hand. "I did, the next morning. But like I said, my father kept me out."

"Why?"

"He said you needed time with yours." He ran his hand through his hair, making it stand up in a rat's nest of soft brown curls. "It just about killed me to walk away, but he was right."

"Did you really discharge yourself against your doctor's advice?"

He nodded. "They wouldn't let me stay with you as a patient, and I didn't want you to be alone when you woke up."

His words weakened the wall around my heart. I turned my hand over, but didn't lace our fingers. It was enough to bring a smile to his face. I longed to run my finger along his strong bruised jaw and tell him how disappointed I felt waking up without him there.

"I went straight to your room after getting discharged."

That had to mean something, right? "Thank you." *How much of what I remember is real?* I wanted to ask, but now didn't feel like the time. We had more important things to discuss.

"How are you feeling? Can I get you anything?"

*That's it? He's ending the conversation?* I pulled my hand away. "Is that all you came to say?" My disappointment filled the room.

"No, it's not, but you're wincing and I'd rather you weren't in pain while we talk."

"Oh." Why was I acting so crazy?

*Because I'm afraid.* Afraid he'll tell me he loves me. Afraid he won't.

And I'm afraid that no matter what he says, it'll hurt my career.

"Where are your meds?" he asked, standing up.

"On the counter."

He made quick work of filling a glass with water and returning to the table. He read the instructions before giving me the pills. "There's no need to suffer."

I took one. Before he could argue, I explained I'd taken one an hour ago.

"What about you? How bad is it?" I asked, trying to make up for being so bitchy.

"Well, I didn't get shot, so I have that going for me." He laughed. "A few cracked ribs are the worst of it. The cuts and bruises are already healing."

"Lucky you."

"If I could go back and change it, I'd take that bullet for you." My eyes shot up to his. "And I always will."

"Don't you dare." I didn't want or need him sacrificing himself to save me.

He stared at me for what felt like an eternity before asking, "Would you do the same for me?"

I answered without thinking, "Yes." *What kind of stupid question was that?*

"So you can take a bullet for me, but I can't take one for you? That hardly seems fair." His teasing grin diffused the tension.

"How about neither of us gets shot?" I bargained.

"I'm on board with that. Getting shot sucks."

I made a mental note to ask later if he knew from experience.

"Yes, it does." My muscles slowly relaxed as the extra medication kicked in.

Jay put his hand on the table, palm up. This time, I accepted his invitation without hesitation.

"I'm so sorry, Cate. I came here today to tell you how I feel. To beg you not to leave. Instead, I freaked out because

I thought you'd already left." He paused. "I didn't handle it well."

Charlie was right. "I noticed. Did you really think I'd leave without saying goodbye?"

"No. Yes." He ran his hand through his hair again. "Christ, I don't know. I tried calling, but you didn't answer." His eyes shifted to my phone. "When I got here and couldn't see your car, well, it scared me."

"And instead of asking me about it, you decided to act like an idiot?" I half teased.

Instead of answering, he laughed and pulled the card out of the roses.

The card said, *I'm an idiot,* in elegant cursive. He didn't write it. Somehow it meant more knowing he'd said them out loud to a total stranger.

I smiled and met his gaze.

"Love will make a man do that," he said. No hesitation. No wavering. Just dropped the damn love bomb on me while holding my hand and staring in my eyes.

I swallowed hard and forced myself to blink. It was my turn. Not to say I love you, I couldn't lead with that, but to admit my fear and to apologize.

"You know, I thought I heard you when I was in the hospital, but I kept slipping in and out of consciousness. You promised to be there, but when I woke up, you weren't."
I sucked in a deep breath, grateful the pain pills worked. I whispered, "I thought I'd imagined it all."

I'm sorry, was all he said.

"It's okay, I understand why now." I paused and looked down the short hall to my bedroom door. "I'm glad my father was there. We needed the time."

He nodded; we both had family issues in need of healing.

"When you didn't come visit, it hurt. I convinced myself it was for the best."

He squeezed my hand and apologized.

"I wasn't leaving. I promise."

He nodded. "But you are going to DC?"

"Yes. Maybe." Probably not, if this conversation continued to go well. "But not today."

He squeezed my hand. "Good."

"I wouldn't have left without talking to you. That's why I went to the store. I needed a phone so I could call you and make sure you were okay, and…"

Following his example, I took a steadying breath.

"To tell you how I feel. To find out if you felt the same." I chuckled before saying, "But you showed up here and pissed me off before I could."

"Sorry." His laugh negated his apology.

"Why do you always have to piss me off?" I asked without venom.

"I don't do it on purpose," he said. "Well, not always." He emphasized the word, always, and followed up with a wink and a grin.

It was my turn to laugh.

"Do you think we would've killed each other if we hadn't fallen in love in the cage?" I asked. Letting him know I loved him in the same indirect way he'd told me.

He squeezed my hand before bringing it to his lips and kissing it. "Absolutely."

His smile melted my insides.

"Just remember, I told you first," he said.

I'd never seen his playful side, but I loved it. "I was unconscious, so it doesn't count."

*I love all of him.* The good, the bad, the scarred, and the sexy.

"So you heard me?" he asked, lifting one eyebrow.

"I did, although I thought it was my imagination," I admitted.

Before I could say it first, he said, "I love you, Catelyn Maxwell."

"I love you, Jaden Sheppard."

He stood and leaned over the table to kiss me. I held my breath as I waited, desperate to feel his lips on mine.

Just before he made contact, he pulled back a little.

I opened my eyes to see him looking at me, mischief sparkling in his eyes.

"You gonna slap me again?"

I reached forward, grabbed the collar of his tee, and pulled him in. "Shut up and kiss me."

He answered with his lips. Unfortunately, neither of us was gentle, and we both ended up wincing in pain.

We pulled back, looked each other in the eye, and busted out laughing.

"Maybe we hold off for another day or two," he suggested.

I didn't like that idea, not one bit, but he was right. We couldn't enjoy the kiss if it hurt.

I could only imagine what Jay's kiss would be like, knowing it had curled my toes when I hadn't wanted it.

"You're blushing." He brushed his knuckles down my lesser-bruised cheek. "Want to tell me what's going through that brilliant mind of yours?"

I didn't need to; his grin told me he knew full well what I was thinking.

"No." I pulled him in for another kiss. "One more." We settled for a soft kiss; one that felt like a promise of more.

# Chapter 49

## Jay

Cate called her dad out of the bedroom. We didn't have to tell him we'd worked out our issues; it was pathetically obvious from the way we looked at each other.

That, and I refused to let go of her hand until it was time to eat.

When I listed off the options, Cate did the predicable thing and chose the Cobb salad. I told her to start while I warmed up the sandwiches and fries.

When I reached for the microwave door, she said, "Heat them in the oven so they don't get soggy."

"Yes, ma'am." I braced for the incoming correction, but it never came. Cate was quiet. Too quiet.

When I turned to see her expression, she said, "Don't call me ma'am."

"Yes, sir." I winked. It was fun riling her up. Images of how a riled up Cate would act in the bedroom flashed through my mind. *Nope, can't think like that.* My body didn't get the message. It didn't care that it hurt to kiss her or that our busted up ribs would make sex painful instead of pleasurable.

Luckily, one look at her father was enough to kill my desire.

During lunch, Cate practically drooled over my fries as she picked at her salad.

I pushed my plate in her direction. "Go ahead, you know you want one."

Her dad chuckled when she grabbed two and shoved them in her mouth.

"Have as may as you want." I said. I'd warmed up all the fries and the third sandwich, knowing I'd eat whatever she didn't want.

"I'm trying to be good. The doctor said I should ease my way back to my normal diet."

I grabbed a knife and cut my sandwich in half. "Here."

She looked at her dad, then back at the plate. "I probably shouldn't."

"Eat as much or as little as you want. I'll finish the rest." My wink brought a blush to her lightly freckled cheeks. *Damn, that's sexy.* I'd never considered a woman's blush sexy before, but I had a feeling I'd be discreetly adjusting my pants whenever I saw Cate blush.

"I don't want to steal your lunch," she said, reaching for it.

Her eyes rounded when I grabbed the other plate off the counter.

"What? I'm starving."

"You're always hungry." She laughed before taking a small bite. "So good."

Her father watched, amusement written all over his face.

We talked until Cate started yawning, and I encouraged her to take a nap.

"Will you come back for dinner?" she asked.

"I can. I'm all yours after I give my father his phone back. It's blowing up."

Cate made a face. "Who's calling that wouldn't know you have his phone?" She realized how silly it sounded and corrected herself. "Right, there are probably a ton of people who wouldn't know."

She was right on both accounts, everyone at SSI knew, but clients and friends didn't. Knowing my family might text me, I ignored the calls and voicemail alerts and opened the text app. It felt weird looking through my father's messages, but my only purpose was to find for the ones meant for me.

Like the family group chat, Jamie started.

> Jamie: Jay, Dad wants to know how things are going.

> Jack: That's what you're going with?

> Meg: We all want to know.

> Ma: Leave him alone so he can focus on Cate.

I typed a quick reply, letting them know I'd fill them in later.

> Jack: That bad, huh?

> Meg: Or that good!

Meg, the resident hopeless romantic, was right. It was that good.

There were other messages meant for me, from AJ and Doug, because of course they knew why I was here, wishing me luck. A small town wasn't so different from a spec ops unit—everyone knew everyone else's business. I replied with a quick thanks, then forgetting it wasn't my phone, I read the next message.

I was halfway through Nathan Blaszek's message when it clicked—*This isn't my phone.* Blaszek was an applicant, so I figured it was okay to read the rest. According to the message, he was okay postponing his interview and wished everyone well.

I'd completely forgotten we'd scheduled his interview for this week. Blaszek was a former Navy SEAL, turned black ops civilian contractor. We all agreed he'd benefit the team, but wanted to know why he was leaving the black ops unit. The job paid better than SSI, but was high risk. I knew because I'd considered signing a contract with one instead of joining the family business.

*I'm glad I didn't.*

I shut off the screen.

"Everything okay?" Cate asked. "You look contemplative."

"Yeah, reading Blaszek's message reminded me of transitioning to civilian life."

"We missed his interview." She stated it as a fact, but it sounded like a question.

"No, Dad asked him to reschedule." Cate yawned. "Go rest. I'll help your father clean up, return the phone, and be back before you know it."

"Okay." She stood and kissed my cheek. "Thank you."

I nodded. "Want me to pick up dinner on my way back?"

"You don't need to do that," her father said.

"I know I don't need to, but I want to," I answered. Turning to Cate, I asked, "How does a T–bone steak sound?"

"Like heaven," she answered. I fell a little more in love when she added, "With a loaded baked potato."

"Of course."

Kissing Cate on the forehead, I promised to be back as soon as I could.

The first thing I did when I got back to the office was give my father his phone. Then, after setting up my replacement, I told a captive audience how things went with Cate. Leaving out the personal details.

"Is she still going to DC?"

Leave it to Meg to ask the hard question. "I don't know. We didn't have time to talk about it." *Yet.* If I had any say, she wouldn't go. *At least not without me.* But we still had a lot to work out.

"But you two are definitely a thing?" AJ asked.

I didn't love the phrasing, but answered anyway. "We're together, yes."

"So no more trying to kill each other?" Jack asked.

I laughed. "I wouldn't go that far." After the laughter to die down, I said, "I'll be at Cate's if you need me."

"Tell her to file an expense report for her phone and I'll reimburse her," Dad said.

"Will do." I grabbed my new phone, shocked at the number of messages. *I'll read them later.*

As I was leaving, Dad said, "Your mother wants you to invite Cate and her father over for dinner before he leaves."

"Copy that." I ordered three steak dinners with loaded baked potatoes, roasted vegetables, and side salads to pick up on my way to Cate's. There wasn't much I could do to help her, but I could feed her and keep her company.

During dinner, Cate gave me an earful when I offered to cut her steak, but then had to eat humble pie when she realized it was a bitch trying to cut meat with only one good arm. I didn't rub it in too much as I cut the fillet portion into bite-size pieces and put them on her plate before cutting the rest.

Her father found the whole situation amusing. After helping her father clean the kitchen, we headed to the living room.

"Have you ordered replacement cards and IDs?" I asked, resting my arm on the back of the couch, behind Cate.

"I did. Luckily, the only things in my purse were my driver's license, PI ID, one credit card and some cash." She yawned. "What about you?"

"Everything except buying a new truck." I winced at the thought. "Dad wanted me to tell you to fill out an expense report. He'll reimburse you for your phone."

"He doesn't have to do that," she argued. Just like I knew she would.

"You lost your phone on the job, so he feels like he does."

"I'd argue, but I know better," she said before looking at the TV. "What do you want to watch?"

"How about a comedy?" I suggested. We could all use a laugh.

"Sounds good. I'm down with whatever, since I'll be filling out paperwork and catching up on emails while we watch."

"Catelyn, I'm sure the paperwork can wait until tomorrow," her father said.

"It can, but I won't be able to relax until I do it."

Her father watched me, making me feel like I was being tested. Only I had no idea what I was supposed to say or do. *What's the right thing to do, according to General Maxwell?*

It didn't matter. I had to be true to myself and do the right thing for Cate.

"Why don't you fill out your expense report, then relax for a bit?" It was a compromise that allowed her to check something off her to-do list while encouraging her not to overdo it.

"Are you two going to gang up on me if I try to do more?"

"I wouldn't say we'll gang up..." her father said.

"But we'll work together to convince you." I finished.

"Fine. Start the movie. I'll be done with the report by the end of the opening credits."

After Cate put her laptop away, I encouraged her to lie down and use my leg as a pillow. She fell asleep less than twenty minutes later as I rubbed her arm and back.

I didn't last much longer.

When I woke up, General Maxwell was reading. At some point, he must have covered Cate with a blanket and turned the TV off.

"How long was I out?" I asked around a yawn.

He looked at his watch. "Just shy of an hour."

Unwilling to disturb Cate, I stretched as much as I could without moving my leg.

When she whimpered in her sleep, I stroked her hair and sang, just like I had in the cage. It had the desired effect, lulling her back into a restful sleep.

"You speak Arabic?" her father asked, after I stopped.

"Yes, sir."

He watched his daughter, tracking my hand as I caressed her back, before saying, "She trusts you."

It wasn't a question, so I didn't respond, but I held my head a little higher at the compliment. I looked back at Cate, grateful pain and fear were absent from her features as she slept. *For now.* Experience taught me the nightmares would not only return, they'd overstay their welcome. My own nightmares had intensified since coming home from the hospital. Pain management wasn't the only benefit of the drugs that knocked me out.

He looked at his daughter, lying battered and bruised on the couch, and my hand brushing hair off her face. He made eye contact before asking, "You'll take care of her? Protect her?"

Yes, sir wasn't strong enough. I held eye contact. "Until I take my last breath." It wasn't a promise, it was a vow. Even though I knew it'd piss her off if she heard me say it.

"I expected a yes, sir." His chuckle woke Cate.

"What's so funny?" she asked, rubbing sleep from her eyes. When she noticed she'd drooled on my leg she apologized.

"No need to apologize." I smiled. She could drool on me whenever she wanted.

Pink colored her cheeks before she smiled and repeated the question.

"Just me, surprising your father," I answered.

"You surprise a lot of people."

*That I do.* But only because I'd hidden who I was. Now that I'd finally opened up, there'd be fewer surprises in the future.

"Your bandage is leaking. Want me to help change it?" I asked as I helped Cate sit up.

She tried looking at the bandage on her back, but the movement made her wince.

"Come on." I stood and offered her a hand. "Let's go."

"Catelyn?" her father asked.

"It's okay, Dad."

Why wouldn't it be?

"The instructions are with the supplies in the bathroom," he said.

He'd helped her before, but it was my job to take care of her now. *Probably shouldn't say that out loud.* Cate would kill me.

"Sit." I pointed at the toilet.

"Don't tell me what to do," she said as she sat.

I smirked.

*God, I love this woman.* Only Cate would tell me off while following directions.

"Can you remove your shirt?"

Her eyes widened in panic.

"What's the matter?"

"I'm not wearing a bra."

The idea of seeing her perfect breasts sent all the blood in my body to the last place it needed to be. She didn't miss me adjusting myself to hide my attraction.

"Did you seriously just get an erection?"

"Are you seriously asking me that? I'm a healthy, young, hetero male, Cate. Of course I got an erection when a gorgeous woman with a great rack tells me she's not wearing a bra when I ask her to take off her shirt."

The un-bruised parts of her cheeks turned the cutest shade of pink. "Well, don't."

"Seriously?" How could I not?

"I look awful." Her whisper low enough that I almost missed it.

"Christ, Cate, just take the compliment."

"Thank you." She looked down at her legging covered legs. "Now think about something else," she insisted.

Like that'd be possible. "I'll try." I said as I washed my hands and pulled on blue medical gloves. I wasn't worried about Cate having a disease, but after years of training, it was a habit.

When she struggled, I stood behind her and helped her out of her shirt. She hugged the loose fabric over her chest with her left arm before sitting back down.

Guilt surged at the sight of the large circular wound on her back. I still felt like I should've tried harder. It didn't matter that the drugs prevented me from protecting her.

I thanked God Franks was a bad shot—Cate may not have survived if he'd punctured her lung.

"You're surprisingly gentle."

"Thanks, I think." I applied the last piece of medical tape. "You're all set."

"It's a good thing." She turned. "You can go. I'll change the front."

"You sure? I promise to be a perfect gentleman."

When she hesitated, I said, "You don't have to uncover for me to help."

She nodded. Afterwards, she watched as I cleaned out the sink before removing the gloves and washing my hands. Unwilling to leave in case she still needed help, I turned towards the wall so she could put her shirt back on.

"Thanks."

When she swore, I asked if she wanted help. Reluctantly, she said yes.

I pulled her up and helped her from behind.

Once she was ready, I said, "You're welcome." I leaned in and kissed her forehead, the tip of her nose, and finally her lips. "Thank you for letting me take care of you."

"Don't get used to it." She huffed out a laugh.

"I wouldn't dare." Never in a million years would I have expected the woman of my dreams to challenge my patience so damn much. *But here I am.* And I wouldn't change a thing.

"Can you stay for a while?" she asked.

"I'll stay for as long as you want."

Before I left, we made plans to have dinner with my parents on Friday night.

# Chapter 50

## Cate

It was chaos in the Sheppard house when we arrived for dinner Friday night. Jay said we didn't have to bring anything, but neither my father nor I felt comfortable showing up empty-handed, so I brought wine, and dad brought a bottle of Scotch for John.

At the door, John shook my father's hand while Mary welcomed me with a gentle, heart-felt hug. It shouldn't have felt awkward or made me nervous, but it did. Before I finished thanking her for inviting us, Jay was by my side. His presence alone was enough to calm my nerves. Forgetting I didn't want to openly display our new relationship, I leaned into him.

"You'll be fine," He whispered in my ear.

"Am I that obvious?"

"Yeah." He kissed my temple. "At least to me."

When John introduced my father to everyone as General Maxwell, everyone being Mary, his two other sons, Meg, and Emily, he insisted they call him Sean.

John and Mary were the only ones who did.

It didn't take long for John, Mary, and my dad to make their way to the kitchen, giving us 'kids' a chance to hang out before dinner.

Jay stood by my side, making sure no one hugged me too tightly when the Sheppard family welcomed me with open arms, literally. They were huggers and there was no escaping it, no matter how awkward I felt. Not that I really wanted to escape. I wasn't a hugger, but I enjoyed the acceptance.

"How are feeling?" Meg asked as she stepped back.

"Better. Doc Greenfield said I'm healing nicely," I said. "I hope to return to work sooner rather than later." There was only so much sitting around I could do without going crazy.

"Good, we've missed you around the office," Jamie said.

"Yeah, it's been too quiet without you two biting each other's heads off," Jack added.

"We weren't that bad," Jay defended us.

I forced a smile. "Yes, we were, or have you forgotten I punched you?"

"That's all on you." Jay rubbed his jaw. "And how could I forget? You pack a hell of a punch." He grinned before adding, "For a girl."

"For a girl?" I asked, with half-hearted indignation.

"Dude, have you learned nothing?" Jack asked.

Jay crossed his arms and held his ground. The sparkle in his eye told me he was having fun messing with everyone.

"I bet he deserved it," Meg took my side.

"Did I?" He asked, winking to let me know it was okay to joke about it.

I didn't answer, but Jack and Jamie said, "Probably," before breaking out in laughter.

Maybe someday I'd laugh at the memory too, but not today. The embarrassment was still too strong.

"Which of those lingering bruises is from Maxwell?" Jack asked, pointing at Jay's face. The swelling was gone, but he still had lingering blue and green patches courtesy of Roman's goons. So did I.

"Hard to tell." He laughed.

After the laughter died down, Jack asked, "What was it you called them, Meg?"

"Enemies to lovers," she answered. "Speaking of, you owe me twenty bucks." She held out her hand. "Each."

"What?" Jay and I asked together.

"Meg bet us you two would get together sooner rather than later," Jamie said with a shrug before pulling out his wallet. Jack made no move to pay her.

"Pay up, Charming," Meg said, using her pet name for her husband.

Emily was reserved but couldn't help laughing as Meg demanded money.

"Princess, we share a bank account," he reminded her with a one-armed hug. "Take whatever you want." The love between them was palpable when he kissed her temple.

"Meg, what made you think we'd end up as lovers?" Jay asked. We weren't quite lovers. *Yet.* We were in love but hadn't done more than kiss. I couldn't wait until I'd healed enough to spend a night living out my fantasies with Jaden's rock hard, tattooed covered body.

"The way you always looked at each other when you thought no one could see you." She grinned and shrugged like it was a given. "It was only a matter of time."

Jay and I made eye contact, staring deep into each other's eyes before smiling.

No matter how much I wanted to be mad at Meg for suggesting it, she was right—Jay and I were a perfect example of enemies to lovers.

The guys offered to refill our drinks, beer for them, and water for the rest of us, giving me an opportunity to talk to Emily and get to know her better. *Not only am I an introvert, I built walls to keep everyone out.* When I apologized for not being friendlier in the past, she confessed she thought I didn't like her, adding to my guilt at shutting them all out.

"I'm sorry if I gave you that impression," I said. I was more like my father than I thought.

Jamie put his arm around Emily. "Told you it wasn't personal. Maxwell just keeps to herself."

"You'll have to come out of your shell now that you're part of the family," Jack said.

Part of the family. I liked the sound of that. *Even if it'll take some getting used to.*

We talked until Mary called us to dinner.

"That's a lot of food," I said as I sat down. The spread included grilled burgers and chicken, Meg's famous bacon mac and cheese, an interesting-looking salad, and grilled vegetables. Everything looked mouth-wateringly delicious.

Finally able to eat like a normal person again, I couldn't wait to dive in.

Mary looked at the table, assessing the spread. "Is it? I'm used to feeding these three bottomless pits–"

"Hey," her sons said at the same time.

"It's true," she said. "But you know I don't mind."

As the Mama Bear of the Sheppard family, Grannie's, and SSI, it wasn't hard to imagine her being the mom who'd always fed the neighborhood kids.

"I can see why you said I didn't need to bring anything," I said with a laugh.

"Anyone want a beer?" Jack asked before sitting down.

"I'll take one," I said.

"You probably shouldn't," Jay said.

"Excuse me?" My irritation flared out of habit. Just because we were dating didn't mean he could tell me what to do.

"You shouldn't drink while you're on pain meds, especially on an empty stomach," he answered.

Did he think I was stupid?

"Who died and made you boss?" I asked, reaching for his beer.

"I'm just looking out for you," he sounded irritated and concerned at the same time.

Ignoring the voice in my head telling me to stop, my hand lifted the bottle to my mouth as if it had a mind of its own.

Holding eye contact with Jay, I grinned before bringing the bottle to my lips and chugging it. At least, I tried to. There was more than I'd expected and I almost choked myself.

Jay's focus never left my face.

Irritated at myself for acting like a fool, I slammed the beer bottle down, causing it to splash out.

Jay put one hand on the back of my chair, leaned in close, and waited for me to recover before asking, "Feel better?"

He wasn't asking about my coughing fit. *Smart ass.* That fucking grin had me responding in ways I didn't want to when I was trying to be mad.

"No." I crossed my arms and squinted at him. "Happy?"

"No." We stared at each other, both fighting grins while waiting for the other to give up in the battle of wills between us.

Staring Jay down gave me a thrill. His hand, now gently squeezing the back of my neck, wasn't helping put out the fire.

His dilated pupils told me he was just as affected.

*This is why I did it.* I liked the thrill of the fight, the fire burning in his eyes when he looked at me, the promise of a passion that could consume us both.

When my dad asked if we were always like this, a chorus of "Yes" rang out.

Jay's lips lifted in a lop-sided grin as his amber eyes sparkled.

I smiled and dropped my eyes for the briefest second, letting him win.

When I looked back up, his grin turned to a full-blown smile. Which promptly turned into a scowl when Jack gave me a fresh beer.

"Thanks, Jack." I said cheerfully, my eyes locked on Jay's. When he didn't thank Jack for replacing the beer I'd stolen, I added, "Jay thanks you, too."

"Do I?"

"You do."

We never broke eye contact.

"Thank you, Jack, for giving my girlfriend a beer when she's on prescription painkillers."

"She's a big girl. She can make her own choices," Jack said. "Even if they aren't always smart."

"Pot," Jamie coughed.

"What was that, big brother?"

"I seem to recall you making the same 'not-smart' choice when you were on pain meds." Jamie made air quotes.

"Shut up," Jack said instead of denying it.

"You work with this?" my father asked, his disbelief laced with humor.

"Every single day," John answered. He raised his beer and said, "To family." Our battle of the wills finished, we turned to John as everyone raised their glasses and repeated, "To family."

We dug in.

Seeing my father relaxed and getting along with John and Mary made my heart happy. When I was growing up, it was just the two of us; the only big family dinners we had were with fellow officers and their families.

*None were as big, or as lively, as the Sheppard clan.* They were a family that lived and loved big, loud, and fierce.

They bickered and teased one another, but if you threatened one of them, you faced all of them. Including those in their extended family. *This is what family should be.* What I'd always wanted growing up. Not that I blamed my father; he did the best he could as a single dad in the Marines.

Over come with emotion, I tried to hide it.

But Jay noticed. Leaning over, he whispered, "You okay?"

*This man!* He challenged me and drove me crazy, but the instant he sensed I felt uncomfortable, he turned caring and sweet. And I loved him for it.

"I'm good." I smiled to back up my words. "I'm just not used to," I looked around the table, "all this."

He snickered, nodding his head once. "They can be a bit much."

"In a good way," I added. Just because I wasn't used to it didn't mean I didn't like it. And maybe, just maybe, someday I'd feel comfortable enough to take part in the crazy. But not today.

Things quieted down as we ate.

"This salad is amazing," I said after taking a bite. The fresh tomato, cucumber, and avocado worked perfectly with the bacon and blue cheese. "Maybe someday you can show me how to make it."

"I'd like that," Emily said with a shy smile. Jamie's was big enough for me to see in my peripheral vision when I asked for an extra helping.

Everything tasted so good. I had to force myself to stop eating, so I didn't make myself sick. My ribs were healing nicely, but vomiting would definitely set me back.

"That was amazing," my father said, leaning back and patting his stomach.

"I hope you saved room for dessert," Emily said.

"No worries there. I'll make room." He chuckled.

"Meg makes the best brownies," Jay said.

Mary put her hand over her heart and feigned offense as Meg said, "Thanks."

"Sorry, Ma, but it's true. Yours are good, but she adds bacon and bourbon," Jay said.

"The salted caramel ones are my favorite," Jack added.

"Mine are the Mexican ones," Jamie said.

"Oh, those are good too," Jay added. "What kind did you make tonight?"

"I made the salted caramel," Meg answered.

"I made the Mexican," Emily said.

"No bacon and bourbon?" Jay asked, pouting. He turned to me, knowing I'd pick up on the fact they'd each made the one their significant other preferred.

*It's a good thing I like brownies, bourbon, and bacon.*

"I guess I'll need the bacon bourbon brownie recipe, too."

Jay's smile doubled in size before he squeezed my thigh. "You'll need all the brownie recipes."

"How much free time do you think I have?"

He glanced at my sling and laughed.

"This is temporary."

"I'll help you bake, Sweetie Pie."

"Don't."

"Snookems?"

Ignoring him, I turned and said, "They both sound too good to pass up. Remind me to only have a small piece of each."

"You should have giant pieces." Jay chuckled when my jaw dropped open. "Don't worry, I'll eat what you don't finish."

"Bottomless pit," his father said, making everyone laugh.

I had two small bites of each before handing the rest over to Jay, along with most of my beer. The few sips I had provided a sense of normalcy, which was all I wanted.

He raised an eyebrow and grinned, but kept his mouth closed like the smart man he was.

"If you have time, we'd love to have you over again," Mary said as we packed up to leave. When she handed us leftovers, I tried turning them down, but Jay vetoed me, and my father took Jay's side.

"I have a feeling there'll be plenty of opportunities in the future," my dad said, smiling at me. "John, if the offer still stands, I'd like to check out the office and the training facility you're building."

"How about tomorrow, say ten?" John asked.

My dad looked at me to verify. "That's fine," I answered. I wasn't like I had anything better to do.

The hugs goodbye were less awkward than the hugs hello.

I wasn't sure when it happened, but at some point during dinner, I'd embraced my new role as a member of the Sheppard clan.

# Chapter 51

## Cate

"Good morning, Mr. Sheppard. I trust you slept well." I heard from my place in the hall the next morning.

Jay and I had stayed up late talking and must've fallen asleep, because when I woke up in the middle of the night, I was curled up in his arms.

"Good morning, Sir." *Damn him.* I could hear the smirk in his voice and didn't appreciate him starting something with my father. "I slept like the dead, you?"

"I slept well on my daughter's couch. Thank you for asking."

*Subtle.* I walked around Jay and put an end to my father's questions.

"Good morning, Dad. We fell asleep talking and I assure you, Jaden was a perfect gentleman."

"That's good to know." He lifted his coffee mug. "Coffee?"

When I turned to the counter, Jay said, "Sit, I'll get it."

"But you don't know how I like it?" I argued.

He scoffed, "Yes, I do."

*Of course he does, just like I know he likes his black with one sugar.* We'd talked about Meg's enemies to lovers theory and realized we'd been obsessively observing each other for months.

"How are you feeling this morning?"

"Better. I think I'll cut back on the pain meds."

"There's no need to be a martyr, Cate," Jay said, setting a cup of coffee, the exact caramel color I drank it, in front of me, along with my bottle of pain meds and a glass of water.

*What the hell?* "I'm not trying to be a martyr. I don't like how they make me feel."

"Pain free?"

Smartass. "No, loopy." The first sip of coffee burned a little, as it always did if I drank it too soon. You'd think I'd learn, but no. I'd suffer the burn to get the coffee every damn time. "I didn't say I wouldn't take any. I said I want to take less."

"I thought you two liked each other," my father said, interrupting us.

We did. Loved each other, in fact.

Jay grinned. "We do."

"Then act like it," he said, standing up. "What time do we have to leave to get to SSI by ten?" He meant nine-fifty-five, because on time to a Marine meant arriving at least five minutes early. *Preferably ten.*

"Nine-twenty," Jay and I answered in unison. I added, "Earlier if we want to stop by Grannie's."

"Nine-ten give us enough time?" Dad asked.

"Nine to make it safe. We can't show up with Gannie's unless we bring enough for everyone."

Dad looked confused. "Why?"

"It's an SSI thing. Remember me telling you about the hazing tradition?"

"Right, I'd forgotten all about it. How many will we need?"

Jaden counted off, "Mom and Dad, Jamie and Emily, Jack, AJ and Blake, Doug and Beth, a decaf mocha for Meg, and a hot chocolate with extra whip for Chase, plus ours… so, fourteen."

"I didn't expect the tour to be such a big event," he said.

"It's not, but it's Cate's first time back in the office since," Jay paused but didn't finish. He didn't need to; we all knew why.

"Understood. Maybe we should go to Grannie's after the tour, so I can actually enjoy the place."

# Chapter 52

## Jay

When we got to the office, there was a huge, colorful banner strung across our door.

Welcome Back Beauty and the Beast.

"Beauty and the Beast?" I asked.

"It was Meg's idea," Jack said, ratting out his wife. "She said just because you work here didn't mean you shouldn't get proper call signs."

"We have proper call signs," Cate said, sounding confused. She turned to Meg and asked, "Why didn't you want to use them?"

Meg smiled. "You weren't working."

"Why would that matter?" I asked.

"Why Beauty and the Beast?" Cate asked.

"The perfect enemies to lovers couple." Meg looked so pleased at being correct about Cate and me I couldn't help but laugh.

"And Beast fits you," Jack added. "Or at least, it did." He clapped me on the back. "Maybe less so in the future." He lifted his head towards Cate.

General Maxwell wore the same expression as my dad as they watched the back and forth—a mix of amusement and exasperation.

"Some days it's like working in a high school," Dad said.

"What about high school?" AJ asked as he entered the lobby from the back, holding Blake's hand. Poor girl practically had to run to keep up with him anytime he forgot to adjust his stride for her short legs. I looked at Cate, glad she wasn't a foot shorter than me. *I don't know how AJ deals with it.*

"Dealing with this crew," Dad said. "AJ Janerek, you remember General Maxwell?"

"Good to see you again, sir." They shook hands. He turned to me. "Permission to hug?"

"Dude, no. I'm not hugging you," I answered.

"Not you. Maxwell."

I knew he meant Cate, but decided to have a little fun at his expense. "I don't think the General wants to hug you either."

"Why are you asking him?" Cate asked, one hand on her hip.

"Because I don't want to get my ass kicked," AJ answered with a grin.

"Who's kicking your butt this time?" Doug asked as he entered with Beth and Chase.

"Great, just what we need, another clown in the circus," I said, rolling my eyes.

After another introduction, General Maxwell said, "It's a miracle you get anything done around here." His tone and smile making it clear he was joking.

"When the crap hits the fan, there's no one else I'd rather have at my back," my dad said, adjusting his language for Chase's little ears.

AJ and Doug each hugged Cate, then insisted on hugging me, too. Chase made his way around the room, hugging everyone. When he finally made it to us, he took one look at our faces and stopped dead in his tracks.

"Hey, Chase." I said, lowering to a knee.

"What happened to your face?" He scrunched up his nose.

Our faces still had plenty of color, but at least we looked better than we had a few days ago.

"Chase!" Beth scolded him.

"It's okay, Beth. I'm sure it's a bit of a shock," Cate said. She used my shoulder for support as she lowered to a knee. "We got into a fight with some bad guys."

"Did you win?" he asked, stepping closer so he could examine our cuts and bruises.

I looked up at my dad. We, as in Cate and I, hadn't, but we, as in SSI, had. I didn't think Chase would appreciate the distinction, so I said, "We did, with help from your Uncle John and everyone else."

"Including my dad?"

It took a hot second for me to remember he'd started calling Doug dad, even though Doug and Beth weren't married yet. They'd marry eventually, and when they did, Doug would sign the adoption papers before the ink on the marriage certificate dried.

Doug sent Chase to hang out with Beth and the other spouses at Meg's desk.

"So, you two are finally an item?" AJ asked Cate.

Cate hesitated, but I didn't. "Yes." It wasn't like they didn't already know.

But I understood why. She was still nervous they'd judge her for having a workplace romance. *Who can blame her after what Gavin put her through?* Eventually, she'd realize I wasn't Gavin and let go of her fear. I just had to be patient.

"You've built an impressive business here, John," General Maxwell said as they came back downstairs.

"Thank you. I've had a lot of help." My father indicated the team.

"Having the local LEOs help cover the cost of the training range helped too," Jamie added. "We're looking forward to the day it opens."

"How much longer?" General Maxwell asked.

"If everything goes according to plan, it should be fully operational in two months," Dad answered.

"You'll have to come back and see it," Cate said. Her tone hinting she didn't expect him to come back so soon.

"That I do. Maybe for your birthday."

"Which is?" I asked, looking down at Cate.

"Dude, you've got to step up your game," Jack said, shaking his head.

"What, unlike you, I can't read her personnel file." It was bad I didn't know her birthday, but in all fairness we'd just gotten together and our courtship wasn't exactly normal.

"True, true. But still, it looks bad," Jack said.

*I should have waited until we were alone to ask her.*

"Cate?" I asked.

"August 14th," she said, putting me out of my misery. "Yours?"

No one gave her shit for not knowing mine. "July 23rd."

"Not long after Jamie and Emily's wedding," she said.

"Yup." I popped the p. I put my arm around her shoulders. "You'll get to meet my sister, Madi. I think you'll like her." I didn't bother asking if Cate was coming to the wedding, trusting she'd be there with me to celebrate.

"I think so, too," Dad said. "She's better behaved than the boys."

"That's a pretty low bar, sir," Cate joked, catching everyone off guard.

Dad laughed, "You got that right. Come on General, I'll show you the range."

# Chapter 53

## Cate

The rest of the weekend was a whirlwind of family interactions and healing. Much of which included meeting up with various members of the Sheppard family at Grannie's. After visiting on Friday, my father had insisted on going back every day. He'd fallen in love with the kitschy decor, the welcoming atmosphere, and of course, the coffee.

Time flew by and before I knew it, Monday morning arrived and it was time to take my father to the airport.

I got up early, but Jay had gotten up earlier. He made coffee and started breakfast. Seeing him and my father chatting comfortably in my kitchen, while Jay scrambled eggs, felt right.

"Morning," I said around a yawn.

"Morning." Jay kissed the top of my head before handing me a cup of coffee.

"Thank you."

"Bacon or sausage?"

"You made both?" I asked.

"No, I was just hoping you'd choose the one I made," Jay said, laying the sarcasm on thick. "Of course I made both."

The exchange caused my father roll his eyes, something I'd never seen him do before. "What was that for?" I asked.

"What was what for?" Jay asked.

"Not you, my father. He rolled his eyes at me." I let my shock bleed through.

"You'll always be like this, won't you?" my father asked, pointing between us.

I laughed. Probably, we still liked to goad each other. Jaden, more than me. Though I bet he'd say the opposite if asked.

We drove each other crazy; we challenged each other, and we loved each other. I didn't see a reason to change.

"It works for us," I finally answered, shrugging my left shoulder.

Saying bye to my father was a lot harder than I'd expected, but we promised to talk weekly. Having bonded with my father over the weekend, Jay extended his leave from SSI so he could drive us to the airport.

Jay went old school and asked my father for permission to date me, earning my father's stamp of approval. We didn't need it, but earning my father's respect meant a lot to Jay.

Who was I kidding? It meant a lot to me, too. I wanted the two men I loved most in the world to like and respect each other.

Watching my father walk away brought an unexpected tear to my eye.

"You okay?" Jay's arms wrapped gently around me as he whispered in my ear.

Saying goodbye had never been this hard before. *But we're closer now.* And I no longer felt the need to hide my emotions around him. I didn't need to hide my emotions at all, which was liberating in a way I hadn't expected.

Having to get shot and almost die for it to happen sucked, but I'd take it.

"I am."

When we could no longer see my father, Jay said, "Let's go home."

Home. Jay had only stayed over three nights, but my apartment already felt like our home.

# Seven Weeks Later

## Cate

Seven weeks. That was how long Jaden and I had been together when I attended Jamie and Emily's wedding as his plus one. I'd received an invitation in my own right, but didn't need it.

Jay spent more nights at my place than he did at Jamie, forcing me to remind myself I loved him as I adjusted to having his stuff everywhere. He wasn't messy, per se, he just didn't put things were I would put them. Jay reminded me every day that I didn't need to be perfect to be loved.

Luckily, the therapist I was seeing for my captivity trauma was also helping me deal with my compulsive need to control everything often reminded me of the same thing.

I was getting better, but still got frustrated when it seemed like he wasn't trying.

Jay'd remind me it was an adjustment for him too, saying, "It's not easy living with someone so uptight."

It always resulted in a fight. The fights always ended with Earth shattering makeup sex.

The sex. Sex with Jaden was everything I thought it'd be. *And more.* He was possessive and controlling, and I found I loved giving up control when I trusted the man I gave it to. Not that I didn't occasionally take charge. *I am who I am, after all.*

Those thoughts were why I was blushing and had an ear-to-ear smile plastered on my face when I walked into Emily's bridal room in the church.

"Oh, I know what you're thinking about," Ashley greeted me with a mimosa.

I laughed. I'd learned it was better to not respond at all if I wanted Ashley to give up on a topic.

"Cate," Emily got up and hugged me. "I'm glad you're here." Another change; everyone called me Cate outside the office.

"Me, too." I made my way around the room, hugging the women gathered with Emily. Meg, Mary, and the only Sheppard sister, Madi. Jay was right; I loved her. And Emily's mom, Anne.

"You look gorgeous," I said when I got back around to Emily. This was the first time I'd seen her in the white silk spaghetti strap dress since she'd had it altered. "Where's the train?"

"Oh, I'm not putting it on until the last minute, so I don't rip it."

Ashley, Meg, and Madi wore dresses in matching shades of baby blue. Ashley's low-cut, figure-hugging dress showed off her athletic figure. Madi's dress had a similar style but was more modest, and the color brought out the flecks of blue in her hazel eyes. Meg's dress showed off her barely there baby bump.

I thought back to the shopping trip when I'd made the mistake of letting Jay help me pick out a dress. His first choice got an instant veto; it was a strappy, second-skin red mini dress. Not only was it inappropriate for a wedding, but there was no way in hell I'd ever leave the house in it.

When he bought it anyway, he said, "It's a good thing you won't leave the house. I'd have to gouge the eyes out of any man who looked at you."

The first time I wore it, he scooped me up and carried me to the bedroom. He insisted I wear it, devouring me with his eyes while he slowly took his clothes off.

"Earth to Cate," Mary said, waving her hand in front of my face.

"Sorry, I was just…" Heat crept up my cheeks. *Thinking about having sex with your son.* I finished my mimosa in one gulp.

While the stylist did Emily's hair, Madi said I should go back to using Max.

"Why?" I asked. When I looked around, I felt like the only one who wasn't in on the joke.

"Because, then all my brothers will be with women who have M names."

I looked at the bride to be. "Emily doesn't start with M."

"No, but everyone calls her Em, which is basically just the letter," Meg said.

It made sense, and I was a little embarrassed it took me so long to see it.

"You can call me Max. Or Maxwell. That's what the guys call me at work."

"Wait, by that logic, you have to marry a guy whose name starts with J," Ashley said, pointing her mimosa filled flute at Madi.

"I'd need to date someone first." Madi answered with a chuckle.

Ashley looked at Meg, then me, and asked, "What's the new guy's name?"

Assuming she meant the new hires at SSI, I said, "There's two, Nathan and Matt." Nathan was starting in August, and Matt a couple of weeks later.

"Sorry Madi, no hunky SSI guy for you." Ashley teased.

"Ew, half those guys are my brothers." And one was her dad.

"Right, sorry. But it's not my fault you have hot, sexy brothers."

"Right." She pretended to gag. "You know, someday they'll be old and gray. Maybe then I won't have to hear about how hot and sexy they are." Madi shook her head as she laughed.

Mary and Anne chose not to take part in the conversation, but they laughed along with the rest of us.

"Then they'll be silver foxes, so you'll still have to hear it," Meg said.

"John's a silver fox," Mary interjected.

"Ma!" Madi cried. "That isn't helping."

After the laughter died down, Ashley asked, "Are the new guys hot?"

"Ashley!" Emily yelled at her maid of honor. "You're incorrigible."

"What, you can't blame me for asking."

"Nathan's tall with dirty blond hair and blue eyes. He has a scar on his face," Meg answered.

"Scars can be sexy," Ashley refused to be put off.

I doubted Nathan would agree. The scar ran from his left temple down his cheek to the corner of his mouth. Nathan had seen some shit, and from the look in his eyes, it still haunted him. Something I could relate to. My nightmares were less frequent, but hadn't stopped altogether.

The traditional church ceremony was beautiful. The look in Jamie's eyes the moment he saw Emily was the stuff romance authors wrote about. Chris, his best friend and Emily's older brother, clapped him on the shoulder to break the spell.

Behind Chris were Jack and Jaden, looking handsome in their tuxes. Jack and Meg kept stealing glances across the aisle, no doubt remembering their own wedding. Madi wiped at her eyes as she watched her brother watch his bride. So did Ashley.

The ceremony was beautiful and there wasn't a dry eye in the house by the time the pastor said, "You may now kiss the bride."

After dinner, and all the typical reception traditions were over, Jay and I danced surrounded by a sea of decorations, the twinkle lights playing on the various shades of blue making them look like ocean waves.

Jay banded one arm around my back and held my hand with the other.

"You look stunning." I'd settled on a fitted, halter style, little black dress that hung just above my knees. "But I still think I like the red dress better."

I felt the heat in my cheeks and was grateful no one was looking at us.

We swayed to the slow country ballad, losing ourselves in each other.

"Do you think we'll have a big wedding or should we elope?" Jay asked.

"Your mother would kill you if we elope."

"Are you saying yes?"

"Are you asking?" I teased, thinking this had to be a joke. We'd only been dating for two months.

His laughter shook his chest. "No, not tonight. Jamie would kill me if he found out I proposed at his wedding reception."

Not tonight? He'd thought about it?

Recovering from the shock, I said, "Maybe we should start with you moving in."

"That ship has sailed, Snookems. I already have a key, and I can't remember the last time I didn't spend the night with you."

"I mean, make it official. You know, change the address on your employee records," I said. "And don't call me Snookems."

"Yes, ma'am."

"You're impossible."

"And yet you love me."

I did. Turning my face, I leaned back so I could look him in the eye. "Against all logic and common sense, I love you."

"Then I accept your proposal," he said, bringing his smirking lips to mine.

Everything—the crowd, the celebration, the cheers—disappeared the instant our lips touched. It wasn't our first kiss, but it was the kiss that finally made Weatherford feel like home.

What happens in Vegas stays in Vegas. Or does it? Pick up TRAPPED to find out.

The next installment in my SSI series includes a scarred hero, a sassy heroine, and a spoiled black cat.

# Acknowledgements

T hank you, Reader, for choosing to spend some time in my world. I hope you enjoyed it.

I want to thank my Proof Reader, Nina, and my Beta readers, Gigi, Kirsten, and Shauna'h. Your feedback was invaluable in helping me polish my story. A big thanks to Maria Secoy, and the mentor team at All Write Well–this book wouldn't be in your hands if I hadn't found them!

A special shout out to my coach, "Flyin" Brian Akins, who helped me with the boxing scene.

I also want to thank my friends, who have surrounded me with love and support while listening to me chatter on endlessly about my characters and plot lines over many glasses of wine.

Thank you all!

# Also by

<br>

<u>**Sheppard & Sons Investigations:**</u>

**TAKEN:** Jack and Meg's story
**BEATEN:** Jamie and Emily's story
**MISSING:** Doug and Beth's story
**BETRAYED:** AJ and Blake's story
**CAGED:** Jaden and Catelyn's story
**TRAPPED:** Ashley & Nathan's story

WebPage

# About the Author

Eveline Rose fell in love with storytelling in a high school creative writing class. Eveline currently lives in the Chicago area with her cat, Prince, where she pours her heart and soul into her characters for your reading pleasure. She's a theatre geek who can swing a sword, and a self-defense instructor who can shoot the bullseye. Eveline spends her free time volunteering in her community, hanging out with her friends, and of course reading. One topic she can chat about for hours: Tudor history. Eveline's promise to you: every romantic suspense novel will include a strong protective male hero who will save the woman he loves, and every heroine will get her Happily Ever After. Eveline is a member of Chicago North Romance Writers Group.